THE ANSWER
IS BIGFOOT LISTENING

PAUL HOWARD JOHNSON

authorHOUSE®

AuthorHouse™
1663 Liberty Drive
Bloomington, IN 47403
www.authorhouse.com
Phone: 1-800-839-8640

Published by AuthorHouse 4/4/2013

ISBN: 978-1-4817-3294-9 (sc)
ISBN: 978-1-4817-3295-6 (e)

Library of Congress Control Number: 2013905220

TABLE OF CONTENTS

CHAPTER 1 1

CHAPTER 2 13

CHAPTER 3 23

CHAPTER 4 33

CHAPTER 5 39

CHAPTER 6 43

CHAPTER 7 57

CHAPTER 8 65

CHAPTER 9 71

CHAPTER 10 77

CHAPTER 11 89

CHAPTER 12 97

CHAPTER 13 105

CHAPTER 14 109

CHAPTER 15 113

CHAPTER 16 121

CHAPTER 17 125

CHAPTER 18 133

CHAPTER 19 139

CHAPTER 20 143

CHAPTER 21 145

CHAPTER 22 153

CHAPTER 23 157

CHAPTER 24 163

CHAPTER 25 173

CHAPTER 26 179

CHAPTER 27 183

CHAPTER 28 187

CHAPTER 29 193

CHAPTER 30 197

CHAPTER 31 203

CHAPTER 32 211

CHAPTER 33 217

CHAPTER 34 221

CHAPTER 35 227

CHAPTER 36 235

CHAPTER 37 239

CHAPTER 38 247

CHAPTER 39 251

CHAPTER 40 257

CHAPTER 41 267

CHAPTER 42 275

CHAPTER 43 285

CHAPTER 44 295

CHAPTER 1

EARLY MORNING IN the Colville National Forest can be a little wet, especially in the late spring. The two scientists and the two Forest Rangers had been walking for about three hours, since just before dawn and everyone was soaked. Rain gear, particularly rain pants, is far too noisy going through the brush and although stealth was really not needed there was an unspoken pact to walk quietly so as not to startle the many forest dwellers. It had rained all night and every leaf and blade of grass was wet. Every plant and tree was quite willing to shower a passerby with sticky fragrant drops of captured rain, but the early morning "after rain" smell was just short of heavenly to the small group of intrepid hikers although not quite a fair trade for being completely soaked in the process. This time of year, after these mountain-soaking rains, the whole Earth smells as fresh as new mown hay. This was only the first day of many, looking forward to an entire summer of research, but all that excitement was quickly waning with every soaked, squishy, step.

Why were these four individuals going through this grueling trek? Yesterday, just as the team was arriving and setting up, some hikers had reported seeing something they could not explain. Although all four of the team were thinking they were going to see a bear, perhaps even a large Canadian grizzly, every lead had to be checked and documented no matter how routine it may seem or how outlandish the report may appear. Since last year there had been several sightings through the fall and winter from hunters and each had been carefully saved and compiled by the Forest Service in their own data base; telephone records and all of that information needed to be cataloged, checked, rechecked and a statistical analysis started. Setting up their lab and research facility had gone on well past midnight but here they were up before dawn doing what they had signed on to do.

"Frank, can we call a halt? I really want to take some samples and an atmosphere density reading," asked Megan Hanley, PhD in Anthropology, with lesser degrees in several other science disciplines, from Washington State University. "I know its background data but if we want something credible we really should go by the book," she had been addressing one of the Forest Ranger escorts who looked at her questioningly.

"OK, Dr. Hanley," replied the Head Ranger, rather over his shoulder, "we'll stop over there in that clearing," pointing to a clearing about 50 or 75 yards up slope, northwest of the deer path they were traversing. Frank took off his traditional Ranger weave hat and wiped his forehead with his faded blue handkerchief. He did not believe in the kind of research these two were doing but the Regional Director had tasked him to help them anyway he could and Frank really felt he had no choice in the matter regardless of how he felt about the whole situation. As the Head Ranger set his pack down and was rummaging through it for a candy bar he looked over at the head of the expedition and asked, "Dr. Paulson, do you really believe in any of this crap?" saying it just as he found his candy bar, opened his canteen and sat back on a oozing wet log that cracked open and sent a cascade of water on the ground making him adjust his position.

"Well, Ranger Leonard, if we must be so formal, I do believe in this crap all of it in fact, otherwise I would be in South Dakota or Montana digging up bones." The man who answered was Jerome Paulson, PhD in Anthropology from Eastern Washington University. Jerry Paulson is a tall muscular man in his early forties who looks more like a football coach than a scientist; possessing a calm manner and an easy smile, "There must be some basis in fact or the myths wouldn't have persisted for hundreds or thousands of years all over the globe and in almost every race of people. Now can we get back to you calling me Jerry, please?" Not waiting for an answer Dr. Paulson took out his notebook and began to write, munching on his homemade trail mix, "as I said every culture on the planet has stories of these creatures and a lot more," Jerry added without looking up from his notes.

Frank just shrugged his shoulders because of the lecture and glanced over at the "leggy professor", which he had dubbed Dr. Hanley, but only to himself. She was standing in the small clearing looking at some curious instrument. Her slightly tight jeans were wet all the way up her shapely butt, which he had also been admiring during the hike. She bent over without bending her knees too much to pick something up causing Frank to stop chewing his candy just for a moment or two, clearing his throat without meaning to as the coarse peanuts went down his throat a little roughly. She must have felt him staring because she looked over at

him as she straightened up again. Frank turned his eyes away
and tried to look as though he were occupied with the study
of trees, rather than female professors, but failed miserably
in his attempt to be nonchalant. His little act made Megan
smile. She knew she was attractive; she continually worked
hard to stay that way. She was in her late thirties and she was
in no mood to let gravity take over her good looks before
she was ready, which would be never if she had her way.
She was really not trying to be alluring but she was always
careful to look her best and that, coupled with her friendly
nature, automatically attracted the males of her species. She
was not terribly interested in gathering the background data
this morning; as far as she was concerned this early morning
excursion was a misuse of her time. They had scoured the area
that the over excited hikers had described to them and there
was nothing, zilch.

"Jerry, this really is a waste of our time. We would have
been better served to have spent a couple of days getting our
data base in order so we would have a few points of reference
and finished putting the lab together."

Jerry put his notebook away and swung his daypack
around so he could put his other arm into the shoulder strap,
"Meg, this is our first day. We'll have plenty of time to sit in
front of those damned computers once we have gathered some
of our own data. Instead of trying to decipher all the material
Stevens and his crew put together last year and of course the
jumbled data that the government threw together to keep us
off track, not to mention what the Forest Service has given
us. Come on let's get a move on so we can cover more of this
hillside. We'll be back at the truck before 1400," he said as he
began walking up hill in a northwesterly direction with his

compass in hand, "we'll have lunch on top of that mountain," he pointed toward Huckleberry Mountain. Frank chuckled and fell in behind Jerry leaving Meg to rapidly pack and then hurry to catch up with the men.

They took another well used deer path up from the logging road by Big Meadow lake and began moving almost due North, to the West slope of Huckleberry Mountain. By lunchtime they were sitting in a small grove of yellow pine just short of the top. The peanut butter and cherry jelly sandwiches really hit the spot. Meg thought this mountain should have been more appropriately named Drudgery Mountain. She sat on a rock with her flannel shirt open trying to catch any cooling breeze and all of the men were trying not to look. She smiled because she knew they were having trouble with her open shirt and she could have cared less if she was wearing a sports bra or not. This time she was wearing a tan sports bra and it was making her feel trust up and completely stifled like the women of the old west must have felt wearing their corsets.

Jerry, as usual, was making notes in his little book when he suddenly but unobtrusively stopped writing. He had noticed something in his peripheral vision on a bush a few meters away waving at him in the very slight breeze. It looked like a piece of Spanish moss that could have fallen from one of the surrounding trees. It had taken his mind a moment to focus but he decided it was worth looking at so, tucking his notepad away, he got up and went over to it. Typically, as a scientist, he already had his 4 inch magnifying glass in hand. Bending down he gently pulled the substance off the bush and examined it closely. He could see immediately it was not plant material, it was definitely animal hair.

"Meg," called Jerry and after receiving no response he called a little louder, "Megan!"

"What?" she looked in his direction obviously irritated at being summoned which was why she had said nothing in response to the first bellow.

"MEG!"

Now she was getting irritated, "What the hell do you want; can't we have a little down time at lunch?" She had been enjoying a siesta in the almost warm sun that was playing peek-a-boo in the clouds and she did not want to be interrupted.

"Come over here please. I think you'll like this," Jerry said in an even tone like he was in his classroom still examining the item and not looking at all in her direction. He had no idea what she was irritated about and really did not care. Her department head said she was easy to work with but added with a wink and an elbow jab, that she was a total iceberg in many other ways and quick to be irritable sometimes.

She came stomping over, rapidly buttoning her shirt and dragging he daypack with her leg, creating a small dust cloud in the quickly drying soil. There were leaves and small sticks in her dark hair making her look like a wild Celt woman, she only lacked the blue skin color, "what is it?" she demanded.

"Look at this and tell me you don't believe in what we're doing out here," he said holding arm out in her direction but still bent down looking to see if there was any more in the surrounding bushes. He did not care for her demeanor but he instantly decided to "let it go".

She leaned over taking it from him rather delicately and sniffed it, "that's just bear hair, so?" she said rather out of hand and finished buttoning her shirt because she was feeling a chill in the shade, "we've got bushels of that stuff back at the cabin that Stevens left for us," although she did smell something a little odd in this sample as she sniffed it again.

"No ma'am, we don't have anything like this," he said as he stood up and looked at her. She pulled out her own magnifying glass from a pouch on her belt. She looked at it silently. She rubbed it through her fingers to check the coarseness of it and then looked back at Jerry, saying nothing. Her right eyebrow rose quickly but she still said nothing. "Well?" said Jerry as the two Rangers Frank and Bryant Baker came over to look. They thought it was bear hair too.

Finally having gained some composure, the irritation gone now in her voice, at least, Meg answered, "You may be right this is not from a bear. It does not seem to be Wolverine although the consistency is close or a tuft of Wolf hair either," she said producing a sample bottle and stuffing the hair inside. "We'll need to test it of course to make sure it is not from some passing human, but the texture seems to be wrong for human too." She shook the bottle still looking at it, "so now are you going to tell me we're on the trail of the mighty Yeti, Sasquatch, the very Abominable guy himself?" her smile seemed genuine, although there was a hint of a giggle behind it. "You know the coastal Indians in the northwest call it Bookwus, the Wildman of the Woods."

"I think that possibly we are, so let's go look for footprints. There ought to be something even in this half muddy dust," Jerry said feeling like a kid that had just started a new and exclusive club. It crossed his mind in a flash "the he-man woman haters club" but he kept it to himself. Jerry was on his hands and knees carefully moving every weed and blade of grass.

It was Bryant, the young Ranger who was just out of school, who found the indention in the grass and a foot print in a muddy spot down the deer trail about ten meters away. "Hey. What's this?" shouted an exhilarated young Ranger. He stood up so the others could see exactly where he was pointing and so he could direct their movements carefully as they approached. "Is this what we're looking for?" he said as he pointed to a large indention in the rapidly drying soil.

The other three approached carefully. Frank feeling instantly uneasy began looking around for any type of movement in the deer brush. There was more of the delicately fine hair dangling from a tree branch that Megan carefully gathered. Jerry went back for his pack and brought out a bottle of the plaster mixture he always carried with him for just such an occasion. Returning to where the young Ranger stood Jerry sank down to a squatting position and began working through his parted knees, deftly picking out as much of the grass and weeds from the print as he could. Then sitting back slightly he took the lid off the jar and poured the entire mixture into the depression. After carefully putting the lid back on the jar and packing it away Jerry crossed his arms on top of his knees, put his chin on his arms, and watched the plaster as it slid into the footprint and began to dry. This was rather quick drying, shouldn't take more than 30 minutes.

Megan had finished gathering all the hair she could find then leaned over Jerry's shoulder, "It's probably just a big barefooted farm boy with a bad haircut stomping around these mountains just to drive us crazy," commented Meg making Jerry chuckle but he did not move or stop watching the plaster.

"I don't think so, that footprint could only belong to a

giant farm boy," mused Jerry without looking back at her, "that farm boy's print took the entire bottle of my quick drying plaster." It had almost not been enough plaster but it covered the entire print in a thin layer ¼ inch layer, and it was all he had brought with him. He would be sure to mix up two bottles next time.

The others had moved slowly up the hill looking for more signs when Jerry heard a rustle in the thick buck brush about five or six meters to his left. Out of the corner of his eye Jerry caught, what he thought was movement of a large dark mass. He noticed that the small breeze had stopped and he had begun sweating a cold, nasty feeling sweat. He looked over his shoulder and near one of the trees, in the buck brush, was something dark; darker that the surrounding area. He felt a shiver run the entire length of his spine because he could not see anything distinctly and could only speculate on what would make such a dark shadow in that spot. At that moment, as if on cue, the sun became partially blocked by some wispy clouds.

Jerry slowly arose. He felt as though they were all being watched by someone or something and he decided to investigate. He put his ball cap on the grass over the casting and carefully backed downhill a few steps, walked across the lower part of trail, into the brush. The sun picked that moment to come out from behind the clouds as he stood there peering into the dense brush but Jerry saw nothing specifically. On the other side of the brush patch were some lodge pole pines that began to sway and he thought he perceived movement again, but again he could not be sure. He was standing now in the sunlight squinting to see into the shadows so he decided to move further into the trees. He half expected to see a brown bear go running up the hillside or charge him, so he pulled his can of bear spray off his belt and had it at the ready, but nothing moved that he could see clearly.

Frank, who had seen Jerry walk toward the brush, had come down to see what he was looking at and as Frank approached Jerry turned toward him and put his finger to his lips in a gesture of quiet. Frank nodded his understanding and they both quietly ducked into the shadows. The flies and mosquitos, attracted by their dark clothing, body heat and sweat, began buzzing around their heads and eyes. One or two tried to go up Jerry's nose and something bit the back of his neck viciously. Jerry swatted it, feeling the small crushed form fall away and he knew he killed it, whatever it might have been. Both men decided it wasn't worth it and went back out into the sunlight where the less bloodthirsty bugs live. Unseen from all four people on the hillside was something large in the pines, having had its sleep disturbed, that kept moving away from them keeping the trees between itself and these noisy intruders.

Finally rid of the mosquitos and the most of the deer flies, Jerry just sat on a rock and sipped from his canteen. He kept his eyes on the area that he had been watching and just beyond where he was sure he had seen the movement, but still he saw nothing discernible. He decided it was his over active imagination. The plaster was usually dry in about 30 minutes but he would give it an hour. Jerry wanted the cast to be perfect and because it was so thin he did not want it to break apart on the walk back to the truck. Before he poured that casting he noticed that there were several large toes, one great toe and four smaller and there was a scar across the heel. The foot measured a full twelve inches across at the widest part just under the toes and the length of the foot was just over twenty inches. Jerry chuckled to himself, "this was one damned big farm boy." This thing had to be a minimum of eight or nine feet tall and weigh in at six or seven hundred pounds, he guessed from the depth of the print, about an inch and a half; but he would make more accurate calculations later. Those huge feet would act like snow shoes in the winter.

Frank broke Jerry's concentration, "What did you see in the brush?" he asked as Jerry was wrapping the plaster cast in his spare shirt.

"I'm almost sure I saw something moving, but it was just a dark mass, nothing distinct, but I also got this foreboding, chilling feeling down the back of my neck that we were being watched by something really nasty and dangerous."

"Um," was all Frank said, he had no words of comfort because he had experienced the same feelings of dread, like he was a small boy in the basement alone.

"Let's get moving, I want to take all the material back to the lab," yelled Jerry as he picked up his pack and headed back down the mountain. "Megan, I want those hair samples analyzed as soon as we hit the door," he did not even look back to see if anyone was following or protesting. It was time to go and he was the head of the project and that was that. Everyone fell into line and back down the mountain they all went.

CHAPTER 2

"**D**ANG, DR. J you've been admiring that cast ever since we got back to the truck. What the heck is so interesting?" asked the young Ranger.

"Well Bryant I'll tell yah," said Jerry with a visible twinkle in his eyes, "I find it interesting because it was not just put there for us to find and no one sent this one to me with a tall tale to go with it. I don't believe this is any kind of hoax. You know we have had some pretty outlandish jokes played on us in the past, now I found this and I believe it is genuine."

"How do you know that this particular foot print is so genuine?"

Turning it over Jerry ran his finger along the bottom of the casting, "do you see this scar on the heel? Do you see these wrinkles and calluses and the weather beaten lines all the way from the toes to the heel? There is way too much detail here. Look here, there is even a mole on the bottom of the great toe, see!" Jerry lifted it up and put it right in front of Bryant's eyes. This was probably not the best thing to do considering that Bryant was driving the truck. "The very first day out and we found something to really sink our teeth into," Jerry said still holding the cast up for Bryant's inspection. The truck weaved back and forth on the graveled mountain road.

"Hey! Dr. J you'd better take it easy," said the startled Bryant as they hit a really deep hole in the road that he might have missed if his vision had not been so impaired, causing them all to bounce up and grunt on downward impact with the hard seats, "I really do need to see the road."

"Oh yeah, sorry, I'll show it to you in better detail when we get back to the cabins," remarked Jerry as he pulled it back and there was a hint of disappointment in his tone. He brought out his magnifying glass while they bounced over the rough logging road and he tried to examine his precious find. Megan just clutched her pack in her lap and tried to relax even though they were being thrown all over the road by the rocks and the ruts as well as all over the double cab, seat belts or no seat belts. She glanced at the speedometer that registered 45 mph. that made her close her eyes. Had she been driving would have been doing no more than 25, just for safety's sake.

After about half an hour of teeth busting, bone jarring fun on the steep and winding logging road they finally hit the more maintained gravel road which, although it still growled under the tires, was somewhat smoother until they hit the water chatter ruts causing the truck to become a huge vibration machine. Bryant had accelerated to about 50 miles an hour as soon as they turned on to the better maintained road because he knew the road better, he said, although it seemed to Megan he was taking some of the corners on two wheels. After another 20 minutes of fishtailing in the deep gravel they finally made it back to the cabins where they had only begun to set up any sort of lab or testing facility. The lab, except for the electronic gear in one corner, looked more like the chemistry set her father had given Megan on her tenth birthday. It would do for what they were trying to accomplish, she thought, as she shrugged her shoulders and tossed her daypack into the corner, her sample already in hand. If there were any delicate measurements or something needing more precise readings, they could always go back to the Spokane area and use the campus facilities of Eastern Washington University, just south of Spokane in Cheney, Washington. In the past this makeshift set up had sufficed for all the preceding research teams so this team will just continue with the same stuff used for the past few years on this very poorly funded project. A project most of her colleagues thought was a joke and had taken every opportunity to let her know it.

Megan took the bottles with the hair samples and began to set them up for testing; to find out what type of animal they had come from or even human. She followed the current protocol by bringing up the data from every known type of fur or hair found in the northwest. She, when comparing the sample, found no matches initially. On a lark she turned on the old Geiger counter and waived the wand over the sampling. It registered 1.7 RADS. She did it again after taking off her wrist watch, just to be sure and it showed the same result. She showed her initial findings to Jerry. He just smiled.

It was pretty late before the two scientists finally got any sleep. Megan was very tired and had expected Jerry to put some moves on her. He had been giving her little side glances all day and she thought he had summoned the courage, but it would seem now that he had not garnered enough fortitude or he just was not interested. She would have turned him down just to toy with him and see how he would react. She was not terribly interested in summer flings anyway, even if the other person stirred her desires just a bit. But he hadn't, so she didn't, and they both got some sleep.

After breakfast the next morning Megan, in her baggiest pajamas, sat at the lab table rechecking her findings and decided to run a few more DNA tests on the hair samples. There was little doubt that these hair samples were not from human or northwest animals, at least not a known northwest animal. She was going to have to rule out animals of the world before they could be sure but the ancient laptop computer was still thinking about that part of it as she sipped her green tea. She lost herself in the aroma of the tea, the elixir of the Gods to the Chinese Emperors.

Coming out of the shower Jerry walked across the small room to the door of his room when he noticed that the answering machine was flashing with the number 3. He had not heard the telephone ring. He threw his towel over his shoulder and went to examine the telephone. The ringer had been turned off. After shooting a glance of disdain in the direction of his team member he turned the ringer back on, he replaced the headset in its cradle and pushed the button to listen to the messages.

The electronic voice droned, "You have three unheard messages. Message one, received at twelve thirty five a.m., "Jerry, if you're there pick up. OK! Pick up. OK! There has been another sighting on Seldom Seen Mountain. Yes, that really is the name of the mountain. Look at your map; you'll see a gray area due west of Ione called Stewart Meadow. Look due west of that meadow for the mountain. There is a good trail that goes to the top so I can meet you at the cabin by eight thirty and we can be there by noon, if we hurry. Oh yeah, this is Leonard, Frank Leonard. Thanks, bye."

"Message two, six thirty a.m., this is Frank again, did you get my message? Where the hell are you two? Call me and we'll get going."

"Message three, seven fifteen a.m., if you two don't call me pretty soon you can find your own way up that trail. Confirm please. Soon! (Beep) end of messages.

Jerry just stood there looking at his lovely colleague. She paid no attention to him. "Meg, I really wish you wouldn't turn off the ringer on this telephone. I told you I'll get up and answer it, day or night," said Jerry looking at the clock with the cock pheasant on it. "It is just a couple of minutes past eight I'd better call him. Let's get dressed we are running out of time."

"If you're going to be in that kind of mood today you can go by yourself. I have other work to do here anyway," she said still not looking at him. She was staring out the kitchen window nibbling on a sour dough English muffin with cream cheese. She could see his reflection in the window and she was admiring, just a little, his muscles and his aging six pack. He was not bad for a stuffy professor. He had the abs of a Greek statue and the arms and shoulders good enough to be a pro wrestler or pro football player.

Jerry, not wanting to start a fight or cause friction on their second day together decided to retreat, "OK, I'll see you later then." He called Frank to confirm he did want to go and then he disappeared into his room to finish dressing.

Megan really had expected him to protest a little. That's fine with her; she was still playing him and trying to figure him out. In her mind she would have him panting to be with her in less than a month and then she would be ruling the project. Her way of ruling the project would be the way many famous women had been ruling countries of hundreds of years, that which made her feminine. She didn't use it often but this time she had made a conscious decision to wrap this guy up in it and keep him there just for fun. Besides, a little tension relieving recreational sex might be OK as long as they did not get too involved emotionally. She still did not like short term flings but this, she thought, would be purely business. She wanted to be the project director even if it had to be by proxy. She would be the captain's lady. She snapped out of her little daydream when the forestry truck pulled up and Jerry exited out the door without a word or even a backward glance.

Just after 11:30 a.m. Jerry and Frank stepped out the forestry suburban and walked up a small dry creek bed into a stand of Douglas fir that the loggers had left alone. Slightly in the lead Frank looked over his shoulder at Jerry and then crouched down to a kneeling position with his back to Jerry by the sandy shoulder of the creek bed waiting for him to catch up.

"So what's the big deal here, Len?" asked Jerry as he crouched next to the Ranger.

"Look at this," replied Frank, his excitement was almost too much for him to keep inside, "look at this track. There are several more headed up the soft dirt following the creek," he pointed in the general direction, more a wave with the back of his hand than an actual pointing finger. "These might be more interesting than the one you got yesterday."

"OK, let's get a cast of one or two of the really good ones and take them back to the lab. We need to take some digital pictures of the rest of them, close up and detailed for computer analysis. You are correct sir, these are good," replied Jerry as he began digging out his casting material containers; he had brought three jars this time just in case. "You know how to do these casts don't you?" he said handing one of the containers to Frank.

"I believe I can figure it out but before we start this dirty work I've got something else I want to show you," said Frank reaching into his shirt pocket with his free hand and pulling out a photograph, "the hiker who took this said he almost crapped his pants on the spot and so will you when you see it."

Feeling a great deal of skepticism Jerry reached over and took the picture. He looked at it but did not say a word. Jerry simply reached into his daypack and brought out his largest magnifying glass and quietly examined the picture, "you say he almost dumped a load in his pants? I have no doubt that he probably did need clean underwear after seeing this first hand. How did he get this printed so fast?"

"The guy says he is a bird watcher. He likes to see the pictures he takes of the birds immediately, large and in full HD color so he has a laptop and a color printer in his vehicle. He printed it in his vehicle on the trail. What do you think it is?" there was a hint of a smirk on Frank's face that slowly expanded into a broad grin.

Ever the scientist, "I am not sure," said Jerry turning the picture in several different angles, "it seems to have the wrong shape for a bear, the profile of the head is all wrong and there also is no evidence of claws; I see fingers and hands. The digits are a little stunted and deformed for the size of the forearm but they are definitely not paws like a bear would have. The head is neither ape like, nor bear like, something in between. At first glance I thought it might be a deformed gorilla, but its posture is too upright." Jerry finally smiled a little and

Frank began giggly like a ten-year-old schoolboy; his eyes were positively glowing as he deftly poured his part of the compound into the footprint before him. "It is either a very elaborate hoax of a man in a furry suit or we may actually have some hard evidence here," said Jerry. He was thinking out loud, but the more he studied the picture the more he convinced himself that someone was probably playing a trick on them. Hell, it could even be Ranger Leonard in the suit. "What is that in the right hand?"

"The bird guy, his name is Steve something, said it is a multi-grain breakfast bar that the thing took right out of his hands and just walked away, eating contentedly. He thought it was a bear at first too, but he thought fast enough to get his camera up and take a flash photo. He said the most amazing thing happened when he took the picture. Steve said the thing vanished like it was made of smoke. He also said that he was going to make another copy, of this and some other shots, and get it to the newspapers and claim the reward. He is convinced this proves the existence of Big Foot and he wants the one hundred grand." Frank gasp just slightly because in his excitement he had forgotten to breathe and his lungs were empty. "Here let me have that," said Frank panting slightly as he took the other two bottles of casting compound and poured them into two other footprints. He could see that Jerry was too engrossed in the picture to remember to pour the other molds.

"Newspapers, that's not good. How much is that reward again?"

"One hundred thousand dollars," said Frank looking at Jerry with a question in his eyes.

"I don't think I can match that kind of money just to keep

this out of the papers," Jerry was still thinking out loud, "we know however that it did not vanish because those foot prints go down the creek bed a little and then straight up the hill and judging from the space between those prints it was on the dead run," Jerry said as he lifted the first cast that had been poured and wrapped it carefully in some bubble wrap that he had acquired from unpacking the equipment.

"Wait a minute; let me see that," said Jerry, "this is the same foot print we got yesterday from Huckleberry. There is the mole under the great toe. This really is something to get excited about. We might actually have something here." Jerry was smiling but there was no mirth in his eyes, his brain was going into hyper drive, "We have got to do two things, the first is find bird man Steve something and keep him from going to the newspapers and second we should set up a base camp around here somewhere and really start looking this place over. I don't know where I am going to get a hundred grand though, this whole project was funded at just under two hundred thousand and none of it in a place where I can lay my hands on any large amount of cash but, I will think of something, come on let's get moving."

The two men gathered up the other two castings, packed them very gingerly into the bubble wrap and then placed them ever so gently in some foam lined boxes, also from the unpacking, in the truck. Jerry thanked Frank for doing the other two footprints although Jerry could not remember Frank taking the jars and pouring them. Still scratching his head the two men got into the truck and drove back in the direction of the cabins.

CHAPTER 3

MEGAN HAD BEEN working in the small, very make shift, lab with the radio on in the background, for no other reason that just something to break up all the quiet and creepy stillness that seemed to surround the old cabins where their little headquarters was now located. She had been testing and retesting the hair follicles DNA profile against everything listed in the computer and it still had not come up with a match. She was pretty sure what the hair was NOT but she could not be sure of what it was, exactly. There were some human and simian similarities but nothing was coming together. For some reason when the news came on the radio it caught her attention enough to actually listen to what the newscaster was saying.

"In late breaking news today in the Colville area a farmer, Mr. Ed Bjornson, reported that two of his cattle had been mutilated. Their eyes, tongues and hearts had been, in his opinion, surgically removed and there was no blood in either bovine. The police have brought in a veterinarian to do an autopsy on the hapless animals. In a related story, residents of Addy, a small town southeast of Colville, have reported seeing a UFO formation of five separate light clusters flying low over the direction of the Bjornson farm and the city of Colville. Authorities are looking into the matter. First reports are calling it some sort of mass hysteria. The personnel from the U.S. Air Force survival school, called upon for their expert opinion are giving the usual cover up story that that it was combination of weather balloons and the Northern Lights. This reporter is reserving an opinion for further developments. The weather for the rest of the week..." she reached over and turned down the radio.

Megan quickly reached for something to write on and wrote Bjornson slash Addy on a sticky note and pasted it to the top of her notebook page. This was something they would all need to check out, she mused. Then she returned to her original task, but just as Megan was dropping precisely 10 drops of a golden liquid into a test tube with one of the hair samples, there was a loud knock at the door. Megan bristled a little at the interruption but put the test tube into a holder and went to see who was at the door. Pulling the creaking old weather beaten door open, having to lift up a little to clear the rug, Megan at first thought it was a salesperson. There on the porch stood a woman, around 35 or 40, smiling at her. She was loaded down with several suitcases and there was a huge pile of instrument hard cases stacked beside her on the porch. This woman brushed past her and set down all the bags and then, without a word, went back out for the rest without any type of explanation, just wry little smile. Finally when there was a small mountain of equipment cases and suitcases piled in the middle of the room did the woman stop and, taking a deep breath, smile a wide photo shoot smile and extend her hand. Megan slowly extended her hand, with some obvious trepidation.

"Hi, I'm Lisa Shields. I'm out here from the University of Michigan," her smile changed to a look of puzzlement, "obviously you were not expecting me, hum. Didn't Jerry say anything? No, of course he forgot to say anything. I am sorry for barging in like this but my ride was leaving and I had to get all the stuff in here before that idiot of a taxi driver went back to Spokane."

"Lisa Shields," Megan was not the best in the world with names, titles or places, in fact she really sucked at Trivial Pursuit, but she was rolling that name around her brain like she was polishing a diamond, "you're neurobiology, microbiology and genetics aren't you?"

"No I'm English with a few drops of Irish and a little Sioux Indian on my father's side," she said taking Megan's hand again and shaking it gently, then letting it go like Megan had Leprosy.

"OK smart ass, you know I meant those are your fields of study," said Megan wiping her hand on her pajamas because Lisa's hand had been really sweaty.

"Yup I'm a smart ass. Would you mind letting me know who you are or should I just call you "meat head" or "baggy pants" or something?"

"I'm Megan Hanley, Doctor of Anthropology from Washington State University. I usually go by Meg rather than meat head," Megan decided she might tolerate Lisa, for a while anyway. Lisa was not sure how to take this because there was no jollity in Meg's eyes when she smiled at her, just leering suspicion of some sort.

Always one to get right to the point Lisa jumped right in with, "Where will I be bunking? Would you like me to bunk here in the lab or do we girls have our own little hideaway?"

Actually she had planned on bunking in with Jerry to make this summer more tolerable. She and Jerry had been on again off again lovers for many years. The distance between Michigan and Washington State was considerable. She had quickly agreed when Jerry had suggested this summer project. Although nearly forty years old Lisa had aged like a fine violin, but one not played too often. She was slim, but not skinny, her legs still turned heads whether in shorts or a flowing skirt and her double D's were twin peaks that gossip and legends were made of. Her short auburn hair set off a beautiful complexion.

"I guess, unless Jerry has other ideas, you'll have to bunk in with me in the cabin next door. The boy himself bunks in back," said Megan gesturing with her thumb over her right shoulder. "The little house in back, actually two chemical toilets are between the cabins marked his and hers. These rustic little cabins do have running water but just sinks, showers and no other bathroom facilities."

"That's fine. Thank you, Meg. May I say those are very becoming pajamas? Who is your wardrobe designer?" remarked Lisa as she picked up her suitcases and was going out the back door, "and those slippers are just what they will be wearing on Martha's Vineyard this year at the height of the season."

Megan could still hear her laughing, about something, in the cabin next door. Grabbing the outside of each leg of her baggy pajamas Megan pulled them out and looked down at her fuzzy teddy bear, anniversary issue, slippers and wondered what was wrong with them. They kept her feet warm. She had already decided she was not going to wear anything sexy or see through for anyone, at least not yet. She went back to her analysis of the hair, "Hey, Lisa, if you ever get finished unpacking there may be some stuff here in the lab you want to look at," Megan yelled through the open, screened, window.

"Thank you, I will be right over," came a lilting reply, like a song, but the sarcasm could not be mistaken, "I am going to take a quick shower. Can you give me thirty minutes?"

"It will take you that long to cake on your makeup," mumbled Megan. Although Med did have to admit that Lisa was pretty well preserved for forty or fifty. Meg shrugged her shoulders and went back to recording her findings. She finished her notes and suddenly jumped up and headed for the "girls" cabin. Lisa was in the shower singing, or trying to sing, some show tune from Cats or something. Megan wanted to put cotton in her ears but she was dressing, in a hurry, so she could change and get back over to the lab before Lisa was out of the shower. Megan was not going to look like the house dog when the boys came back. Megan put on a fresh, crisp pair of faded jeans that were just a bit tight here and there; a khaki shirt that she had tailored to fit in the right places. She replaced her warm slippers with her clean pair of hiking boots. She had time to quickly run a brush through her dark hair and put on a baseball cap from WSU, putting her pony tail through the hole in the back of the cap. She then ran back to the lab. She felt better now, although she had really been comfortable in her first ensemble she refused to look frumpy.

In about thirty minutes, as promised, Lisa came into the lab looking like an ad for an outdoor magazine. She had on light green bush pants, also a little tight, and a matching light green shirt, tailored like Megan's to fit just right. Each woman sized up the other without commenting. "May I see what you are working on Meg?" asked Lisa. She secretly decided to check Megan's credentials and abilities.

Megan sensed immediately that this was some sort of assessment of her abilities so they began testing one another for competency in the lab, competency of the job that lay ahead and probably this would be where the rivalry would begin to grow, if there was going to be a rivalry, to see who would be the alpha female of this pack.

"We went hiking around Huckleberry Mountain and Profanity Peak yesterday because a hiker saw something. While we were checking some interesting footprints and we made a cast, which is on the desk over there, Jerry found these hair samples on a bush," explained Megan watching for any reaction from Lisa. Lisa showed no emotion, she remained cold and clinical.

"What kind of analysis have you done, so far?" asked Lisa as she picked up a test tube, held it to the overhead light and shook it a little.

"I have run all the standard chemical tests; I've examined it through the microscope, the spectro-analyser and run DNA tests that so far I can't tell you what it is or where it is from but I can say what it is not. It is not a hair sample from a northwest animal that has had this type testing done on it since scientists began keeping records. I think the most interesting thing is that it is slightly radioactive, more so that the surrounding area anyway."

"Thank you. I think you have been watching too much science fiction or space programs. Wasn't the spectro-analyser on one of those T.V. series space programs?" Lisa looked at Meg and smiled, "may I have a look please at the sample in the microscope and then look over your DNA findings?"

"Yes Frau Doctor, the slide is still there. Just turn on the light switch," said Megan as she got up to pour another cup of tea. "Would you like some green tea? I have kept the water hot for moisture in the air and to keep the tea flowing."

"Yes, I would love some," said Lisa as she twisted the dial on the ancient microscope. She had not used one like this since she was in grad school. This is going to be a primitive expedition, she thought, looking at the hair. "Just for the record that is Fraulein Doctor. Did you find any odd chemicals or substances in any of these strands? Did the dye tell you anything? Were you able to isolate where the radioactivity was coming from?"

"Well, if that old computer ever gets around to showing us I'll let you know. Initially I thought there was an odd color in the first test so I put the data into the computer. We'll have to see if that poor old thing can sift through the data in our lifetime. It is currently on dial-up which really slows things down. Would you like anything in your tea?"

"No thanks, I drink it straight for the medicinal refreshment quality," said Lisa taking the cup of steaming tea from Megan. "What data have you gotten from the DNA sequencing? Have you had a chance to do that yet, or am I just in time to give you a hand?"

"Well we are still waiting for some data from the computer that I have nicknamed the ancient oracle, but we can do another DNA sequencing if you like. I couldn't hurt anything at this point.

"Jerry told me about this old stuff we would be working with so I took the liberty of bringing some equipment from my lab in Michigan that might help. I have an up-to-date laptop with satellite interface capability so we can use the ancient oracle to keep our records on, if you like. We have some room over in the corner so why don't we get it set up and really tackle his hair problem. I cannot identify it either and now my curiosity is really getting the best of me," said Lisa, the last words trailing off as she went over to un-stack the mountain of hard cases still in the middle of the room.

That evening the two scientists had finished setting up the instruments and the more up-to-date lab gear that Lisa had brought with her. Neither of them had even thought about food but there was a nagging hunger beginning to sneak in, making them somewhat edgy. It became even more protracted when they heard the vehicle pull up out front. Megan suddenly remembered it was her night to cook. While Meg went looking through the cupboards for a can to open, Lisa went out on the porch to greet Jerry.

The Ranger took a double take as he got out of the driver's side. His initial reaction was WOW! Jerry got out and went right for the rear of the truck without a glance at who was on the porch. He was too interested in getting the specimens and casts into the lab. With box in hand and one foot on the steps he did finally look up. He almost dropped his precious box when he saw who was standing there and how good she looked. He was genuinely happy to see Lisa.

"It is about time you noticed me," she said with a mirthless grin, "you haven't changed a bit, you still can't take your mind off work long enough to say hello to an old friend."

Setting the box on the top step of the porch, Jerry swept her into his arms and gave her a long, lingering and slightly hard kiss. This was not a peck to say hello to an old friend, this was a kiss promising some very interesting future nights, and it was a kiss to say how happy he truly was to see her and how much he had missed her. They enjoyed the kiss but Lisa, now feeling a little embarrassed, broke the kiss and pushed him away slightly, to look him in the eyes.

"Well, I am happy to see you too! Been in the woods all day have you soldier boy and feeling your oats," she said somewhat out of breath. She leaned back against the porch railing.

"I am so happy to see you. I wasn't sure you were coming at all. How long has it been, about three years this time?" Jerry asked grabbing her again and holding her tight against him.

"Closer to four years," said Lisa over his shoulder. She could feel something else that told her he had missed her a great deal. "Jerry, it is great to see you. I never expected a greeting like this, but let's get your items unloaded and we will have time, later, to have a little home coming get together, OK?" Pushing away she bent down and picked up the box and with a quick smile to the Ranger went inside the cabin.

Jerry, a little embarrassed but smiling, went back to get the rest of his stuff. Frank, who was carrying a box too, had waited at the bottom of the star for the greeting to get over so he could take his stuff inside. The Ranger smiled; this meant that there really wasn't anything between Megan and the professor, so he might just give the "Leggy professor" a whirl.

CHAPTER 4

AFTER A SUMPTUOUS meal of grilled turkey paddies, green beans, bread and butter pickles and sourdough bread two of the researchers retired to the porch to sit in the cool night air of this mountain environment. Lisa sipped her diet drink while Jerry drank a cold beer, "damn, that's good," he said quietly, he had been looking forward to an ice-cold beer all day. He was enjoying it almost as much as he was looking at his companion. She looked good enough to have for dessert, which was precisely his plan.

Lisa, for her part, was not at all opposed to the idea of having each other for dessert; she could see a look in his eyes that she had seen in him, and a few other men, before. She lowered her eyes and smiled to herself, "So tell me about the point of this project, Jerry?"

He reached over, lifted her head gently by the chin and looked into those beautiful eyes. He did not want to talk about work; he wanted to throw her over his shoulder and head for his room. This was no time to talk about the project. There would be plenty of time for that in the morning and days to come. Now was the time to rekindle an old relationship and make it new again.

Jerry stood up; reached for her hand and she reached for his, "Let's talk about work later. Right now all I can think about is you."

"OK," she said, "why fight it. You can brief me tomorrow on some of my "other" duties. Megan isn't going to be jealous is she? I mean you two haven't…" her voice trailed off as they went through the door.

"No, Megan and I haven't done anything. She is just a colleague nothing more. All I have been able to think about is you," he said opening the creaking inner sanctum door to his bedroom. "Well it was mostly true," he thought to himself.

"Oh right, and I believe you too!" Lisa said with a smile. As the door closed she said, "I hope that bed doesn't squeak as much as that stupid door." There was no more talking to be heard only the audible click of the door lock.

Megan and Frank had been doing the dishes and were planning on joining Jerry and Lisa on the porch for some refreshment and to take in some of the cool night air. Looking over her shoulder Megan saw the two go into Jerry's room and heard the door lock. The cabin was not that big or well insulated and the wooden walls echoed the slightest sound. "Well Frank it looks as though those two are set for the night," she said knowing almost exactly what Frank was thinking and probably would say next. Part of her hoped he would try something and a small part of her was perhaps more eager than she was outwardly showing, but then again she had rebuffed him a few times and knew he wouldn't have the nerve to make much of a move. "Men are always so predictable," she thought to herself. She was desperately trying to think of something clever to beat him to the punch, to let him down easy, but not scare him completely away. Megan felt like a cat with a catnip mouse just out of the package. She finished the last of the silverware, rinsed it and put it in the drainer. "I'll see you on the porch," she said grabbing a cold soda form the small refrigerator and going quickly out the screen door.

"OK," was all Frank had a chance to say before she was out the door. His mind had gone into overdrive trying to figure a way to get Megan interested enough to consider him. He finished drying the silverware and put it all in the drawer. He snapped the wet towel once and threaded one end through the handle of the oven door and pulled it down so the two ends were even. He opened the refrigerator, reached in and found a long neck, popped the top and stepped outside onto the porch. Megan was seated in the chair as far away from Jerry's room as the wood porch would let her, laying back slightly with her head on the back of the aluminum chair staring up into the sky.

"Do you want me to leave?" asked Frank. It was all he could come up with at the moment. He did want her to know he was interested but he did not want her to think him desperate either. Frank had "been around the block and seen a few calf roping's" and he had initially thought that Megan may have been thinking of putting the feminine whammy on Doctor Jerry, but those plans were now out the window because Lisa seemed to have sewn up the market. Frank was watching her face for any reaction to the creaking bed, but he saw very little.

"No, stay a while if you like," she said moving only her eyes to look in his direction. She caught him staring and she smiled, "Frank, I really hate playing games, don't you?"

At first he thought here we go with the let's be friends speech. He had no idea how to answer that question. He knew he had only a 50/50 chance to blow the whole thing so he did the only thing he could think of, he hesitated.

She smiled, "Frank relax. I have no intention of dragging you off to my room or you dragging me, so relax; even though this mountain air makes me as horny as a heifer sometimes." She was still looking at him and he had to shift his position a little in the chair to be more comfortable. She found it amusing and now she was feeling playful and wanted to tease him a little just to see him squirm. She took another sip of her cola and noticed a slight breeze with a strange musty but flowery flavored mist moving across the porch. Megan closed her eyes and then opened them slowly. There seemed to be a different man sitting on the porch with her now, one with more appeal and bringing out some of her most guarded emotions. "Frank," she said, "how long does a girl have to wait in these mountains before a guy will stop wishing and actually make a move?" She was surprised at her sudden boldness, but she was feeling "very" playful all of a sudden and it seemed like a good idea now to entice him. The direct approach usually got some type of action whether it be caveman style or running for cover.

Frank almost dropped the long neck, which he set on the porch next to the leg of the chair, "Not long at all," he said grabbing her hand and gently tugging her to her feet as he stood. If he had not been moving a little slowly he would have missed her mouth entirely. He kissed the side of her mouth and then immediately repositioned and kissed her firmly on target.

At first Megan was not sure if she wanted to respond but there seemed an actual spark passing between their lips and she, to her own amazement, did respond in spite of some misgivings that she had never been this wanton or ready for action, more of a slow burner. He held her tight and tightened up just a bit more. She could feel his manhood pressing against her. She was impressed so she did something that made him jump slightly; she grabbed his ass with one hand and pulled him closer. He responded to the game by grabbing hers with both hands and they ground together for several long moments. They stopped kissing, a little out of breath, and still clung together. "Frank is this true attraction or are we giving in to the panic of last call at the bar?" Before he could answer the question they melted into another lingering kiss, initiated by Megan. They were both unaware that the musky, flower mist was clinging all around the cabin and seemed to further intoxicate them both. Neither had any idea it was a very powerful, natural, not from this world, aphrodisiac.

"I don't know," he said not wanting to loosen his grip, "you knew I was attracted to you. Are you attracted to me or just having a little fun?" He kissed her again before she could answer. She responded in kind. Her flame had been kindled and she instantly made up her mind she thought he had asked a very honest question and considering where his manhood was currently grinding away and her responding with each push, she pulled away from the kiss and whispered in his ear, after she playfully bit it, "I wanted to have a little fun and see what might develop. You have got to understand I am not this easy but now you have started something you've got to finish," she said as she grabbed him by the hand and led him across the small patch of land between the two cabins, up the steps and quickly inside. "Yes sir, you started it and now you've got to finish it, even if it takes all night."

"Oh, poor me," said Frank, "you know what Smokey Bear

says don't you, put out all fires." The door closed as Megan reached for Franks belt buckle.

Unseen by any of the participants now in amorous pursuit, a huge shadowy figure moved back into the wood line and disappeared when the cabin door closed.

CHAPTER 5

THE BREAKFAST TABLE was quiet except for all the eating going on, forks hitting plates, yummy sounds with cups and glasses put back on the table. Megan and Lisa had cooked up waffles, scrambled eggs and sausages. All four people had healthy appetites and were making the most of the hot and quite delicious food.

Not one person had both hands above the table and there were a few giggles and knowing looks and a lot of smiling. Lisa, still curious about the project, between mouthfuls asked, "Jerry, now that the sleeping arrangements have been decided would you please tell me more about this project? I mean, why the hell would a university fund a research project looking for Big Foot?"

Squeezing her hand, under the table, Jerry answered, "There have been a lot of sightings in this area lately and of course the legends from the Indians to the pioneers fill volumes with their accounts. They, the University, had some extra fund money and the Dean is a nut on the subject, so here we are. Dean Connelly is getting too old for the field but he is still very interested. The one thing I did have to talk to him out of was bringing a bunch of students. I wanted to relax instead of herding undergraduates around the woods," he said stabbing a piece of sausage and then a bit of waffle and shoving it in his mouth. Jerry now reached for Lisa's leg but she had other ideas at the moment.

"Whoa, we've got work to do. We can't spend the whole day romping here at the cabin. We have a couple of months, don't we, so let's not wear out a good thing," said Lisa as she demurely pulled her robe back over her legs. She also quit holding his hand and moved her arm up to the table.

Similarly Megan and Frank were "playing" a little. "I think that is a good idea, we have time for things," said Megan straightening her own robe and closing the top just a little, also giving a little furtive look around the table but kept eating.

"What we have here, ladies and gentlemen, is what is known as a hirsute," said Lisa, wiping the corners of her mouth with a paper towel and smiled.

Frank looked at Megan, then the others, but he just had to ask, "OK I'll bite what the hell is a hirsute?"

Megan sat back in her chair, took a drink of her warm green tea, and smiled just a little, "What the lady is trying to tell you is that we have a manlike animal walking around that is covered or coated with hair. It is usually a term used to describe the Yeti in the Himalayas, but I guess it could work here."

"Exactly," added Lisa, "the people in these parts have been seeing something that they think looks hairy and manlike. Jerry has some good footprint impressions that discount a bear walking on its hind legs, which bears cannot do for any distance anyway. Megan, you have those hair samples that have no reference to any animal species, at least on this planet."

Turning to Jerry she asked, "Where does that leave us and where, and how, do you want to continue this investigation professor?" slapping his wandering hand again.

Jerry leaned back in his chair and reached over to the stove to get the simmering pot of coffee. Bringing it back he pours a half cup of the aromatic liquid, "That leaves us with getting our butts out into the woods and doing a lot more investigation. We don't have enough data yet or hard evidence to make any sort of conclusions. We've only been here two days."

Frank got up and began clearing the table, "You folks are really serious about this aren't you?" He asked as he stacked the dishes and began running hot water in the sink, "I'm already, mostly, dressed. So I'll clean up while the rest of you get ready. Where are we going Jerry, same place?"

"Yup," said Jerry as he and Lisa went into his room and closed the door. Lisa emerged a moment later still in her robe carrying her clothes and heading for the cabin next door where Megan had already gone. Lisa's clothes were still in the girl's cabin.

Just as Frank had finished the dishes and was putting them in the drainer Megan and Lisa came back dressed for a day in the woods, and both, in his humble opinion, were ready for the cover of any outdoor magazine. Jerry came out a couple of minutes later, throwing his daypack on the floor with a loud clunk. They all clustered around the computer that had been running information all night. Just then Megan remembered and located the sticky note she had written the day before.

"I wrote this note yesterday while I was listening to the radio. There is this guy Bjornson, I think his first name is Ed,

41

over around Addy, in the Colville area, who reported a cattle mutilation yesterday. It was just a snippet of a news item but there was something about seeing UFO's the night before by bunch of people in the area, four or five light clusters. The Air Force is claiming it is a hoax or mass hysteria, or something, but it might be worth our looking into it. Perhaps there was a landing in the area where the dead animals were and some hard evidence for a change," said Megan looking at each person in the room with her eyes finally stopping with Jerry.

Jerry was busy tapping on the computer keyboard and kept muttering something about out dated equipment. He grabbed the mouse and clicked it two or three times and then went back to the key board and hit the enter button hard with one finger and the keyboard almost leapt off the table, "This thing still does not have any useable data. It is still processing something and it will not respond at all so we'll just have to let it run while we're gone. What was that, Bjornson over in Addy? Let's get over there before they trample all the useable evidence into oblivion. Why didn't you say something last night about this Megan?"

"Excuse me!" she said hefting her own rucksack on one shoulder, "I believe you were a little distracted to work or drive over to Addy, so give me a break!"

Jerry shot a glance to Lisa, who just shrugged her shoulders, "Let's get moving then," he said as he was going out the door with the others following in behind.

Frank fired up the government Suburban, "We'll have to go over the Flowery Trail to get over to Addy. It is the quickest way," he said as he stepped on the gas throwing gravel against the chemical toilets and the east end of the two cabins.

CHAPTER 6

THE TEAM FINALLY got over the mountains to the Chewelah side and out to Addy. It was nearly 1300 and it was getting hot. They stopped at the little hardware store, grocery store in the town of Addy to get directions to the Bjornson farm then drove the three or four miles out there. The directions consisted of go to the old barn about half-mile out of town, turn left at the old creek bed (they believed it was the old Arnold place so it may say Arnold road). Go about three miles and you will see the Smyth Hereford ranch; go another half-mile, then turn left right on a the very next dirt road with the red mail box. Even with these explicit directions they arrived, in a cloud of billowing dust off the lightly graveled dirt road, onto the creosoted road leading to the farm house. They immediately saw that there was at least one other government vehicle and a news van, with its antennae up. The Forest Service vehicle was greeted by a young 3 stripper airman with a .45 caliber side arm on his pistol belt and then by the Bjornson's dog that looked like a border collie with one blue eye and one brown eye and gray patch across its forehead.

The airman, whose name tag said "Taylor", at first, waived

them to stop and then seeing the government plates waived them through. He waved and smiled at Megan who returned his smile, half-heartedly, and nodded her head. After they drove past, "He's a confident fellow isn't he", remarked Megan that drew a chuckle from everyone.

Frank pulled the suburban around by the pole building that seemed to serve as the farm's main garage, turned off the engine and they all piled out and headed toward the house. An Air Force Captain, whose name tag said "Chapman" immediately came out of the house and tried to block their way at the gate to the yard.

Frank obviously bristled at this attempt, "my name is Frank Leonard, and I am the Head Forest Ranger in this area. This is Dr. Jerry Paulson, from Eastern Washington University; Dr. Megan Hanley from Washington State University; Dr. Lisa Shields from the University of Michigan. I have been tasked to help them in investigating any type of unusual activity in the vicinity of eastern Washington and northern Idaho. We are all here on federal government business to study…"

At this point Captain Chapman held up his hand to stop the introductions and speech, "it is very nice to meet you all but I must insist that you have no business here. This is a U.S. Air force project and we have authority," he said turning his head to the side and closing his eyes, as if to emphasize his point.

"If you would let me finish, Captain, these professors are here on a government grant, therefore government business, to study this type of phenomena and have the full authority of the Department of the Interior," said Frank, there was an edge creeping into his voice, "this is my forest and my jurisdiction. The U.S. Air Force does not have the authority to keep us out of any investigation that we may wish to conduct, in fact I will get the authorities out here to arrest you and escort you and your little group off this site. May I remind you that your survival school is on Forestry land," Frank finished and he was looking steadily into the Captain's eyes whose head had snapped back to the front. Neither man was giving an inch of ground.

Just then a "Full Bird" Colonel came out of the house, "Gentlemen, there is no need for such bristling, I am sure we can work together. Captain Chapman, these are not tourists they are researchers and may proceed," he said. His name tag said "Petrovitch".

"Yes sir," was all the Captain said as he stood aside and opened the gate to let everyone into the yard and make their way to the house. Frank kept eye contact with Chapman while his three companions passed between them and did not break contact until Megan grabbed his arm and escorted him inside. It looked to her like the main event was about to start but they were not going to their separate corners. Frank was ready to "throw down" with the butt-head Captain; he did not like him or his attitude; a decision he made when he first saw him. In Frank's nostrils was that musky, flowery smell he remembered from last night and his blood was ready to boil, an instant flame like striking a match.

Mr. and Mrs. Bjornson were inside seated at the kitchen table. The farmer got up and there were introductions made all around and then he finally introduced his wife Janice. Colonel Petrovitch asked if he might remain and Jerry said, "Of course," and then Jerry asked if the scene of the event was cordoned off or if there had been people trampling all through where the animals were found.

The Colonel answered quickly, "Well, the news crew is out there on the edge of the site right now. I told them to be very careful and not go inside the taped off area. We are expecting our own investigation crew out here very soon," he said as his eyes darted to the faces of the team to catch their reactions, "so we have not let very many people out there." The Colonel glanced out the window, "they seem to be on their way back."

"Would you tell me please why a news crew gets to go in and your watch dog Captain stops official investigators?" asked Frank, his eyes flashing enough to make the Colonel react by stepping back.

"Captain Chapman objected to them as well, Head Ranger," said Petrovitch, "I think he was taking some frustration out on you and your team here, I am sorry."

Frank audibly growled but Megan grabbed his arm and looked into his eyes. The musky, flowery smell was still in her system too and she communicated her feelings with her hands caressing his arm. Frank mellowed somewhat and as a couple they moved away from the Air Force personnel that Frank so obviously did not like.

Jerry turned to look outside and saw two people walking toward the house just to the left of the barn and then turned his attention back to Ed and Janice Bjornson, "What did you see last night, or day, when it all happened? Oh, sorry, do you mind if we record this interview for our research?" he asked as he sat at the table.

"No, go ahead. We have already been recorded twice this morning," quipped Ed.

Jerry pulled the small recorder out of his daypack and, pushing the record button, set it on the table. "Mr. and Mrs.

Ed Bjornson, Addy, Washington," he said glancing at his watch, "it is 1345 on June 11th. Thank you sir, and ma'am, now can you tell me please what happened?"

"Well, last evening the wife and I were on the porch just enjoying the cooling down and we saw some lights moving in the sky. At first I thought it was a plane or something but there was no noise to speak of, just a low humming sound. Then the lights changed to, well, a "V" formation and then stopped and I mean totally stopped in the sky. I rocked forward to look up at them; there were five distinct balls of light changing colors from white to yellow to orange to a real bright blue."

"Could you see any particular shape to the objects or just the lights?" asked Jerry.

"No, I could only see the lights. It was really dark outside, about 1030 or 11 o'clock."

"OK, then what happened?" asked Lisa, her interest was growing. She sat down next to Jerry and smiled at the Bjornson's putting them a little more at ease.

"Then the lights hovered for a few minutes and began to get closer. All of the lights seemed to be coming down very slowly, so slowly it was hard to see, but the lights did seem to get bigger. Then two of the lights, one from each end of the top of the "V" broke away and flew up higher and hovered again. Well, the other three kept slowly going down and ended up in the trees just on the other side of the pasture, east of the barn," he pointed toward where the news crew had been walking from, "and they went behind the tree line, setting that whole stand of trees aglow."

"What did you do then, sir?" asked Lisa, kind of taking over for Jerry without asking, which drew a furtive glance from him but no comment.

"Janice and I just sat and watched. We did not really know what to do or if we should call the sheriff, but we did not know if the sheriff would believe our story so we just kept watching. Sometimes the survival school helicopters fly around here and land, doing field exercises," said Ed, with Janice nodding in agreement. "I was in the Army, in Vietnam, and I just figured that the survival school was out there playing around, but we usually get a call for something like that. The really eerie thing was that there was almost no sound, just that humming sound, like a generator a long way off in the distance. Choppers usually make a hell of a racket, but I have heard that the military have these quiet stealth helicopters; the school has never used anything but Huey's to my knowledge. Finally, we heard a hissing sound, something like a hydraulic brake being released or a release of steam, something like that, so I decided to call the sheriff."

"What did you do Mrs. Bjornson?" interjected Megan who was also feeling the zeal of the investigation.

"Please call me Janice," she said with a demure smile, "I just sat there and watched as Ed went inside to make the call," she said, "and then I saw something moving between me and the lights. I thought that our cattle were moving in there or something, I really couldn't be sure. Anyway, the lights toned down a little bit, like someone dimming the headlights on a truck and there was a lot more movement. I got a little scared and called to Ed to come back outside. The Air Force usually don't use anything when they are doing landings except small red landing lights and then turn them off when they're on the ground; I've seen them do that lots of times right out in our pasture. But like Ed said they always call so we can get our cows out of the pasture."

"What scared you, Janice?" asked Jerry.

"The shadows against the lights did not look like cows or horses, not four legged, two legged things walking around. It is difficult to tell at this distance so I asked Ed to bring the binoculars."

"What did you see specifically?" asked Jerry as he looked over at his recorder to make sure there was still tape recording what Janice was telling him.

"I am not sure what it was but there were more than one and they were kind of running all over the place. Ed looked through the binoculars but he couldn't make anything out distinctly, just a lot of moving around," she paused to ask, "Would anyone like some lemonade or coffee?" There were two or three yeses to the lemonade so she got up to fix it and kept talking as she moved around the kitchen. "Those lights were in the trees for about 15 or 20 minutes, and then the sheriff came up the road with her lights flashing, no siren, and the three balls of light lifted quietly into the air, where they were joined again by the other two and in a split second they were all gone. By the time the sheriff deputy was at the house they were all gone. The show was over but we did not know what the performance was about," she laughed a little and there were chuckles around the room for a few moments.

"Did the deputy or you go out there to investigate?" Jerry asked Ed, then he added "wait a minute while I turn the tape over. And by the way thank you for the lemonade, it really hit the spot. This is real lemons not a mix, it is delicious. There the tape is on," said Jerry as he sat back in the creaking kitchen chair.

"The deputy and I went out there and found two of my two year old heifers laying there. There were pieces of them missing. Their tongues, eyes and some of their internal organs were missing. There was no blood but some very precise cutting had been performed. The deputy decided that we should not contaminate the scene anymore so as soon as we got back to the house I called Dr. Faulkner, our vet. He came out early this morning to take a look. He is the one who called the Air Force and then the local radio station. Dr. Faulkner was an Army veterinarian and said he had seen this type of activity in the desert areas in Colorado and Arizona.

"It was quick thinking by the deputy not to contaminate the scene. What is his or her name?" asked Jerry.

"Her name is Deborah Kent. Nice girl, she's been working here in Stevens County now for 3 or 4 years."

"Why did the vet call the radio station?" asked Colonel Petrovitch.

"He had heard something on the station last night about some lights in the sky and he wanted them to follow up on the story from this angle. Because of his military experience he did not want any of this to be covered up or hushed up. He also said he wanted it out in the open so the government wouldn't lie to use about what we actually saw," said Ed.

"Can we go out and see the site now, Mr. Bjornson?" asked Jerry turning off his recorder and repacking it, "I would really like to run some tests."

Ed, for some reason looked over at the Colonel before he answered but the officer said nothing, "Yes, of course, I'll take you over there."

As they walked out the back door everyone noticed that Captain Chapman was talking with the news crew. They were T.V. news from Channel 4 in Spokane. Whatever he was trying to convince them to do the two news peopled seemed unwilling to cooperate. They put their gear away, lowered their remote antennae and drove off, with the Captain just standing there, hands on hips, looking after them and eating their dust. Whatever they had seen and gleaned from the scene was going on the air without the approval of the good Captain and probably the Air Force. The Colonel, who was also walking out to the site with us seemed impassive to the prospect of a news release.

"Colonel Petrovitch, you don't seem nearly as upset or bothered by any of this. Why is your Captain having such a hard time?" asked Frank.

"He is the public affairs officer for the air base. He deals in this sort of thing and although he is young he probably thinks in terms of the old Project Blue Book where everything was kept from the public, for their own good. He is overly concerned with the Air Force's image in this affair. I, on the other hand, am from base operations and I was individually briefed by the base commander before coming out here. Brigadier General Flaherty feels that there should be no cover up or the appearance of a cover up. He disagrees with the public affairs people and his own G-2. The G-2, security officer, a Lieutenant Colonel Malcolm Smith, is trying to play it safe with Washington D.C., just in case. Say, I bet everyone would be satisfied if you and your team were able to certify this site as an actual extra-terrestrial landing," said the Colonel glancing around at the team as if it was a good idea he just had, "or are you just looking around?"

"We are here studying something else, but we feel this could tie into our research. We probably couldn't certify this as a landing site and frankly until we have had a chance to look it over it is just as big a mystery as crop circles. I don't know if you know this or not but there have been a lot of reports of cattle and horse mutilations over the last 30 years in the west and southwest but seldom does it happen up in this area, unless that too has been part of the overall government effort to cover things up," stated Jerry as they reached the police barrier tape and ducked under it. The Colonel would not look him in the eyes.

Standing just inside the tape Jerry stopped to talk to his team, "everyone please move slowly and spread out. Let's get some useable data here and some samples, if there are any. Megan did you bring a digital camera?" asked Jerry looking over at her he got a thumbs up. She was already snapping pictures. The Colonel stayed just outside the tape, taking notes as the three scientists moved slowly around and worked their way into the site. Frank stayed near the Colonel and both men were watching Megan do her work.

Jerry turned on his small Geiger counter to check for radiation. He decided to look over the carcasses of the cattle first. There was a slight ticking coming from his daypack. He lifted the flap to see the reading and was happy to see it was quite within the safety limits. He noticed that the grass had been disturbed around the dead animals, footprints. He carefully brought out his magnifying glass. He expected to see the prints of Air force boots and shoes, but he found something small, not unlike a goat or a pig track but with three pointed toes, not exactly hooves. He found some other prints, probably from Ed and the vet. The smaller prints were indistinct, hard to read until he found one in a mound of dirt around a ground squirrel hole. It was distinct, three toes of equal size and a heel with wrinkled skin markings. He was excited, so much so that he almost dropped the bottle of his special casting solution. He poured it in carefully, oh so carefully so as not to disturb the loose dirt. He had bent himself over so far to watch the pour he could smell the damp dirt and dewy grasses. Jerry glanced at the Colonel who seemed to be locked in conversation with Frank. They were both probably getting bored, but still watching Megan.

Jerry looked around from his kneeling position after he resealed the jar and caught Megan's eye. She had been snapping pictures of the depressions in the taller grass. He silently motioned to her to take pictures of the dead animals and the footprints around them. Her brow knit momentarily but she quickly understood what Jerry wanted done and did not say a word. She just nodded to the affirmative and took pictures all the way over to Jerry's position.

Jerry turned his attention to the dead animals. He was careful to walk only in the boot and shoe footprints already there. He examined only the closest animal to him. Clearly he could see that the eyes, tongue, heart and lungs had been removed with surgical precision. There was no evidence of blood on the grass or on the hides. There was an odor about the animals that was almost antiseptic.

When Megan finally worked her way over to him he whispered, "Try to walk in the boot and shoe prints. Take pictures of these animals from as many angles as you can, thanks."

Jerry could see Lisa, about 30 yards away, squatting down and putting something into a small sample jar. She looked at Jerry and then he nodded and slowly made his way to her. Kneeling beside her he asked quietly, "What did you find, Doctor Lady?"

She gave him a puzzled look but let it pass, "I found more

of the same type hair we have not yet identified. I also found some footprints that will dwarf those number 13 clod hoppers you call feet."

Jerry smiled, "I'll take a print casting with the quick drying stuff and we'll get the hell out of here. This site gives me a very uneasy feeling and it is slightly radioactive but not dangerous." He opened another jar, mixed in some water from his canteen and poured the contents into the closest print.

Lisa leaned close and kissed him on the cheek, "Have you been keeping an eye on that Colonel?" she whispered in his ear, "he is watching us closely but trying his damnedest not to get caught doing it. Frank is trying to keep him distracted but the Colonel is a little sly.

Jerry kissed her back, "I thought he just didn't want me to see him checking out your cute little butt."

"He's been doing that too, my dear," she smiled and hit him on the shoulder.

After about thirty minutes Jerry and Lisa walked slowly back toward where the Colonel and Frank were standing. Megan was already walking back toward the house. Jerry could see that the Captain was standing on the back porch, just watching everyone. His fists seemed to be clenched at his side and it looked like he was biting his lip like a middle school teenage girl.

"Well Dr. Paulson what do you think we have here?" inquired the Colonel, who was smiling pleasantly. His notebook was nowhere in sight. Frank had gone to catch up with and walk with Megan.

"I am not sure Colonel Petrovitch. The scene is pretty contaminated by all the people walking through it. I took a couple of footprint casts, but they look more like animal tracks, so it was probably a waste of time. We found something that looks like dog hair or maybe coyote hair, on the grass further in, so off hand I would say this was some sort of hoax."

By his reaction the Colonel seemed pleased with the news. Jerry couldn't help but get a real oily, smooth to the point of being greasy, feeling from this guy. There was something certainly not genuine about him. "We're going back to our lab now, but I think this was a waste of time," added Jerry hoping the guy would buy it.

They walked back to the farmhouse with only the sound of the dry first cut hay stubble crunching under their feet. Jerry and Lisa held hands and put on a show for the Air Force dudes, trying to make them think that they had a lot more on their minds than going back to their lab for research. They kissed and hugged all the way back and Lisa was giggling like a teenager. They had agreed that deception was the name of the game on this little outing.

Megan and Frank, in the spirit of deception, also kissed a few times just to irk the Captain and seemed to be accomplishing their goal. Megan knew for a fact she had already broken the heart of the airman at the gate. It made her smile to think his ego was so easily bruised. Both the Captain and the gate guard were wearing wedding rings with no reason for their actions, what hypocrites, and that drooling Colonel Petrovitch character scared her a little. He smiled with everything in his face but his eyes. He was a little too accommodating and he was actually pleased when Jerry said it was probably a hoax.

Everyone breathed a sigh of relief when the Bjornson farm was rapidly vanishing in the rear view mirror.

CHAPTER 7

BACK AT THE cabins, the camping trip had been called off for a while; Jerry was listening to all the telephone messages. There were three. One of them was from Bryant Baker, who had been holding down the fort at the Ranger Station while Frank had been cavorting with the scientists.

"Dr. Paulson pick up please this is Ranger Baker. That guy, Steven Jansen, the bird watcher who took those weird pictures, called to say he is going to sell them to the National Star or the National Scandal, one of those supermarket rags. He left a number if you want to get in touch with him its 555-6179. He is staying in Newport tonight but he's headed into Spokane in the morning. I gave him your number too. Uh… well okay…thanks," and he hung up.

The second, "Dr. Paulson, this is Steven Jansen, you never called me like the Ranger said you would about the pictures I took, so I did some calling around and I found a couple of very generous and eager bidders. I'm going into Spokane in the morning and meet them at the airport," click.

The third, "Dr. Paulson, this is Colonel Petrovitch. You all left in such a hurry I couldn't finish my report. Would you call me please so I can fill in the blanks and get General Flaherty off my tail? I got your number from the Ranger Station, they were most helpful." Jerry did not remember giving anyone at the Bjornson farm the telephone numbers for anywhere he could be contacted. The clever Colonel must have just figured we were available through the Ranger Station because Frank was acting as the chauffer and it is in the phone book.

"Sounds like we've got some trouble," said Frank as he finished filling the old coffee pot with water and set it on the stove to brew. "Are we going to see Steve, what's his name, or are you going to stay here and analyze whatever it was you found at Ed Bjornson's place?"

Somewhat lost in thought Jerry answered, "Uh…Len…I mean Frank. Say what the hell should I call you anyway?" shooting the Ranger a dagger filled glance and then smiling.

"I go by either. Megan calls me Frank and so does my mother but people I work with call me Len. Take your pick," he said sitting down at the kitchen table. Frank cut a big slice of an apple with his pocketknife and shoved it into his mouth, giving a full cheeks smile and chewing away. The apple crunched and the freshly cut apple gave the room a pleasant scent.

One eyebrow went up a little but Jerry was too tired to be amused, "OK, Frank I think we had better go over to Newport and talk with Steve Jansen. I really don't want him selling those pictures. We could always slap a gag order on him due to an ongoing investigation but I don't think he would believe that. Do you know a good lawyer around here who could pull off a stunt like that?" said Jerry as he got up, grabbed an apple for himself and headed for the door.

"Yah, there's a guy right in Newport who might be able to convince old Steve to keep his mouth shut and his hands in his own pockets, instead of someone else's. Let me give him a call and then you call our newest buddy Stevie and find out where he is staying. There is that motel by the high school on Highway 2," quipped Frank as he pulled his cell phone off his belt and hit speed dial.

While Frank was talking on his cell Jerry picked up the regular landline telephone to call Steve Jansen. "Hello? Yah, is this Steve?"

"You've got him, who is calling?" was the reply, sounding a little muffled for reasons unknown.

"This is Dr. Paulson. Do you remember me?"

"Yeah, I remember you Doc. What can I do for you?" there was a slight laugh and a clearing of the throat, "you are of course calling me about those pictures I took, right?"

"Uh…right, yes I am, can we get together and talk, maybe over dinner?"

"Sure, there is a pretty good Chines restaurant right here close to the motel, I'll meet you there about 7 o'clock."

"That sounds just fine Steve, my treat. We'll see you at around 7 o'clock," said Jerry hanging up very gently, although he really wanted to slam the receiver down. Turning to Frank, who was still on his cell phone, Jerry looked at him with a question on his brow.

Frank nodded and held his hand up in a gesture of hold on a second, "Great Jason, we'll meet you at the Pagoda at around seven. Yeah, his name is Steve Jansen. OK, super, we'll see you there." Turning to Jerry, "It's all set. He says he can invoke a little known State ordinance and put a gag order on this guy, but if he leaves the State there is nothing you or anyone can do about it."

"That will have to do. I was really hoping for something a

little more Federal, but I can live with it for now. It's already 1730 so we had better get moving," Jerry was once again headed for the door.

Lisa came over from the lab table quickly when she saw the two men were actually about to leave. "This sample you just brought in is the same type hair that you found on the mountain. So, offhand my good doctor, whatever happened in the woods at the farm was no hoax, unless it's all a huge, elaborate one with tons of people involved," she said giving him a quick kiss and heading right back to her laptop to input some additional data.

Megan came in the back door from the toilets, was quickly grabbed by Frank who laid a good-bye kiss on her that curled her toes. When she opened her eyes all she said was, "Wow". The two men shuffled out the door leaving her blinking her eyes in amazement. "He may not be young stud anymore but he sure knows how to say good-bye." She ran to the door and called after them, "Hey bring us back some Chinese food, will you?" and she got a distant OK and a partial waive from both men as they climbed in the rig and pulled away, which probably meant they would not be bringing anything back.

Lisa raised her eyebrow and smiled but did not stop typing until she hit the enter button to put the data in the system. She then turned to Megan, "You two sure hooked up fast. Is that your normal style or do you want to talk about it?"

Megan just looked at her; there was a long pause before she answered, "well, I really had no intention of hooking up with anyone this summer. I was looking forward to an uncomplicated summer and no, it is not my style to jump in the sack with the first Forest Ranger or man in uniform I see."

"Sorry, I didn't mean anything bad by the question I was just curious."

"Last night when you and Jerry started squeaking the springs on his old bed, I guess I had a weak moment and let him kiss me. I actually goaded him into kissing me and before I knew what was happening I was hotter than a stick of dynamite. I do remember a lingering mist suddenly forming around us that had a musky flowery scent and suddenly my fire was lit and blazing. We abused the springs on my bed for the better part of three hours. He's, what I would consider, a little old for me but he's got the stamina of a much younger man."

"I think we have ourselves a couple of bona-fide wild men," remarked Lisa as she watched the dust settle from the forest service suburban, "yup, the days are going to be long but the nights are going to be even longer," she said as she went over and turned the now boiling coffee down, "to tell you the truth it was a little painful to walk this morning."

"Tell me about it," said Megan as she was jotting some notes down in her trusty notebook.

Before the conversation could get into really risqué girl talk there was an odd noise outside, a kind of hooting howling noise from the nearby wood line causing Megan to reach over and turn off the low playing radio and the table lamp, "What the hell was that?"

"Got me," answered Lisa as she picked up the small, but ancient, tape recorder from the table, turned it on to record and put it in the window sill over the sink next to the open screened window. She put her finger up to her lips to signal quiet and waited. They could hear the distinct, although faint, sound of brush breaking as though something large was moving through. Then there was another strange howl, this one seemed closer giving them both a strange chill. Just as peculiar as the first howl it seemed to be an answering howl from a different place.

Megan came closer to Lisa to whisper in her hear, "that second one sounded like it came from a different direction." Lisa nodded her agreement. There was more brush breaking and something seemed to be coming closer to the cabins. The tree line was only about 50 feet from the back door. There were several more howling's, hoots and whistles and snapping of tree limbs. At one point they thought they heard a tree falling. After about 15 or 20 minutes the sounds began to fade away in roughly a northern direction.

Finally feeling as though they might be able to relax, "Jerry's going to love this," said Lisa as she got up from the kitchen table, where both of them had been sitting in the dark and retrieved the tape recorder. "Let's get back to work, I believe we are going to make some really astounding discoveries this summer and I don't mean just in the love department."

"Megan do you know about crypto zoology?" asked Lisa as they both continued their tests.

"All I really know is that text book answer. Crypto zoology is the study of hidden creatures and animals that appear where they should not be, like a wooly mammoth in Florida. I know that the field does not get the respect it should, like paleontology or zoology."

"You are as smart and talented as Jerry said you were," said List with a smile, still not looking up from the microscope. "The crypto zoologists do search for creatures of legend, but they insist on hard scientific facts and conclusive evidence before letting anything be known of their research. I think we are going to have to do the same thing. We still don't want to discuss anything with anyone who is not in our little circle of friends. Sasquatch, as the Canadians call it, is looking more and more like a real creature to me and believe me I am the original skeptic."

"That's it. I cannot classify this hair as corresponding to any living creature in this area or even on this planet," said Megan as she put a test tube into the wooden holder. "There is slightly more radiation in this hair than is considered normal and there are trace minerals, some of which are in the wrong proportion to the norm, but some of these minerals are totally unknown to the data base.

Even if we don't have Big Foot, we do have a creature that is probably extra-terrestrial in origin and has the intelligence to have figured out how to travel vast distances in a short amount of time. As I understand it to get to the closest star from our solar system, Alpha Centuri, it would take nine of our lifetimes. Either these visitors came from our own solar system somewhere or they can actually "warp space" somehow to travel in large chunks of space in a fraction of time." Looking around, with a long lingering gaze at the kitchen, Megan added, "I can't wait for those guys to forget to bring us any food, let's eat, I'm starved."

CHAPTER 8

LATER, OVER TEA, the coffee was still on low heat for later and after eating a sumptuous meal of fried hotdogs with chopped onions, relish, catsup and baked beans right out of the can, Lisa picked up her oversized cup with both hands, savored the aroma of the freshly brewed green tea, with her eyes closed and took a long drink. "Did you know that Teddy Roosevelt believed in these damned Big Foot creatures?" she said finally letting herself relax and sat back in the kitchen chair.

"How did you know that?" asked Megan as she cleared the table of the paper plates and plastic utensils. "Where did you come up with that little tidbit of information?"

"I did some reading before coming out on this, what I should call it, expedition," said Lisa waiving her left hand in the air in a grandiose manner, "I thought I ought to learn something on the subject before I really came off looking or sounding stupid or uninformed. Oh, I know my way around a lab and all that, but I do not share the passion for this subject like Jerry does. I came out here to be with him," she squirmed in her chair causing a creaking sound.

"Well what did Roosevelt have to do with these creatures?"

asked Megan as she sat down after pouring her own cup of tea that she was letting steep a little.

"The old boy wrote a book called *The Wilderness Hunter*, back in 1893 or 1894. In it he recounts a story about an old mountaineer named Bauman who lived all of his life on the frontier," Lisa got up and moved to the rocking chair, Megan moved to the only other comfortable chair, an old recliner, "Bauman was trapping with another guy in the mountains around the headwaters of the Wisdom River. They weren't having much luck and the place had a bad reputation because another trapper had been mauled by a wild animal and half devoured, in the same area."

"They came back to their camp one night and it had been torn apart. There were strange tracks all over the place but they didn't pay much attention to them for some reason, figuring I suppose that it was a bear. They put their camp back in some sort of order and went to sleep after cleaning their catch. Around midnight Bauman was awakened by a noise and he could smell a strong retched odor, a wild animal smell. He saw something large standing at the opening to the lean-to, so he fired at it, heard a short grunt of pain and he could hear it running for quite a ways. He figured he missed it because there was no blood anywhere. They decided to leave the area after hearing some really strange noises way out in the brush that night. The next day they discovered they had trapped a few more beaver; consequently Bauman was forced to prepare them before they could leave and it was after sundown before he finished. His partner had long since gone back to break camp."

"When Bauman got back to camp he found his partner dead with a broken neck and four fang marks on his throat.

He abandoned everything but his gun and left the area in a hurry." Taking another sip of tea Lisa sat back and just looked at Meagan for some type of reaction.

"Not a bad story," mused Lisa, "I figured that there must be some credibility because it was written by a U.S. President to be. These things range all over the Northwest and into Canada. There are stories galore. There was a guy named Albert Ostman, in 1924, who said he was captured and held for six days by a family of Bigfoot, until they got bored with poking and jabbing him and he seized an opportunity to run away. The story goes that he kept running until he hit a town and never left it again." Megan chuckled and sipped her tea letting Lisa continue with her stories. "There was an Indian from the Nootka tribe from Vancouver Island, British Columbia, who claimed to have been kidnapped by Bookwus, the Wildman of the forest. Even the Russians and the Chinese have had their stories over the centuries."

"Cultures have been spinning these tales for hundreds of years but there has never really been any hard evidence to support any of them. Oh, there have been skull caps, in Tibet and Nepal, made for monks to keep their heads warm from, they say, Yeti skulls, skin and hair, but this is still not the evidence we need," said Megan, "and the pictures of the footprints in the snow at eleven thousand feet were pretty convincing I must admit, but didn't the guys in northern California finally admit that the film they made was a hoax?"

"Yes, one of them did," said Lisa, "I read an article about one of them making a death bed confession that they had staged the whole thing. Everyone looking at that film was pretty convinced that they were looking at and analyzing the real thing, for years. It still boils down that there is no proof, no hard evidence. I think that hair we have been analyzing is a start to what may be a break through."

"Yeah, we've got some hair and some plaster casts of huge feet and some frightened campers, hikers and one very greedy bird watcher. We need to analyze what we got at the Bjornson farm. Let's get those digital pictures on the computer and take a good look at the plants from the mutilation site. I think we may be adding some really credible stuff to our data base," exclaimed Megan as she reached into her pack and brought out a plastic bag jar of flora setting it out on the lab table. Putting down her mug of tea she got out the Geiger counter and began recording the readings. Some indications proved higher than she expected, almost to a slight danger threshold. She decided to put on thick plastic gloves and use tongs and tweezers to separate the different plants. Meanwhile Lisa was loading the photos into her laptop computer directly from the digital camera.

"Megan, come over here and look at these poor cattle," said Lisa her fingers deftly moving over the mouse button on the computer, "these animals have no sex organs, no blood, no eyes, and no tongues. There is a hole in the cheek muscle where something was obviously inserted. I wonder what was removed through there?" said Lisa pointing at the screen.

Megan came over and was leaning on Lisa's shoulder, "Look at those incisions they are absolutely precise," Megan said pointing to several spots on the carcass, "that is not a scalpel; it was a laser or something like that. I've seen pictures of these type mutilations but I have never been able to look up close. I noticed that the flesh was folded back, like something really hot had been applied. Those incisions are straight, very mechanical," she added pointing to the areas around the where the genitals used to be and in the jaw area as well. These cattle were both female I believe. Only imperial storm troopers are so precise!" she said with a big grin.

Lisa nodded her head acknowledging the pun but continued her thought process, "This is the butcher in the delicatessen using his tools of the trade," she glanced at Megan who looked at her and nodded in agreement. "This does not smack of a government cover up, unless they have been given permission to let this happen, this is someone or something coming in and ordering dinner."

"I have always felt that way about these and the other mutilations I have seen pictures of," said Megan as she went back to the lab table, "it seems strange that these grasses have been irradiated. These readings are borderline critical and we're going to need a lead container for storage. Let's put them back in the jar and put them outside anyway, away from us." She said as she wrapped the plants in foil and put them in the empty glass jar; into a foil lined box and took it outside and put it under the cabin, at the far end.

CHAPTER 9

THE LADIES HAD been in bed about a half hour; it was just after 1 in the morning, when they heard the door slam and the yelling begin. Jerry and Frank were back and Jerry was angrier than he had been since WSU beat his Eastern Eagles in last year's football game. He was so mad he was ready to toss in the towel on the whole project.

Lisa came out of their room wearing his only pajama top, looking a little sleepy and not trying to very alluring. Frank smiled and whistled a small, light, wolf whistle. Jerry, nearly ready to throw something across the road stopped in his tracks to gap, totally losing his train of thought. She looked fantastic, even though she was half asleep and a little rumpled. "What seems to be the trouble here, Doctor Paulson? Is this the professional demeanor we are all supposed to display when, obviously, there has been some sort of set back?" Lisa yawned, "Calm down and I'll reheat some coffee or something," she said walking into the corner of the room that served as the kitchen. She felt two sets of eyes watching her barely covered butt as she walked, also being careful not to bend over; but it only made her smile because, although a little revealing to Frank, it had a calming effect. She had heard some curse

71

words, which she had never heard Jerry say. She thought better of coffee and just got a long neck beer for each of them, sat down at the table and asked, "Now, do you want to tell me what's wrong? Obviously your meeting with the bird watcher was a little less than productive. Oh, by the way, you forgot to bring us any Chinese food."

"That butt-headed bird watcher, uh…sorry, Mr. Jansen was totally unreasonable. He showed us all the pictures he took, he even gave me copies of them free of charge, but neither of us could talk him out of going to Spokane and meeting the sleazy media. I offered him thirty thousand dollars for the rights; he turned me down flat," Jerry almost spit on the floor in disgust. "He made me promise not to sell them or publish them, in fact I had to sign an agreement promising prosecution, if I did use them in any way until he got his money from the media. As it turns out Jansen is a Notary Public and a county clerk in Whitman County, somewhere. I am sorry about the Chinese food, but I really got so angry with the guy and I did not want to stay any longer. The lawyer Frank got in touch with, Jason, didn't show up until it was too late so we couldn't get the gag order on Jansen either."

Reaching across the table, "May I see the pictures?" asked Lisa in a calm aloof, coldly professional voice. She did not want to agitate Jerry any further. She really knew how to calm him down if Frank would go over and see Megan, but he seemed content to stay and finish his beer and listen to Jerry vent.

Jerry handed her the envelope with the pictures and then came over and sat down next to her with a heavy sigh. She took them out of the envelope and looked at them carefully; there were only four with any type of discernible images of something. In one she saw a haunting dark eye, surrounded by a yellowish eyeball with huge streaks of red, very bloodshot in fact. The face was almost in focus and she thought she could probably computer enhance it, Jansen probably had already done so. There was a hint of a nose, cheekbones and thick lips that were definitely not apelike features. The dark hair was matted with dirt and leaves, like it had been rolling around on the ground, probably just sleeping on the ground. Another picture was a total back shot of the creature, a fairly good outline, giving the impression it was totally covered with thick filthy hair; no discernible neck. The other two pictures were just the creature going into the woods, up a small grade. "Just does he think he can get a hundred grand for these? I don't believe anyone would be dumb enough to pay that kind of money for these awful pictures. You were being generous at thirty thousand," said Lisa as she put them back into the envelope and laid them on the table.

"That's where you're wrong. He says he already has an offer from one of the gossip rags for one hundred thousand, sight unseen. I don't care if some movie character said it was the "best investigative reporting on the planet" Jansen is being totally mercenary about the whole thing," said Jerry then he took a long pull of the long neck, glancing over at Frank who seemed to be nursing his beer. "I offered all the money from our petty cash fund up front before I looked at the pictures and Jansen wouldn't even consider it. We talked, and then argued for the better part of two hours. The waitress even came over and told us to hold it down. If I could have I would have had him arrested, but neither Frank nor I could think of a good reason to call the police. Frank couldn't arrest him because it would seem it is not a crime to take pictures in the National Forest," said Jerry as he upended the long neck and drained what was left down his throat; it didn't look like he swallowed it, just poured it down.

"Do you have your copy of the statement he made you sign? We might have a way out of this," said Megan who was standing in the door wearing a half T-shirt and baggy sweat pants, "we may be able to put these pictures into a scientific paper first before they get into those so called newspapers, although one he mentioned is a T.V. gossip reporting program, but I have to see how the statement is worded."

Jerry pulled a waded piece of paper out of his coat pocket and tossed it to her, "Good luck. Frank already looked at it and he couldn't find a loop hole, but that doesn't mean you can't try," said Jerry as the paper was in the air. Megan caught it and opened it up then went to the refrigerator to grab a long neck of her own. Jerry pulled a kitchen chair across the linoleum with a powerful scraping noise and threw his feet up on it, "I'd really like to shoot that guy."

"I really didn't hear that," said Frank as he sipped his now warm beer. He then looked at Megan, still sexy even in this current fashion statement, "what do you see, babe?"

Megan flinched; she really hated being called "babe" for any reason. Ignoring the remark until later she continued to read, "I think we may have him on a technicality." Three heads jerked around to look at her, "this entire thing says is that you, Dr. Paulson, agree not to publish these pictures in newspapers, journals, scientific papers, magazines or books. This is written to you personally Jerry not the expedition, the college or any foundation that may have contributed money to us, so," she looked up to see if she had their attention, she did, "we have Lisa publish it in a scientific paper on the Internet under the name of her college, her department and name this expedition as consultants. What do you think?"

Jerry looked at Frank, who was supposed to have all the legal training of a police officer, which in fact he did from two separate academies; one local and one federal. Frank looked back and nodded to the affirmative but added, "It would be tired up in litigation for years anyway."

"So let's get to work on this thing. Get your notes out, this could take a few hours," said Lisa with a heavy sigh. She had planned to spend the wee hours of the morning doing something else with Jerry, not writing a paper on any subject.

Seeing the disappointment in her eyes, Jerry reached over to her, grabbed her hand, kissed it, and said, "I'll make this up to you, I promise," then he winked. Lisa smiled knowing he always kept his promises. They both looked up as the back screen door slammed. Frank and Megan were walking hand-in-hand down the back steps toward the other cabin.

After two tedious hours of working on the paper they both had edited and re-edited it several times, compared all the data they had to ensure accuracy and also to make sure they could prove their findings and have some evidence to back up their theories, Lisa saved it all on a disk, then she called up the Email address of the Smithsonian, but decided against that. She called up the Email address of her own department head and sent it to him with instructions, read it, then to publish it in a department paper immediately then forward it to his friend at the Smithsonian for publication in their next magazine. She added in her text to perhaps send it to the National Geographic Society for their perusal. Lisa looked at Jerry for his final approval, which was a nod of his tired head, she hit send with the mouse click and everything was set into motion. The clock on the wall had the pheasant's wings pointing to just after three a.m.

Lisa stood up, grabbed Jerry's hand and said, "Come to bed big fella, its way past our bedtime," and he allowed himself to be led away. All of a sudden though he wasn't as tired as he thought he was, the door closed and they melted into each other's arms.

CHAPTER 10

THE MAIL TRUCK seemed to have an engine problem as it huffed and puffed outside the cabins; the fan belt was screaming very loudly. The mailman sounded like he was tearing the screen door off the hinges as he knocked trying to get someone to answer the door. What he was delivering held something that later proved to be quite surprising. The mailman was glad to leave after the big guy had opened the door, yawned 5 or 6 times while trying to sign his name on the clip board, mumbled thank you and closed the door in the face of the postal officer.

"Lisa get up we just got a package from Nepal," said Jerry as he stumbled to the water faucet to get the coffee going. The pheasant said it was almost 9 o'clock. He poured some grounds into the filter when he finally got all the mechanical guts into the coffee pot, set it on the old stove and turned the button to HI.

Lisa came out of the room putting the pajama top back on as she walked and plopped down at the table. Jerry marveled how she could look so good after just rolling out of the sack. She took the little box and just rolled it around in her hands while she too yawned.

"This is from Bob Phillips. Isn't he on the same kind of research mission in Nepal that we are working at here? Look at this box, it has taken almost three weeks to get here but somehow it made it. Look at all those weird stamps and there are so many rubber stamps one can hardly see the paper.

Jerry threw a pound of bacon in a pan, 6 eggs in another pan and toast in the toaster, "well open it up, let's see what he thought was so important."

Lisa carefully opened the paper wrapping; she wanted to preserve the odd stamps and all the rubber stamp images. When she got the box open there was a short letter enclosed with some pictures and a sample bottle with some hair in it. The letter read:

"Hey Megan, I heard you were looking around the Northwest for Sasquatch. We found these footprints at 24,000 feet and the hair we found frozen to a rock with a small amount of blood. We also found some really deep footprints at another location about 12,000 feet in a pass between two very high mountains. No people around up there.

Our little expedition is in the village of K'u La K'a. The hair and first set of footprints were found near Ganesh (7,406 meters) 24,296 feet high on the southern border between Tibet and Nepal. Ganesh Himal is northwest of Katmandu.

I hope you have found something at least as exciting there.
All the best, Bob."

Lisa took a small bite of toast, "there sure is a lot of activity, there and here," she said looking at Jerry, "it must be high tourist season for these things," she quipped.

Jerry's bite of egg stopped in midair momentarily as he looked across the table at her, "are you becoming a believer, finally?"

"I'm still not sure, it just seems odd that all of a sudden there is so much activity and all this hard evidence is beginning to surface. Bob even got a blood sample. We seem to have gone beyond circumstantial evidence and I do hope our little composition proves that to the scientific community. I think that even Hamilton Berger could win this case," said Megan and she Frank sat down at the table amid the reserved chuckles. "Got any more chow there mess sergeant?"

Jerry smiled, "yes ma'am, take all you want but eat all you take." He finished cooking the turkey bacon, scrambled 6 more eggs and had a pile of toast in no time.

The telephone rang, making everyone jump just a little, and Jerry leaned back, stretched his long frame and reached for the receiver, "Hello, yes this is Dr. Paulson, what's up?" He listened a few moments, looked at his watch, "who the hell is this anyway?" the voice on the other end was loud enough for everyone to hear it as the caller said, "Turnbull, Mike Turnbull."

"Do I know you? Are you reporting something to me or what? National Star!" Jerry looked at everyone in the room quickly, his eyes flaring as he listened for a few moments, "No I will not do an interview with you, now or later. Why should I..."he listened a little more," that is Steve Jansen and no I will not authenticate anything he has to say or anything he has to offer you," still listening Jerry stood up quickly, but sat down again, "Yes I know you try to interview experts, but... no...no none of my team will talk to you either. Ranger, what Ranger?" a pause to listen to the loud voice, "Max Delecourt. He at a lookout tower according to the head Ranger," Jerry looked over at Frank who nodded to the affirmative, "What's going on with him?"

Frank motioned for the telephone, "Mr. Turnbull? This is Frank Leonard, I'm the head Ranger for this district, what's going on?" he listened. "No, I'm sorry you will not interview any of my Rangers or any of our support personnel without my approval. That's my policy and the district policy for the entire Kanisksu National Forest area, thank you," he handed the telephone back but the line had gone to dial tone.

"He probably picked Max because he's one of the newest guys on the staff. Bryant or Mary wouldn't give him any information, I'm sure of that," said Frank, putting cherry preserves on his toast and downing it in two bites. He drank the last of his coffee and got up from the table, bent over and gave Megan a lingering kiss, "I'll see you tonight, OK?"

"When you put it like that, OK," said Megan opening her eyes to look at him up close.

"I'll get Mary over here with the other suburban as soon as I radio her from my truck. I've got to get over to the station and talk to Max at the fire tower. What are you all going to do today?" asked Frank over his shoulder as he took his dishes to the sink.

Jerry looked at the two women for their feedback, neither woman had a discernible reaction to the question, "I want to go set up camp where Jansen got his pictures. I have an idea we might be able to see something," he said still getting indifferent stares from both women.

Frank waived as he went out the door. Megan looked at Lisa, "what was the name of that trapper who kept having his camp torn to pieces?"

"Bauman, I think. Why?"

"OK, let's go set up Camp Bauman. Anybody superstitious?" laughed Megan, "we had better get moving or we'll be spending all our time pitching those old canvas frame tents and everything else we'll have to set up in the dark."

It had taken them some time to get their supplies together and to wait for the Forest Service truck to arrive but they were finally on Huckleberry Mountain. Just after darkness was caressing the mountain the tents were up, a small fire was burning in a portable fire pit and there was coffee and tea water on the boil. Megan had set up a third frame tent with the assistance of Mary Degenhardt, the Ranger who had brought them up to the site. This third tent was to be their lab. The portable generator was running quietly and everything seemed to be in readiness for something to happen.

Jerry was busy setting up trip wire camera traps and motion detectors around the hillside, to catch creature movements during the night. He wished he had more motion sensitive camera equipment but it was not in the budget so the old trip wire technology would just have to work.

Lisa had finished setting up, what she called the love nest, and went over to the lab to help put it together. She hoped she and Jerry would not scare the animals during the night and it made her inwardly chuckle. It did not take long to get the lab in order and both Lisa and Megan had a slight feeling of foreboding as they watched the suburban turn the corner of the mountain road and disappear in a cloud of dust.

"Let's make it a simple meal tonight. What do you think about hot dogs and beans?" asked Megan as Lisa exited the lab tent.

"Can we do something a little less lethal than beans? Jerry wouldn't last two minutes in that tent with me if I eat beans again tonight," said Lisa smiling, "what else goes with hot dogs?"

"Well we have a two pound container of potato salad on ice or potato chips, maybe both," suggested Megan looking through the coolers.

"Sounds just right," said Lisa, "when are we to expect the leader of the expedition for dinner, do you think? Does white or red wine go with hot dogs?"

"Beer," commented Megan, not being able to tell if Lisa was serious or not.

"Aah yes, beer. Why don't we have one right now while we are preparing this glorious repast? Let's see what we have," as the top of the cooler squeaked and scraped open, "oh, both light and regular beer, it is such a well-stocked cellar. What will you have Lady Megan?"

"Make mine regular please, only peasants drink light beer, my Lady."

"So true, so true; then I too will have a regular beer," smirked Lisa. The entire hillside could hear the creaking of the cooler lid as the two women got their long necks and settled around the small fire. "Do you know the fire danger today?"

"We are in luck today it's at moderate. That is why we are using this above the ground fire pit to keep it small and get good coals for cooking," replied Megan as she reached into the cooler again for a package of turkey dogs, "should we cook these on a stick or grill them? We do have a grill around here somewhere," she said as she rummaged through the kitchen box.

"I don't care, it would probably be easier and quicker to grill them, but we'll have to let the fire go down to coals so they don't burn on the outside and stay raw on the inside."

Megan finally found the grill and set it up on the top of

the metal portable fire pit. She also set up a small table and put all the condiments that she could find on it, along with a package of potato buns. "Do you want me to dice an onion or a tomato?" asked Megan as she found the battery-powered grinder.

"Do both, I like them on a hot dog," said Jerry as he walked into the camp. Both women, although trying not to show it, were startled, "sorry I didn't mean to scare you. I'm finished with all the camera stuff for any visitors and I am famished," he too reached into the noisy creaking cooler and retrieved a long neck, "now all we have to do is sit and wait." He sat down with a sigh, took a long drink of the golden brew and laid his head back on the top of the folding chair, just looking at the stars. Taking another long gurgling drink Jerry closed his eyes and just threw out a question, "Have either of you ever heard of Stanislav Szukalski?" He got no response but the looks he got were as if he had grown another arm. Finally there was a "no" almost in unison.

"Who the hell was or is he?" asked Megan as she poured the chopped onions and tomatoes into a small bowl.

"He was a Polish artist who immigrated to the United States back in the early 1900's. He was rather gifted as an artist but that is not his only claim to fame. He wrote a 39 volume work on Zermatism," said Jerry, without moving, but there was just a hint of a smirk on his face.

"Where to you get all of this obscure information and what the hell is Zermatism and why does it have anything to do with our little research project?" asked Lisa just before taking a big bite of her hot dog, catsup and mustard dripped down her chin and into the dirt at her feet.

"He made up Zermatism, I guess," answered Jerry, "one

of my students referenced old Stanislav in a paper he wrote on the origins of the human race. It was so far out in left field that I just had to look up the guy and find out what it all meant. Our buddy Stanislav said that all human culture derived from Easter Island after the flood that destroyed all living creatures except those on Noah's Ark." This immediately received a groan from both women. "That's not all, this guy was very religious. He also said that all languages derive from a single source (the Protong) and all art is a variation on a few themes that can be condensed to a single series of universal symbols." Jerry could feel he had their attention now because there was no sound except chewing and the crackle and popping of the fire. "Yup, he developed Zermatism to explain the differences in the races and cultures by claiming that are due to the cross breeding of species. He also said that the first humans were nearly perfect but they mated with Yeti, with abominable results."

"Jerry up to this point I had no idea you were so full of crap," said Lisa and both women had a good chuckle.

Jerry opened one eye and turned his head toward his lovely companion, "I can't believe you don't believe me. Stanislav lived from 1893, they think, to 1987. He was a real guy. I went to one of his art exhibitions at the Laguna Art Museum back in December 2000. I never said I believed his theories, I just asked if you had ever heard of him, learned colleagues, I was not asking you to believe his 39 volumes of his extremely boring rhetoric. My point is that he contends that humans have mated with Yeti, now where the hell do you think he got that idea?" he said turning his head back to the relaxed position, closing his eyes once more.

"He was a nut case, obviously," remarked Megan,

"people will come up with all kinds of explanations to justify or quantify how everything came to be the way it is. If he was so religious he was way out there on a limb by himself, probably with the serpent from the Garden of Eden, with this stuff. Darwin probably starts spinning in his grave whenever anyone discusses this guy," said Megan as she threw her head back killing the last of her beer. "Another dead cowboy," she said, as she tried to hit the trash bag with the empty but missed.

Just at that moment one of the cameras flashed, about one hundred yards away on the hillside, slightly up from the camp. A few seconds later a second flashed, showing something was coming in the direction of the camp. Jerry did not see the first one but Lisa and Megan saw both of them. Jerry sat up and unsnapped the holster of his .357 magnum pistol and took a bite out of his hot dog, more than half of it disappeared, two or three chews and then the second part disappeared. He downed the rest of his beer on a straight pour again without swallowing. All three then sat there and listened for any type of sound. There was no sound except for an occasional pop from the wood on the fire, a small breeze swaying and rustling through the bushes; silent as a tomb.

All three grabbed their one million power flashlights, although Jerry put up his hand to keep them from turning them on too soon. They waited a little longer. Then a third flash went off, further up the hillside, as whatever it was seemed to be now moving away from the campsite.

"I'm going to check out the first two cameras. They are all digital so I can get an image right away," said Jerry his eyes still scanning the dark wood line, "anybody want to tag along?"

"I'll have a go," said Lisa looking at Megan, "I am not shrinking away from a moose running up the hillside, although a very quiet one."

"You two kids have fun, I'll stay here by the cheery campfire," responded Megan, "Make sure you have your radios on, just in case I have company or you have a problem."

"The radio is on Channel 1, we'll see you later. It is a little early to be checking these cameras, I mean we should let them alone until morning, but I am curious and I will probably have to reset a trip wire or two," said Jerry as he switched on his powerful light and started up the hill. Walking right behind him Lisa just carried her light. She thought she would save it until they needed extra light for those unexpected something's that may go bump in the night. She too was wearing a pistol; her choice was a 9mm automatic. No wheel guns for her.

Jerry had put small light reflectors on the trees where he had placed the cameras so they were not too difficult to find in the dark. It only took a few minutes to get to the camera closest to the camp. Jerry reached up and unsnapped it from the mount on the tree; hit the button to see what image it may have captured, if any. Together they both saw the image of a small brown bear, its eyes glowing green in the flash. Jerry reset the camera and loaded it into the mounting device. He had to reset the trip wire too. They did the same for the other two cameras. On the third camera, where the bear was moving away, they both saw evidence of a cub walking at her heels.

Megan was sitting at the campfire with Frank, who had finally made it up the mountain. Neither Jerry nor Lisa had heard the vehicle come up the road, but they were happy to see him.

"Hey Frank, what's the good word?" asked Jerry as he and Lisa came into camp and sat down. Lisa threw Jerry a beer and opened another for herself. "Did you make contact with your new Ranger or the newspaper guy?"

"Yeah, I talked to both of them. They…" he stopped talking when Megan interrupted him.

"I want to know what tripped those cameras, and then we can talk about the stupid newspaper problem."

"OK. We saw the image of a momma brown bear and a cub moving through. Cute but not very spectacular," answered Lisa.

Looking at Frank, "What is the bear population in this area?" asked Megan.

"About average I'd say. In this area around the lake there are about thirty adults. That's in a 10 square mile radius," answered Frank who looked at Jerry with a question in his eyes but neither man said anything.

"Pretty sparse for bear isn't it? There is a lot of natural feed here. I saw several thickets of huckleberry bushes. Is this an open hunting area then?" asked Megan, she did not want the subject to drop until she had some information for her report.

"This is an open hunting area, but there is logging in here too. That's the main industry around here," said Frank as he looked into her eyes across the campfire. He liked the way the fire reflected and danced in her blue eyes. "As for your question about the new Ranger and the newspaper guy I told them both no story and not to talk to one another."

CHAPTER 11

"**JERRY,**" **WHISPERED LISA** as she levered up on one arm, in a rustle of nylon sleeping bags, "we have been here for two days. All we have to show for our time is that we all stink; we have pictures of that momma bear and her cub, some Elk and Deer, a Raccoon and some Gray Squirrels. When are we going to get out of here, I need a shower?"

"I've never known you to complain so much about needing a shower. We set up that portable one and Frank keeps bringing up water for us to use. Do I need to make you scream some more and scare all the animals away in this vicinity?"

Lisa smiled at the thought. Their lovemaking had not slowed down a bit; thank heaven for that portable shower. In truth she was bored out of her mind. There was no action here on this mountainside. Whatever had been here has gone. She could hear Megan and Frank rustling their sleeping bags in the next tent and it brought her mind around to fooling around again. With a couple of light touches she knew Jerry was interested too. But of course that's when everything went to hell in a hurry. Flashbulbs were going off all over the hillside and there were several of the same eerie howls that she had Megan had heard back at the cabins. There was a massive amount of breaking brush and it sounded like some of the small trees were being knocked over.

Jerry was up trying to get his pants on. Lisa pulled her pants over to her and was trying to get hers on while still lying on top of her bag. They both finally got some clothes on and went outside to see what the ruckus was about. Frank and Megan emerged shortly after and they were all standing around in a complete state of confusion. There was a lot more screaming and howling coming from just up the hill where a flash kept going off, as soon as it recharged. All four people went to investigate this disturbance; no one wanted to be left behind this time.

As they approached they could hear something noisily breaking brush and trees and swiftly moving away from them, but going straight up the hillside like a bulldozer. Jerry and Frank were sprinting up the hill and the women were not far behind. When they finally got to where one of the cameras had been up in a tall pine there was now a clearing of freshly fallen lodge pole pines. Some of the trees had been torn out of the ground and thrown down the hillside; the shallow roots in evidence. Everyone stopped at the edge of the newly cleared space and spread out in pairs to survey the area eager to recover the camera, hoping it was still in one piece. Even if the camera were broken the disk should have some images on it.

Although it was dark it was easy to tell where something very large had bulled its way through the brush. There was a fresh trail, but more like an actual bulldozer had done it, going straight up the hillside. It looked as though the Army Engineers or the Navy Seabees were trying to clear a quick landing strip for a helicopter. In the now very soft churned up dirt, where there used to be buck brush and low bushes, Jerry could see the foot prints he was looking for. He was certain there would be more hair samples on the fallen trees and maybe some blood, which he pointed to for Megan's benefit and she got the hint, with specimen jar in hand she began putting samples inside it carefully. Jerry found the camera by the method of first find one end of the trip wire and follow it to where it had literally been stomped into the ground. The camera was beyond help but the disk was still very much intact and he put it in his shirt pocket. He did not bring anything to take footprint casts, but at this point he did not care about that.

"Jerry, look at those footprints," said Lisa as she pointed to a very distinct print in the loose dirt, "this has the same scar on the bottom as your others casts. This is the guy you were waiting for isn't it?" She said holding her nose, "what is that smell?" She started to gag, "didn't the Indians call these things skunk apes or something?"

"No, well maybe, Skunk Ape was the name given to these creatures in the Everglades, probably by the Seminoles, but it would sure fit this one wouldn't it? Whew, it's like we jumped about a dozen skunks and they all sprayed us at once," said Jerry still looking around holding his handkerchief over his nose. "The Indians around here just called them the wild men of the forest, nothing about their odor," said Jerry as they both stumbled through the soft churned up dirt and ripped up brush.

"Well this thing does stink but we did not smell this odor at the cabin when there was hooting and hollering there along with the same busting trees and beating the brush. Are you sure this is the one you're looking for?"

Jerry gave her a quizzical look because they had not told him about their cabin experience until now but he let it go for the moment, "This is the guy. Stay here a minute or two I'm going to get one of the other cameras and take some pictures of these tracks in case it rains and they get washed out," said Jerry as he left her and walked into the darkness guided by his powerful flashlight. He was following what he would describe in his next paper, that he was already writing in his head, as the "path of destruction". Small trees had been ripped out of the ground and smashed against some of the larger ones, breaking some of those trees in half. The military could use this creature to clear landing zones that's for sure, Jerry thought, as he looked for another camera.

The first camera he came to was smashed just like the first, but he retrieved the disk and kept going. About 120 yards away, traversing the hillside, he finally found a camera that worked. He looked at his watch; it was two thirty in the morning. As he turned to walk back to the others he felt at least one pair of eyes watching him and the hair on the back of his neck stood straight out. An immediate cold sweat covered his whole body causing a chill that made him shiver uncontrollably. As he walked back toward Lisa he kept spinning around but he saw nothing at the edge of the powerful beam. Jerry expected to see at least a flash of eyes, but there was nothing. The feeling did not leave him even as he rejoined Lisa and snapped a few pictures. "Lisa," whispered Jerry, "we are being watched by someone or something. Keep watch while I finish these pictures, please."

Lisa stood up and swung her light around when suddenly she topped and let out a groan. She was facing Jerry and her light was going over his back. He turned to look in the direction of her light and almost dropped the camera. Shining in the beam of her light was a pair of purple luminous eyes, about 30 or 40 yards away and quite a way up from the ground. Jerry almost relaxed thinking maybe it was some sort insects until both eyes blinked together and then disappeared.

"Uh, can we go now?" asked Lisa. She could see that Megan and Frank were already headed back toward camp, their flashlights trailing down the hillside.

Standing up very slowly Jerry said, "by all means. We don't want them to tear up our campsite the way they destroyed these trees." He grabbed her around the waist and spun her around toward camp.

"Have you ever heard about a mountain man named Bauman and what happened to his camp on the Wisdom River?" queried Lisa.

"Who?" asked Jerry in a low voice.

"Never mind I'll tell you later," said Lisa quietly over her shoulder.

Megan peered into the lab tent and then went inside. Frank began walking around the campsite, his .45 caliber pistol in hand, putting things back up where they had been, like the chairs and the small picnic table that had held the condiments that was now on the ground.

"Hello in the camp," yelled Jerry, something he had seen in lots of western movies and Frank stopped to look in the direction of his voice, "hello in the camp, we're coming in," because he had not heard a response to his first call.

"Come ahead," signaled Frank putting his pistol back into its holster. Frank then went over and put the portable fire pit back right side up he poured water on the coals that were strewn on the ground then quickly buried them. After that he set about building another fire. Jerry and Lisa went directly into the lab tent. Pretty soon all four of them were in the lab, just looking at the mess and picking stuff up off the ground and filling a couple of garbage sacks with the unsalvageable items.

Fortunately the laptops were not damaged so Jerry booted up the newer one and inserted the first camera disk. Lisa and Frank were on the other side of the small table looking at him, "You'd better come over here and look at these babies. Whoa, this is really heavy," Said Jerry who had a habit of reverting back to his days in college and the language of that era.

The best Frank, Lisa or Megan could muster, almost in unison was, "Oh my God!"

On some of the pictures there was a discernible hairy, humanoid face, not at all apelike. One picture had a perfect image of a huge palm, with lines and finger print images reaching for the camera. The fingernails were broken and very dirty at the top of the fingers. In yet another picture were teeth in a huge gaping mouth. The teeth were not the fangs of an ape but more suited to a vegetarian diet in other words very Homo-sapien in appearance but in severe need of a good dentist. The eyes were haunting and eerie, with dark gray pupils and the eyeball itself being more light yellow than white. The nose was not a flat ape nose either; it was more pointed and stood out. The nostrils were large and open. It was impossible to tell the color of the hair as it blended into the background even with the powerful flash. Another startling fact was that there seemed to be two of these beings. While indistinct on the first disk the second disk revealed two faces, similar in body style, but it became evident that one of them was certainly a female. In one side shot, with a lighter grassy background there was evidence of what could only be described as breasts.

Now it was Jerry's turn to just sit there and look, he was at a loss for any intelligent speech. Where the second camera was destroyed there was a shot of the hand reaching for the camera but in the flash the eyes of the other being were luminous purple. He had to endure another instant cold sweat, a half dozen quick shivers coursing through his body and a bolt of fear that went from his stomach to his throat and bounced back again. It took him a few moments to recover.

"Frank," said Jerry, "we need to follow their trail and find out where they are going or where they live or maybe both."

Frank and the two women looked at Jerry like he had two heads, "You want to follow those two things in the dark, in the brush, going straight up a hillside? You sir have lost your sense of reason. They could tear us limb from limb while we are screaming for help," was Frank's reply.

"Uh, excuse me Tarzan, but we are not staying here in camp. Either we all go or no one goes, take it or leave it," said Megan, who had popped the clip on her .45 caliber pistol, looked at it and slid it back in again with an audible click. "That scream we heard from these things is exactly the same sound we heard back at the cabins when they must have run through there. I was scared them and I am leaning toward petrified now".

"I came on this trip for some fun, I never thought we would actually see one of these creatures or be asked to track the damned things in the middle of the night. I agree with Megan though I am not staying here while you two go off in the woods after them," said Lisa as she was looking through her large rucksack. She found her second pistol, a .44 magnum that she put into a small walking pack, with a box of bullets for each gun, as a back-up.

"Ok, ok," said Jerry trying to smile, "we will wait until first light to start tracking them. I'm not suggesting an orgy or anything but I think we should all sleep in the tent that was not damaged, so one person can keep watch while the others try to rest."

There was murmuring from everyone but they all finally settled in the least damaged wall tent. "I'll take the first watch, I am not sleepy," said Jerry as the others, still murmuring lay down in their clothes, just taking their boots off, and tried to sleep. It was three in the morning and first light would be in a couple of hours anyway. "Now, before you turn in I keep hearing about the noises at the cabin. Were you able to record what happened?"

"Yes, as a matter of fact we did. I will dig out the recording for you so you'll have something to listen to on your watch," said Lisa as she handed him the small although ancient recorder. Jerry found some earphones, plugged them into the machine and sat there listening as the others lay down.

CHAPTER 12

ARLIER, IN THE city of Newport, Washington, Michael Turnbull of the National Star newspaper was calling his editor. He had the meeting with the bird watcher and had copies of the pictures that Jansen wanted to sell, evidently these were the ones he had been promised. They were pretty good making him a little more excited about the scoop and he was sure it would finally be his chance to write a cover story.

"Max, I have the proof we were looking for, yeah I've got the actual pictures. Expensive, hell yes they were expensive, the guy wouldn't sell for less than 10 thousand apiece. After I looked at them I bought five of them. Yes, I know, but the others were too blurry. I don't care about them anyway. Yes, I got the disk. No, I don't know if he made a copy, he said he didn't. I figured he'll sell the fuzzy ones to the Scandal. Yes, I know that Dennis Graham is in town. Ok, yeah, I have made an appointment with one of the Ranger boys, but I guess the head Ranger doesn't want me to do it. Max, all I had to do was mention that we pay good money for a good story, with proof of course, and this Ranger, uh…" he fumbled through his notebook, "Delecourt, who is up at a look out station on Cook's Mountain said he would see me. Yes, as soon as I get off the telephone with you I'm going to go find him. The head Ranger is at another site with some scientists and should be out of the picture for a few hours anyway. No, it won't be that expensive. I offered five thousand and Delecourt accepted. I'll call you and Email the story as soon as I can."

Hanging up the telephone in the motel Mike got into his rental Explorer and headed toward the fire watch station on the top of Cook's Mountain. He followed the directions he had been given, which seemed to be fairly accurate, and was soon going up the hill by the city dump, winding his way to the top, actually enjoying the view of the valley and the city of Newport in the near distance. Mike marveled at how clear the air seemed, crisp and clean smelling out in the trees, with just a hint of damp rotting leaves. Several deer jumped out of his way on the way up the mountain logging road which made it more enjoyable, although he did not see a buck anywhere.

It only took about a half hour to drive to the top and he could see the lookout tower about a quarter of a mile along the ridgeline from the radio tower and microwave array. As instructed by Delecourt, Mike parked at the radio towers and walked the short distance to the forestry tower. He found himself enjoying the quiet of the forest. There were flutters of the small birds in the trees and brush; somewhere out there a squirrel was chattering its annoyance at his passing. Mike could see the young Ranger watching him from the top walk around through binoculars, so Mike waived at him. Delecourt waived back and pointed to the stairs that wound their way up thirty-five or forty feet to the top.

Ranger Delecourt shook his hand and ushered him inside after meeting him at the top of the stair. "It would be better if we talked inside," said Mason Delecourt, "would you like some coffee or tea or something?"

"Some water would be nice, thanks," responded the winded reporter, "that's quite a climb you have there."

"I use it for exercise; I do about ten laps a day, just like my cross-country days of running stadium stairs when I was in high school and college."

Taking the tall glass of water and downing about half of it in one gulp, Mike set the glass on the small table and sat in one of the government issued desk chairs, "what college was that?"

"I went to the University of Idaho. I majored in Forestry with the intention of working for the government. I have always liked working outside," said Mason as he put his coffee cup on the same table and eased into another of the office chairs.

"Do you mind if I record our conversation? It really speeds up the conversation when I don't have to scribble notes constantly," asked Mike as he reached for his pocket recorder. Not waiting for an answer he clicked it on record and put it on the table.

"No, I do not want any of this conversation recorded. You'll either have to remember what we said or take notes but I do not want anything recorded. In fact I want what I am saying now to be erased."

Mike casually reached over and clicked off the recorder, took the small tape out and threw it over to Mason, "Here you go; I want you to be comfortable. Now what have you got?"

Mason put the small cassette tape in his shirt pocket, "I can tell you that Frank Leonard, our Head Ranger, has been tasked to work with some scientists from the Universities of Washington State, Easter Washington and I think the other one is from Michigan. They are here to study Bigfoot sightings and gather what information they can on the subject for the duration of the summer."

"Ok, so what have they gotten so far?" asked Mike scribbling his own version of short hand.

"They have a lot of reports of sightings and some birdwatcher got pictures of something. They took a trip out on the Flowery Trail outside of Chewelah following up on a UFO sighting where Frank tangled with a couple of Air Force types."

"Do you know what they found?"

"No, Frank didn't really let me know anything he just said it looked as though there had been a landing of some type of craft and there were some cattle mutilations."

This information drew an "Umm" from Mike as he just kept writing, "Don't you have any more details? Do you know the location of the landing or the sighting? Was it the Bjornson's farm that I heard about on the radio?"

"That sounds like the name, yeah, Bjornson, they live around Addy. I figured they found something because Frank came around and told everyone to keep quiet about it."

"So why are you talking to me if your Head Ranger said to keep it quiet?"

Mason thought for a moment, looked at the ceiling, looked at the floor, then said, "I do not believe in government cover-ups. I believe the public has the right to know this kind of stuff. I knew it was a cover-up when the radio station retracted their original story saying something about a weather balloons coming down. What in a weather balloon is going to mutilate cattle or glows at night?"

"Good point. I am going to write this story quoting a government source, but you may still get into trouble, because your boss may think there was a leak somewhere in his jurisdiction."

That comment drew a smile from Mason, "I'm not too worried. I got a call from a Dennis Graham, from the National Scandal T.V. magazine, following up on a U.S. Air Force statement that skimmed over the details and treated the public like a bunch of ignorant fools. He said he talked with some of the students at the survival school before the Air Force put the hammer down and they said it was definitely UFO activity, not weather balloons. So you can add military sources to your story as well. If he traces anything back to me I will deny everything. When do I get my money?"

"I am prepared to give you the money today, but frankly I was hoping for something a little juicier. What else have you got?"

"Juicier, Ok, let's get juicy," said Mason with a gleam in his eye as he leaned closer to talk as if they were in a crowded room, "Frank has gotten himself mixed up romantically with one of the scientists. Her name is Megan, I think, and he has been jumping her bones for the last few nights. I've seen her and she is gorgeous. Anyway, that's why he has been spending all of this time at their camp over on Huckleberry Mountain, outside of Ione."

"Isn't that the same place the birdwatcher got his pictures of the alleged Bigfoot?" asked Mike glancing up to see the reaction of the young Ranger.

"Yeah, that's what he told us."

"Would you happen to know Megan's full name and which university she is from and whether she is tenured faculty or just a new professor?"

"Her last name is Manley or Hanley, or something like that. I think she is the one from Washington State. I don't know anything about tenure.

"Do you know the names of any of the other scientists?" asked Mike. He was on a dirt dealing fishing expedition now. He did not know how many people he was up against; it was time to get a count.

"Dr. Jerry Paulson is the leader. I think he might be from Eastern Washington. I don't know the full name of the other one, Frank just calls her Lisa, but I am pretty sure he said she was from Michigan."

Mike knew from this limited information he was going to have to shell out more money to more people, but at least he had some leads and some traveling to do as well. Just to catch Mason off guard and make him feel not all of this was important he steered him away from the subject they were just discussing, he wanted Mason to feel important, a little tactic Mike always uses to conclude an interview, "Have you ever seen anything unusual up here?" he said moving his head back and forth to indicate the tower, he needed some filler information for the article anyway.

"I've heard some weird howls in the middle of the night and I found a mutilated white tail doe, but I think a grizzly probably did that. Other than that there hasn't been too much around here. I really have never believed in Bigfoot, although I do believe in UFO's and the fact that the military and all the governments around the world have been covering things like that up for years."

"Thanks, I think I have what I need," said Mike reaching out to shake hands with Mason, "your money is on the table." Mike had let an envelope fall from his note pad. Zipping his coat as he stood to depart Mike made the long trek down the stairs and back to his vehicle, his mind was racing on how he was going to put this entire story together and get it published while it was still hot.

CHAPTER 13

FOLLOWING THE WELL-LAID trail straight up the mountain was only difficult because of the terrain. The path was very easy to see but the climb was steep and energy consuming. Jerry had an uneasy feeling and looking at the others he was sure the others had inkling that something was not right. As they were climbing and struggling up the path through broken trees and uprooted brush Jerry kept wondering why a path, so easy a blind person could follow it, had been put there in the first place. He was still not exactly sure what the creatures were that they were following, but he was sure that their being native to this area or even this planet was severely in question. The loose shale and the buck brush still standing made the actual tracks more than difficult to follow; it looked like a small herd of elephants had just wandered through. The only good thing in all this struggling was that there was an abundance of hair samples, now in two different shades, and Megan had several sample jars brimming with samples. There were no good blood samples or other bodily fluid samples readily evident but they were looking for them none-the-less. Didn't these creatures ever stop to pee or defecate?

Reaching the top of a small rock outcropping Jerry

could see just a hint of where something large and dark was scrambling over the top. After a brief moment of looking at each other all four of them added to their efforts and tried to scramble after it, now more determined than ever, but Lisa had the misfortune of scrapping her hand on a sharp piece of shale. It was not serious and she just wrapped it in a clean bandana as they continued to struggle up the mountain side. At the top of the rock, where they had seen the elusive figure, Jerry stopped and turned to Frank, his brows knit together in a look of incomprehension; Frank shrugged his shoulders in total bewilderment. The trail seemed to end abruptly and there were no fresh or even old evidence of any creature passing on the either side of the outcropping, except for a faint deer trail winding along the hillside. All four were sweating and covered in dirt, so after a brief rest, they fanned out to look for clues. The mysterious creature had vanished, evaporated like rainwater on a hot rock. Actually Jerry had expected to lose the trail much sooner than they had.

Then by happenstance they got a break, Lisa found a rather large tuft of hair, which she carefully lifted and put into a plastic sandwich bag. It had skin and blood attached to it so she was being very careful. Turning around she tripped on something and fell forward landing on the hard ground between two large rocks. One of the rocks actually moved, or at least that was Megan's perception so she put her finger to her lips for everyone to not make any sort of noise. Lisa made no move to get up from where she lay and just observed. There was an almost imperceptible humming coming from the rock Megan thought she had seen move. Lisa was feeling a slight vibration on her elbow.

Quietly Megan, up on her tiptoes, moved over to the

rock and put her hands on it, it was vibrating almost like the vibrating of a cat purring that's sitting in your lap. Megan motioned the others over to have a look. Lisa got up and quietly dusted herself off and joined them. There was a trickle of blood running down the front edge of her scalp and down her cheek. Jerry gave her his clean handkerchief and a kiss on the other side of her forehead. Out of his first-aid kit he also produced a Band-Aid that he quickly applied.

Everyone put their hands on the rock, only Frank recoiled and then again placed his hands back where they had been. Frank lowered his eyes to keep everyone from seeing the twinge of fear he was experiencing, this was not an adrenaline fear but a hair rising on the back of the neck fear with cold beads of sweat forming on his forehead and running down his chin like a cave drip. This was a flee type of fear welling up in his throat. When Frank looked down he saw a big toe print in some soft dirt that was partially under the rock they were all touching. He pointed. Jerry's eyes followed Frank's arm all the way to the end of his finger and beyond, then he too pointed.

Gently Megan and Lisa, the men watching in rapt awe, began moving their hands deftly all over the rock, near a vertical crack, which had formed just a few moments before. No one said a word. The term "grave robber" came and went through Jerry's mind as he watched them gently probe for a hidden latch or sensor. This was more fun than any Egyptian dig he had ever been on or read about. He was just hoping there were no curses to befall them if they got the thing open.

Suddenly, so suddenly it made Frank jump back which in turn startled Jerry, there was a gush of air, dust flying everywhere and a light scraping sound. The crack in the rock began to slowly widen. Cupping his hands beside his eyes Jerry tried to see inside but it was darker than a murder's heart. His favorite author would have said "stygian blackness prevailed".

Lisa and Megan joined Jerry trying to look inside; everyone now had flashlights in hand. The opening was large enough to squeeze through and suddenly Frank found himself standing outside alone. Looking around he grabbed his flashlight and turning sideways and bending over slightly backward squeezed inside the orifice. Just as he got inside the door swiveled open to allow easier access. Frank kicked some dirt in the direction of the door.

Initially they all saw nothing but a rock wall that looked as though it had been chiseled and a well-used dirt path leading down a short tunnel. The only sound was their excited breathing and a low, machine generated humming sound that got louder as they descended. After about thirty feet their descent stopped at a blank rock wall, the path showed signs of use, although nothing very discernible in the soft powdery dirt, but the footpath seemed to go under the wall. Again they searched for a catch mechanism or a sensor of some type. Dr. Paulson now felt like Dr. Jones searching for artifacts.

CHAPTER 14

MIKE TURNBULL HAD a good start on this story, but he didn't have quite enough to call it in to his buddy Max, the editor. Some of the locals in Ione remembered the summer scientists and gave him directions to their cabins in an area where all the locals referred to as the old Walsh place. He found it easily.

There were no vehicles in evidence but he felt he should knock to see if anyone was at home. He received no response to his knocking or his calling out, so he tried the handle, it was locked. "How shocking," he thought, "they don't trust anyone." He looked at the old lock a moment, pulled out his plastic medical plan card and slipped it into the rotting door jam, past the door latch, and in he walked. He smiled, very pleased with himself. Putting on his driving gloves he began to sift through the papers on the desk, reading about the reported sightings and the rough assumptions of the researchers. These items only raised his curiosity further.

He looked at the old computer and read the screen but all he could figure out was that they had analyzed something and found an unknown element or something like that. He went into the adjoining bedroom where he found a picture of, who he perceived to be, the two of the Scientist's together under the Arch in St. Louis. He liked the woman's features and build, mostly her build. Leaving no stone unturned in the pursuit of a story he went through their luggage like a seasoned professional thief and he paused at some lacy undergarments; he smelled her perfume; her soap and her shampoo. He wanted to meet this woman.

Mike turned his attentions to the brief case finding a valid, although well used, passport. He thought this Dr. Paulson looked more like a football coach than a geek professor. Mike was really going to make up some juicy stuff in his fermented little brain about this "scientific love fest" article, but that was going to be saved for the next issue.

He moved to the other cabin and went through Megan's things thoroughly. He found a picture of Dr. Hanley on what appeared to be a mountain climbing expedition, probably in the Himalayas, and he liked the way she filled out her hiking gear just fine. There was a clean Forest Ranger's uniform in the closet, which just added fuel to the fire. Mike could have cared less if they found evidence of Bigfoot, he had enough stuff for a Penthouse Letter or a "My Lover is a 9 foot hairy monster" article or an orgy of scientists and a Bigfoot super baby creation by the mad lustful scientists. Mike was seriously thinking of making a career out of this group.

He had found enough information about each of them, their colleges, universities, where and what their doctorates were in and the fact that both the lady doctors were D cups.

A car went by on the dusty gravel road out from, but it did not stop. Its passing brought Mike out of his writer's fog and back to reality. He had obtained the Bjornson's names and

location from the notes of the report and he was going to talk
with them real soon.

Checking his GPS Mike concluded that Addy was too far
to go today, he had an appointment with the bird watcher who
had the pictures of Bigfoot. Mike knew he could not pass up
those pictures. He figured he already had enough for a series
of stories about orgy's, lust, monsters, government cover-ups
and UFO's to keep his gin soaked imagination going for six
months to a year. Mike had never been happier.

He carefully re-locked the door, got into his rental Explorer
and floored it toward Newport and his next interview. He had
taken pictures of a lot of the items in the cabin which he would
enhance here and there for the desired effect, especially the
lady scientists.

CHAPTER 15

OWARD THE BOTTOM of the wall Megan noticed, what was supposed to look like, a small round polished rock. To her it looked more like a button than its intended disguise as a rock. She reached toward it waving her hand but nothing happened. Continuing down with her hand she pushed it and still nothing happened. Thinking a moment or two she reached for her flashlight and focused the bean on the small object, it reflected a green luminous interior but still nothing happened. Then she got the bright idea to look for a pattern of some sort and asked the others to turn their flashlights off, which they did, as the other three stood there in fascinated amazement watching Megan work. She then directed her light straight at the wall in an ever increasing circle. Then Megan saw the button on the top of the wall. It looked like a failsafe key system, she surmised, maybe they needed to be pushed at the same time, simultaneously. Putting the toe of her boot on the lower rock and stretching up to touch the higher button caused the rock door to swing out, just like an old gothic castle with a hidden passage. She immediately thought of the movie "Young Frankenstein" and the hilarious "put the candle back" routine that had her howling with laughter when she had watched the movie, in fact every time she watched the movie she laughed at that part. Peering inside they all saw the path go downward again, so they followed it like rats in a maze.

Just as the wall swung closed behind them there was a blood curdling, heart stopping, grab your ass and kiss it good-bye, scream. Blue, red and yellow strobe lights flashed twice and then stayed on. Their vision was altered and everyone was temporarily blind as a white light flashed several times and then there was complete darkness. They could not even see using their flashlights because their vision had been altered so harshly. Then another horror of hands, gigantic hairy hands, seemed to come out of the wall and pull them forward. All of a sudden the small space smelled like they had been accosted by a whole herd of skunks. Fortunately the smell dissipated quickly and a more antiseptic aroma gratefully began to fill the chamber.

The four were guided to stone hard chairs, which they later discovered, were hewn out of the living rock. A bowl was placed on their heads with an elastic strap fitted with a strap under their chins. Lisa and Megan both groaned; Frank was cursing; Jerry just kind of went through the rough ordeal rather without comment, other than a low groan now and again.

Each of them was still totally blind from the rapid series of flashing lights; lights designed just for that purpose. Then they heard clicking and screeching and a few sounds that were very difficult to describe or even identify. This definitely was some sort of speech, a language, inside their heads directly into their brains along with a few rapid pictures, too rapid to make any sense of anyway. Instant migraine headaches caused everyone to groan in unison and be on the verge of passing out. Frank could feel the welling of vomit, but was able to choke it down again.

The talking was too fast to understand, Jerry put his hand up in front of himself to motion for them to slow it down. The sounds stopped a few moments and then resumed, somewhat quieter and slower but still unintelligible.

In each helmet bowl the speech was becoming more understandable. At first it was just random words rapidly passing through the human speech centers like "you, we, I, talk, you, we, I with, why are, what are, where is, are you, what can…etc." as if learning the language directly from and then back into their brains. There was a sudden feedback like a microphone at a rock concert but much more intense and all four passed out quickly. They were each caught, gently and held in their seats until consciousness returned.

When Jerry awoke his eye sight had begun to return. He could see dark shapes and smaller lighter shapes moving around. Lisa whispered into Jerry's ear, "What the hell have we gotten ourselves into? I'm scared."

"Me too," he replied, "I think we're at home with the forest people. I just hope their friendly and receiving guests today."

"Me too," she said squinting to try and focus her vision, "can you see anything?"

"Just blobs of light and dark shapes, large and small, at the moment, how about you?"

"About the same," she squeezed his hand. Lisa was comforted that there was no evidence of restraints in the chairs. Lisa leaned the other way, "Frank? Megan? Are you two there?"

"Yeah, we're here," answered Megan as she squeezed Frank's had.

"Can you see? Are you two OK?"

"We're alright," answered Frank, "Megan and I are just fine. Can't see a damned thing, but I think we're fine."

All four chuckled which made the movement in front of them stop for a moment. In the helmet bowls, a voice, "Is there understanding?" all four just sat there looking around trying to focus their eyes, blinking with tear filled eyes.

"Is there understanding? Can you hear myself?"

"Yeah, I hear you," answered Jerry, with a mumbled agreement from the other three.

"This is good. We have not tried these on your primitive persons…uh…species before. I/we were not sure how it would…uh…functions…uh…work. Your brains are so… odd…we were…scared…no…afraid this might…terminate… cease your…kill you. Are you understanding?"

There was more screeching and grunts and then, "I am sorry. We are working…adjusting…this machine to adapt to your primitive brain waves to…translate our language… brain emissions…to match your primitive speech. You have most unrefined speech patterns. It has been 50 thousand… crandor…uh…years since we tried to…verbalize…talk with your kind. I am pleased you can at least talk now. Who is your chief…uh…leader…uh no…speaker for…"

"I am," answered Jerry adjusting the bowl on his head, "for now, if everyone agrees." There was a mumbled OK from the other three. The migraines were increasing with every word.

"Oomglat blo-ga sathcha," Came a loud reply into each helmet bowl. The humans recoiled in severe pain. "Oh, I am…

sorry...I am still...adjustment...uh...adjusting...uh...tuning this machine. Are you Ja-er-old?"

"Yes. Can you say Jerry easier?"

"Jarry"

"That's close enough."

"Thank...you...Jarry."

"Why did you bring us here," began Jerry without further introductions or diplomacy.

Ignoring the question, "I am Gesroh."

"OK, nice to meet you, Gesroh. Now, why did you bring us here?"

"Oh yes, to the pinnacle...ah...point. We did not bring you here. You...arrived...came...stumbled upon our lair... home because of rebellious...wild youth.

Jerry's eyes were beginning to clear; he could almost make out a more distinct blob than before. "Explain please."

"Explain...extrapolate...further define...yes...we brought several youth here for a seasonal outing...vacation. They are young and...impetuous...strong willed...and wishing to see more of your world than just the...beautiful... pristine...lovely forests and mountains. In the process one of our, uh...maidens...young females...ah yes...girls has gone missing. We of the higher cast, no...clan...maybe tribe...no... clan have sent out search parties to find...she...her."

"What was that entire racket last night and why the plain trail leading up this mountain home of yours?"

"Racket...not a game implement...noise...yes, you were scared and angered by the young ones. They were going into the forest to mate and frolic...play...mate. You interrupted their fun with all those flashing lights and image holders... uh...cameras."

"They scared the hell out of us!"

"Hell…metaphor…extreme feelings. I am sorry for that perhaps you can get your hell back."

Lisa elbowed Jerry, "who cares about all that crap last night. Can we hear more about their lost girl?"

"I am sorry I do not understand. What does crap… excrement…spore have to do with losing your hell?"

"Forget the comment. Can we hear more, please, about your lost girl?"

"Her name is Aaah. She was frolicking with Ustra and he returned quite unhappy without her. He left her sleeping in a cave in the lower forest. When he went back for her she had gone. We have been…looking…searching almost since our arrival two…weeks, no why can't this device operate properly…months, no…days, yes, days ago."

"Didn't Aaah leave any tracks or spore?" asked a skeptical Lisa.

"Your females are strong headed…independent…hard to control."

"Yes they are, please go on and answer the question," continued Jerry rubbing his temples hard to try and relieve the pain.

"Tracks? Spore?" murmured Gesroh playing with some dials and switches, "no she left no tracks. She left no…spores…or any signs of passing. She is mature enough for that," he said looking at the other creature in the room, a huge female, who grunted a few syllables and fell silent, not taking her eyes off the four humans.

Unable to restrain herself any longer, "Where do you come from and where did you arrive on this planet?" asked Megan, her eyes finally were starting to clear but the pain in her head was still quite severe.

"I have forgotten how interesting your females are," said Gesroh, "we landed in 3 small vessels near a meadow a few nights ago. There were crude buildings made out of tree material, inhabited by two of your kind…human…Homo sapiens…no, human is correct. We Teer are from not only a different planet but another plane, time and space. I cannot explain it yet in your language. We call our planet Kleek, which means the place of the Teer. It is a very old planet and there are nothing but dwellings there now, no beautiful woody plants or high rocks and white frozen water…you call it snow…a strange name."

"Okay," Frank chimed in, a slight irritation in his voice, "we know where you landed. Why did you kill those cattle?"

"Cattle? Oh yes…the domesticated food beasts of your planet. Our pilots, the Kev-tah'esh, the gray people, find parts of these animals very tasty. We allow them such small pleasures when we visit because they hunger for flesh and the red liquid…no…blood. We take our pleasure from green leaves and your wide choice of berries."

"Come again?" snorted Frank as he tried to stand, "you let them slaughter animals as payment for the trip? How long has this little arrangement be going on anyway?"

"A moment, I must calculate in your primitive mathematics," said Gesroh as he deftly punched some oversized buttons on his console, "yes, I believe it comes to 30 thousand years."

Jerry almost fell off his chair and had to stop Lisa's reaction as she sat up very quickly, the helmet almost falling backward off her head.

"We have the ability to fold…warp…manipulate space and time. We are an old race as are the Kev-tah'esh. I, myself, have been visiting this blue planet for over 500 years."

CHAPTER 16

DENNIS GRAHAM, OF the National Scandal T.V. program, was sitting in the main street diner in Newport, Washington going over his notes from his interview with Jansen, the bird watcher. He was also looking at the photograph's his paper just paid 50 grand for and was formulating his byline when he looked up to see a familiar face stroll in and sit at the counter. "Mike, come over here and join me. I have a feeling we're both working the same story."

Mike smiled at Dennis and, grabbing his fresh steaming coffee, sat down in the squeaky plastic covered cushion of the booth. "I see you've talked to Jansen. What did he soak you for those?" asked Mike gesturing at the pictures Dennis was putting back into the manila envelope.

"50," replied Dennis sealing the envelope.

"He got me for 50 too. Jansen, for a bird watcher, is turning out to be quite a crook. He probably told you they were exclusive?"

"Of course, I made him sign a statement to that effect so he will see us in court if you publish them and vice versa I imagine. What else have you acquired?"

Mike and Dennis used to work together at the Star but

never really trusted each other, "not much, I am kind of running out of angles on this one. I can't get in to see any Rangers and I hear there are some research types in the area but they aren't talking either. What have you gotten?" asked Mike out of courtesy not expecting any information.

"Not much," hedged Dennis, "I just talked with our swindler Jansen. I was going to contemplate my next move over lunch." Just about that time a pretty waitress, whose name tag said Doris, brought out the meatloaf special, with mashed potatoes, gravy and succotash.

"That looks and smells good Doris, can I have one too please and a refill on the coffee?" She smiled and wrote the ticket as she went to the kitchen window.

"Another special, Howard."

"You got it," was the reply from the unseen chef in the kitchen.

Mike had no intention of sharing his interview he had with the young Ranger, the information on the Bjornson's or his ransacking the research facility. Friend or no friend he was going to publish this story as exclusively as possible.

"I've got an appointment with an Air Force Colonel about some UFO sighting but to me it's not really related. I may be able to file a couple of stories instead of just these smudged pictures." Dennis was lying because the pictures were sharp and pretty detailed. "This Colonel wants 10 or 20 grand to leak his input, unofficially of course."

"Of course," pulling out his pen, "who did you say this Colonel was and his name?"

"I didn't Mike. Knowing you I'm not going to give you a lead any more than you are going to give me one. I know you're holding out on me, you always have, so let's just eat and talk about your secretary's moral attitude or maybe Doris' legs.

"Okay, my favorite subject, women's long beautiful legs," smiled Mike as he put catsup on his steaming meatloaf and gravy.

CHAPTER 17

THEIR VISION QUITE clear now all four humans were looking at a group of beings of huge proportions. The male was easily 9 or 10 feet tall with arms the size of a weight lifters legs. The female was just slightly daintier than a school bus but did have some feminine features and each breast the size of a cow's udder, with very little sag.

Gesroh continued his story, "We met the Kev-tah'esh when they invaded our planet to try and subjugate us as another food source. That struggle lasted for almost 1,000 of your years. The Teer abhors violence but only to a point and we finally overcame the Kev-tah'esh only when alternate food sources were discovered on parallel planes. As I already told you we warp the time and space for them, our technology; for the use of their flying machines, their technology."

"Are their appetites only for cattle and horses from our planet?" inquired Megan who was feeling a good deal of revulsion for the grays, one of which was standing in the back of the room.

"No, they have taken some humans for study and for human breeding stock for their farms on their home world of Kev-tah, but they do prefer the other delicacies from this world. They far prefer the four-legged variety so abundant on this planet. They have been taking humans for hundreds of years and cloning them for the best product to care for their food herds of four-legged stock.

For thousands of years they have also taken other stock, cloned and bred each of a particular taste, the horse and cow a particular favorite. Their appetites know no limits for the fluids and the organs. They do, although seldom, eat the flesh of their stock," Gesroh stopped to regard his listeners but continued, "I am surprised that you do not ask about the Clot-tor or the Effe. They too have been visiting your world, although they have other reasons. The Effe have seeded many planets through this Galaxy by taking…by kidnapping your human brethren for nearly 300,000 years. They take thriving cultures and place them in safe, nurturing environments for future planet relocations. The Effe have populated several hundreds of thousands of planets." Gesroh stopped to adjust another machine. He seemed to have learned the rudiments of our primitive language now and could communicate with much more ease.

The Effe, after several generations, go back and harvest the results of their seeding expeditions to fill their need for constant nourishment. Beings of pure energy must feed all too frequently. The Effe have degenerated into nothing more than flesh farmers. However, this planet was not supposed to be one of the Effe farming planets. It was seeded by the Bastra Nok with one of their seeding meteors.

The four humans just listened, looking with questioning eyes at one another and the being that could not stop talking, now that he has learned the primitive language. Although it was all talking with his mind not his mouth.

"We have shown the Effe how to warp space and time to suit their purposes. They are a barren, dying race, who was evolving to space when we Teer were still just creatures contented with our once forested planet."

"The Clot-tor are a war-like race of cold-blooded creatures who just like to travel from their home planet of Tor. Unlike the Effe who, as I said, are creatures of almost pure energy and light, the Clot-tor are not friendly to anyone and will fight at the least provocation. Including declaring war on a whole race, with no provocation, other than their planet was in their way as they moved through space."

"The Kev-tah'esh had a war with the Clot-tor but their captured breeding stock was distasteful to them because the Clot-tor are not carbon based but a silicone based reptilian race," as Gesroh was finally taking a breath the female finally began to speak. She had been standing nearby, almost motionless, just listening with some sort of device in her right ear that looked like a cell phone earpiece but it was the size of a curling iron.

She stumbled over the words at the beginning, just as Gesroh had, trying to get used to using her brain to communicate with the humans in their primitive dialect, "My name...my name is...my name is Keai (pronounced Key-eye). My daw...daughter is Aaah and we...I...we...require, uh...need your...aid...assistance...to help to...seek her...find her," at which point she stopped and barked and grunted to Gesroh, who adjusted the settings on a console near him. Satisfied with what Gesroh had done she again turned to the four humans, "I am asking you for your help in this matter of my lost daughter."

Jerry leaned forward, "What would you like us to do

exactly? We had a very hard time finding you and the trail was extremely easy to follow."

"Yes, your deductive reasoning has come into question, but you did finally find we…us and I've read your thought patterns and I believe you can be…trusted? Yes trusted to help." She pointed to Megan and Frank, "You were the ones that Aaah sprayed with our mating enhancement compound. I can still sense it in your hair follicles."

"Sprayed us with what?" Megan did not like the sound of it and she especially did not like being treated like a lab experiment.

"Our mating compound; we use it to fire the blood; to make our frolicking special and remembered. It also helps the male to stay in the rutting mood much longer. Instead of a short mating…uh…you say a quickie…coupling time… it lasts through the night and keeps up both of the partner's enjoyment while keeping them at the highest peak of performance," making Keai actually seem to blush and smile with her dirty yellow but nicely aligned teeth.

Frank cast a sideway glance at Megan, "I wondered why you warmed up so fast, but I am not complaining one bit," and he took her hand. She smiled wearily but knew she had developed feelings for him too.

"It has a lasting residual effect that can remain for many of your years. She sprayed you just for fun because the smell in the air indicated you both wished to couple and frolic. We have sprayed it on many species here on this world to test their reactions; yours were most interesting to be sure. Now, can we discuss Aaah and how to find her?" Keai pursed her considerable lips like a mother scolding a child.

"How can we find her? Your species has been eluding us

for thousands of year. How do you suppose we can overcome that?" asked Jerry whose eyes were finally focused and could see the room and all of its occupants clearly.

"Yes, we have been able to elude almost all human contact when we wished it. Your minds, although strange, are easily fooled, at least at short distances."

"Okay, so how would you like us to find Aaah?" interjected Frank.

"Each of us has a location sensor implanted in our neck, just below the skull. It monitors health as well as working as a location device. This is what it looks like," said Gesroh as he extended his huge open hand with a small marble sized object that blinked with an internal power source and a wire, about 4 inches long, protruding from it. He handed it to Jerry in the other hand he had a device that looked like a small computer game, although it looked smaller in that enormous hand and he gave that to Jerry also. "On this you can find her. The terrain is superimposed as the object is carried. The device, as long as it is operational, will always show a location. This is set only on Aaah's frequency and her device still seems to be working, although at a very low output."

"What would cause the device not to work?"

"Should her life force cease to function, which is where the power source is most taken from the individual brain patterns after its insertion. The original power source only keeps the device working until it is inserted; they are made for each individual, not made in large quantities.

"Does this thing also make you invisible?"

"No, we have the ability to blend in completely with our surroundings which might make it seem that way."

"Why would you have this power source then, if you only

make them when you intend to use them? I mean, with your technology why is such a thing needed at all?" asked Lisa as she took it from Jerry and twirled it in her fingers. She noted that the wire seemed to have a life of its own, as she moved the marble sized device the wire kept moving away from touching her skin.

"We are of a mind to give each of you one of these and chart your movements. We could communicate brain-to-brain at any distance; I believe with some buffering, you might call it telepathy, to help in the search. I'm sure you can appreciate that we would not be able to accompany you."

A tear formed in Keai's eyes as Gesroh spoke as if pleading her case. Both Megan and Lisa looked at Jerry for a response. Frank just sat in stunned silence. Jerry looked at his companions contemplating the situation then Gesroh spoke again, "There is one more small problem I need to tell you about." All human eyes turned to Gesroh.

"What is that very slight problem you need to tell us about?" inquired Jerry feeling that all was not right in the merry old Land of Oz.

Loosing eye contact with the humans or Poc-cin in his language, Gesroh continued, "It has to do with two of our kind. We have a crime...criminal...yes, criminal element even in our society. We usually imprison them on your high mountain range on the other side of this planet. Him... Himal...Himalayas, you call them. Yes, that is what your brain is telling me, an interesting name. We call them Na-tok-lum-ta, the place of imprisonment."

Jerry sat back on his rock chair and flicked the bowl helmet to one side with his thumb, "How does that affect us and this problem," although he had an idea where this was going like an episode of "X" Files.

"Two of them, their names are Grious and Tic-Nar, were locked in prison transit cell accompanying our group. With some help they have escaped the holding room from this safe place and are currently at large in this area."

"Do you think they have something to do with Aaah and her disappearance?" asked Frank, the law enforcement side of his training now kicking in.

"Yes I am sure of it. They must have convinced her to let them out and then they picked her up to take with them, at least we think they took her. She may have gone with them because of a slight element of danger. She enjoys "frolicking" with males and sometimes older males. This was her discovery trip now that she has come of age."

"Come of age?" was the reply from all four humans, sounding remarkably similar to the 3 Stooges. Although no one was sure which one was Curly?

"She is prime breeding age now, 150 of your years," replied Keai, "she is searching for a mate. She and Ustra tried but she became angered with Ustra's immaturity, he is just 200 now. Our females mature faster than our young males and she wants more staying power in his prowess and performance. Aaah has regrettably always had a liking for older males. These two criminals seemed to have led her away or taken her as a hostage from the cave where Ustra left her sleeping; they deactivated their own locator devices so we are having difficulty tracking their movements. We are having difficulty with species scans, infrared sensors and other conventional means. Aaah is still very much alive but has not moved from her, rather precarious, position for two sunrises…ah…days."

"I just have to ask," Smiled Lisa, "How can you follow these two outlaws if they disabled the thing in their heads?"

"Outlaw…oh, same as criminal…slang…meaning outside the law, I like it. These outlaws of our planet must undergo many tests and a few tortures before we bring them here. One of those is a brain inventory, of sorts. We can trace them through their profile, although it is much more difficult. We are programming our machine now but it will take perhaps two of your days to configure to brain patterns instead of the implanted device.

All four Poc-cin looked at each other and after a quick conference Megan and Frank went into another chamber with Keai. Lisa and Jerry stayed with Gesroh, although they were all becoming extremely mentally fatigued. The interaction between the two species, Poc-cin and Teer, was fatiguing for everyone but mostly the Poc-cin because of the powerful minds of the Teer.

CHAPTER 18

ENNIS LEFT THE more devious Mike as he was trying to get to know the lovely Doris, at least for a short time, and Doris appeared to be having none of it. She was small town but not stupid. Dennis was heading to the courthouse. Jansen had told him about the city official who had gotten pushy with him. He quickly found the auditor's office and went inside. Dennis noticed it was 1:35 p.m., 1335 hours in his mind. He was greeted by a lady whose desk name plate read "Betty" and it did not escape his attention that she was quite attractive. She had big brown eyes, light brunette medium length hair and obviously working hard to take care of her assets.

"May I help you, sir?" she asked with a nice smile. He could tell she was a smoker but that did not bother him too much.

"Yes, I'd like to talk with Jason Gordon please."

"Is he expecting you; do you have an appointment?"

"No, I work for an out of town media source and I just have a couple of questions for him, if he has the time."

"A moment please," she went into an office on the side, kind of out of sight from the counter area. Dennis was mildly surprised to see a black man emerge.

Extending his hand, "I'm Jason Gordon, what can I do for you?"

"Hi, I'm Dennis Graham. Do you have a card sir?"

"Yes, of course," Jason reached over to a card holder on the front counter and handed one to Dennis.

"You are an attorney and the Pend Oreille (pronounced Pond or Ray) County Auditor, very nice, thank you.

"Would you like to come into my office, Mr. Graham? Would you like some coffee or tea?"

"Yes to both. Coffee black, if you please."

"Betty, would you mind getting us two coffee's please. Thank you.

"Yes sir."

They both went into the office, followed almost immediately by Betty and two cups of hot and very aromatic coffee. It smelled like French Vanilla. Jason gestured Dennis to a seat and then sat down smiling wondering where this was all leading.

"Thank you for seeing me on such short notice. I just wanted to ask you about Steve Jansen, the bird watcher, who happened to take some interesting pictures."

"I can only answer questions that pertain to the county auditor?" asked Jason.

"Well sir, word has it you tried to slap a gag order on our bird watcher. Is that true?"

"I was doing a favor for a friend, nothing more. I offered some legal advice to the man and my friend and that was the extent of it. I am afraid you have wasted your time."

"May I ask what you advised your friend and Jansen to do regarding the photographs or at least who your friend is so I can talk with him or her?"

"No, you may not. Is there anything else I can help you with outside of attorney client privilege?"

"Well when you put it so formally I guess not. I do want to thank you for your time," Dennis arose, shook Jason's hand and walked out. He caught Betty's eye and said thank you, quietly, just moving his lips. She smiled and went back to her work. Out on the street Dennis made a few notes and walked slowly up Main Street. Suddenly someone was walking next to him; he looked up from his notes and saw it was Betty.

"Hello," said Dennis trying to hide his astonishment, "going my way?"

"Yes, let's go up to the drive in and get a sundae," she grabbed his arm with both hands and pulled him in that direction, up the hill, north.

"Okay, I guess I can take a sundae break with such a charming companion," agreed the ever skeptical Dennis. It was a short walk to the old drive in.

Seated and eating a pretty good banana split, Dennis looked over at the lady, "Betty, why did you pick me up?" which brought a smile to her pretty face.

"I picked you up to see if you wanted some information for your money."

"Oh, I see, purely mercenary huh. How much information and how much money are we talking about, exactly?"

"I could use twenty thousand."

His eyebrow lifted a little, "and what will I get for my money?"

"I can tell you what they talked about and who was in the conversation. Does that earn a little money?"

"It may be worth something at that. I'm not sure I can promise twenty thousand for it though."

"Okay, well I have to go, my break is almost over, I guess if you don't want my information I'll talk with the other fellow in town, Mike isn't it?"

"I'll see what I can do…"

"No, it's twenty or nothing, good-bye," and she got up to leave. Dennis grabbed her arm gently and decided he never wanted to play poker in this town. He also decided that she wasn't too bad either; he might even try to negotiate a roll on the bed springs. He had to get more than just a couple of names for the twenty grand though.

"If you have a little more time perhaps I can pay your fee."

"Okay then, let's go outside," she said getting him to stand, pay the check and she pulled him outside where they sat at the most remote picnic table. "I know you may not like this but let's act a little like new lovers and cuddle a little," she said moving closer, "then no one will think twice about us out here talking low and intimately." There was a musky odor of flowers and slightly fermented berries in the air, very thick and heady but pleasant.

"A fine idea," said Dennis as he grabbed her around the waist and pulled her to him. He planted a kiss on her neck, "why don't we continue this at your place, I could really get into this role," whispered Dennis suddenly losing his eland for an interview.

Betty snuggled closer, "Okay, I'll take the rest of the afternoon off. My children both have an after school game today. What is that strange scent it smells like musk, berries and flowers? It's giving me such thoughts."

A pair of yellow eyes looked out from under the drive-in. Aaah had been scavenging for food from the dumpster and had fallen asleep under the crawl space, that she had dug out a little to fit her girth. She smiled, in her own way, as the endorphin spray swept over the Poc-cin. She thought they could both use a good frolic.

Hand in hand Dennis and Betty walked to her house. She called in on her cell phone that she had some urgent business to take care of and fortunately for the local populace her house was close. No sooner did they get through the door when clothes were thrown in all directions and the queen sized bed began to protest from the abuse. It was easily two hours before the fire died down.

Sweating and out of breath it was difficult to remember why they had together in the first place. Dennis, just recently divorced, had not had this kind of combat for a while. Betty had enjoyed herself too, also having had a bit of a dry spell lately.

"I had no idea you'd turn out to be such a rutting bull."

"Wow, me too that fire was hot. I really hate to break the mood but can we get back to the information you wanted to sell? By the way we're not finished yet this is just the end of round one. Smiling she grabbed his manhood and began to play, it began to respond almost immediately to her touch, to their mutual surprise and delight.

"Now can we get to the names please? Yes, that feels nice, but not so vigorously right now, thanks."

"Fine, I can wait a few minutes if you can. Well let's see Jason talked with the head Forest Ranger Frank Leonard and a Doctor Jerome Paulson from Eastern Washington University about how to stop the Jansen guy from selling some pictures to any newspaper people. Paulson wanted the pictures for himself and his research. Jason tried an old law that is still on the books, to enforce a gag order to keep from causing public panic. Your little man here isn't so little is he?"

"Could you slow down just a little please," she did slow her actions a little but she kept up the manipulation. She felt herself becoming more aroused.

"Was there anything else they talked about?" Dennis was having a little trouble concentrating on the interview.

"Yes, Paulson wanted to cut a deal for 30 thousand but Jansen wasn't having any of it and told all three of them to pack it "where the dun don't never shine" and he stormed out of the restaurant. Interesting choice of words don't you think?"

"That's nice," and Dennis rolled over as neither of them could hold off any longer. The bed springs were soon protesting loudly once again.

CHAPTER 19

"**DO YOU KNOW** where Aaah is exactly?" asked Jerry as the two giant beings helped him lie face down on the table that looked like a chiropractor's torture rack.

Still having some difficulty translating in his brain Gesroh answered, "she is located in the…village…town…city…no, town, under a small food hut on the edge of this town called Newport. It could be a café or restaurant, take your pick. Your brain is not exact on the type of building or place. I do not know what "fast food" means, there is so much clutter it is hard to isolate the correct terms in your speech. This will cause you no pain but you may be unconscious for a few…hours."

Just before completely laying down Lisa looked at Jerry, he managed a smile and squeezed her hand in an effort to assure her that they were doing the right thing although it seemed like this was like all the stories of alien abduction. Unexpectedly a mist caressed their faces and into their nostrils. Both humans lapsed into a deep dreamless sleep; it did not take too much as they were exhausted. Frank and Megan endured a similar procedure and just as painlessly. All four humans rested for several hours in a very deep recuperative sleep. After all they had been through this sleep was welcomed. The little wire was shortened somewhat to stay outside the skull and skin looking a little like an errant hair on their neck, something that is not noticeable at all on a Teer.

Meanwhile, the two fugitive Teer hovered on the edge of the forest, on the hillside of Cook's Mountain. Although eating some of the June plants, some insects and the new sprouts of the pine trees growing on the end of the branches had kept them from starving, they had killed a hapless deer and devoured it in its entirety in great mouthfuls. The Teer have evolved over the centuries to be vegetarians but criminals are reprogrammed to live off anything at hand. The Himalayan environment does not have enough plant life to sustain their great appetites, especially at the excessive altitudes where they choose to live away from the bothersome Poc-cin. Although not spoken of in most Teer circles the criminal element could, and on occasion has, eaten the unwary Poc-cin that might venture into their harsh environment.

These two criminals were determined not to get recaptured and equally determined to take Aaah with them for their pleasures. They had made plans to start a colony of criminals and begin terrorizing the Poc-cin and this seemed to be a good place to start that type of venture. Both of these individuals are relatively young for their species at 750 and 800 Earth years old, not quite middle aged. They also were hatching a plan to take over a safe haven and contact the Kev-tah'esh to transport them to other planets where there are more interesting animals and indigenous life forms if their plans did not work out in this place. Although they would not need to move off world too fast because the animal providing their current feast was quite tasty with iron rich red blood giving it a tangy, interesting flavor. Both figured they could stay on this backward planet for a few hundred years before moving on.

Grious and Tic-Nar finished the feast, buried the little that was left and curled up in a depression under an exposed root of a partially uprooted tree and slept the rest of the day. Absolute masters of disguise they both resembled dark mounds of dirt.

Aaah had wedged herself under the primitive structure where all the noisy Poc-cin were when daylight had come. She dug out more of a space for her own comfort and covered herself with the dirt in an effort to cover her scent. Comfortable at last she decided to sleep the day away and run for the forest when the darkness came. The people inside the restaurant kept remarking how bad the skunk population was becoming or that someone must have hit a whole family of skunks on the highway. The owner went over the hardware store and bought a whole case of air fresheners. He also put a call into the city animal control to come out and eradicate the skunk family that may be living under the building, but they were busy and would not be available until tomorrow.

Aaah awoke to see the two Poc-cin sitting near her. She sensed their attraction so she sprayed them to heighten their experience. The carefully mixed compound only works if there is an attraction, the pheromones will only match to the natural pheromones already being produced in a chemical attraction. If there is no attraction then there is just the pleasant odor of musk, berries and forest flowers. Aaah giggled to herself when they left in such a hurry. She thought back to Ustra and the fun they had together. She still thought of him as immature and a little pitiful but she decided she loved him anyway.

She was tired of being abused by the two older Teer she had helped get out of their holding cell.

Finally, in her own mind, she figured out why they had been imprisoned. She liked the frolic generally but they were cruel and mean during and after. They wanted to subjugate her and keep her around only for their pleasure not hers.

CHAPTER 20

DENNIS AND BETTY had somehow survived the pleasant night, neither got much sleep. Betty sent both of her high school aged children to friends' houses to stay the night. She fixed a quick meal for herself and Dennis and then right back in the sack. They had strong feelings for one another and the fire at this point in their budding relationship seemed unquenchable. Given time it would eventually mold its way into love, a true long lasting love.

For now though, Dennis left her sleeping. He got up, dressed and departed like a burglar. He had mixed feelings, but he left for his motel room to clean up and to get a much needed change of clothes. He couldn't help thinking that he had never given himself to a woman so completely, he felt unlike himself in a strange alternate reality, like he was standing in the room watching everything unfold before his eyes. When he finally got into the shower he had to wash himself very gingerly because he was a little sore and even raw in a very sensitive place.

In the restaurant his over easy eggs looked at him with a smirking glint, the bacon was smiling. He chased the sausages all over the plate and the hash browns were giggling. When he was in college he had similar trips smoking marijuana but not the day after getting lucky. That was one of the many reasons he had given up marijuana completely.

Betty was glad it was Saturday because at this point she was having difficulty walking. She was sure she was in love but realistic enough to be just as sure that the creep would probably never call her or see her again. She showered and put on loose fitting sweats to lounge around the house nursing her sore body parts. She curled up in a big easy chair with some black oolong tea and began reading the morning paper. She felt tired, of course, but a good feeling crept over her and the hot tea warmed her throat and stomach. Betty couldn't stop smiling and thinking of their night of unbridled passion.

Dennis, the cool calculating hard hitting reporter he had always been, could not keep his mind on anything except Betty and the lovemaking that had lasted well into the wee hours of the morning. He couldn't help but smile, as he drained his tomato juice, because he was actually proud of himself. Proud that he could keep up and keep going back for more. He had never even imagined a night like that in any fantasy he ever conjured. He was sure he would see her again and soon. Sore or not he couldn't keep his hands off of her for very long.

CHAPTER 21

RESTED NOW AND in touch with the safe area and Gesroh through directed telepathy, the four made their way back to the camp site. It took less time to go downhill, naturally, and soon they were actively breaking camp.

All four of them suddenly stopped what they were doing and came to a standing position and began receiving a message from Gesroh. Their eyes glazed over a bit and they all resembled secret service agents guarding a V.I.P. and listening to instructions from the agent in charge. Jerry even had to resist the urge of putting his finger next to his ear even though there was no ear piece to hold. They all felt a little foolish because the power of these types of communication seemed to immobilize them. It would take practice to act more natural during communications with their alien friends who are now their benefactors. The message was that Gesroh had lost Aaah's signal for the moment. He gave reference coordinates and a mental map image of the area north of Newport on the east slope of Cook's Mountain. All four had the instant headache from the powerful beings rich mind transmission. After it was over they all passed around a bottle of pain killers and took them with beer for a more lasting effect.

The plus side to being linked to the aliens and the alien computer, and all of its subroutines, was that they all have firsthand fascinating information about the Teer home world, some of their technology and a lot of information about the Kev-tah'esh as well as some of the other travelers of the galaxy that, at least Megan was sure, had never been seen or heard of in Earth's recorded official history. They all hoped they could remember half of the stuff coursing through their gray matter.

After the transmission ceased Lisa contacted Gesroh and asked that he send less powerful data streams. She said it almost blew the back of her skull off and all of them were suffering a great deal. All Gesroh said was that he would try. He also added that the next prisoner transport was due in a few days and he would like to relocated Grious and Tic-Nar too, what he called the high mountains (Na-tok-lum-ta in their language), what we call the Himalayas.

They all now understood, because of the colorful thought transmissions, that the Himalayas on this world have been the prison without bars of the Teer for Centuries. It is a place that barely sustains their existence and teaches quite a lesson to the criminal element both in humility and being forced to spend all of their time searching for food instead of harming other Teer or taking others possessions. It did not however keep them from harming the Poc-cin who inhabit this desolate area where the Yeti is both revered and feared.

The Council that passes sentence does not care if they kill one another or that they must be programmed to eat flesh; it only cares that it is a fit punishment for any crimes committed. There are female criminals too and sometimes families were started in the old times, now, just before drop off they neuter the males. This is the fate Grious and Tic-Nar do not look forward to and why they seized the opportunity to escape.

There have been occasions where a sentence was paid in full and the criminal was actually brought back to Kleek, the home world. These returning criminals told stories and wrote of their adventures and usually became wealthy in their declining years. The average life span of a Teer is 1 to 2 thousand Earth years. Having conquered most disease, both their own and several Earth strains, their lives tended to linger in their robust, gargantuan bodies.

A typical prison sentence can last 4 to 5 hundred years so there are only a few survivors of the prison planet, but it is also a favorite excursion planet. Families of high officials, scientists and the wealthy come to this planet they call Strig'et ocouts (excursion planet 3) for study, rest and just to live among the trees again. The Teer have far over populated Kleek and can only visit parks or set aside exclusive sanctuaries to live among trees in their home world. There are far too many Teer and every sanctuary is overrun. Even the estates of the wealthy cannot stop the ebb of Teer looking for solace in the trees.

The research team and the Park Ranger have had this knowledge thrust upon them along with other facts about the Earth's climate changes, ice ages and volcanoes just to mention a few items of interest. The Teer seem to know far more about our planet than the people who live on it, but they have been here longer so that really shouldn't count.

Jerry and Lisa just threw their gear into their room and headed for the shower. Megan and Frank finished their unpacking, putting everything away meticulously, and then headed for the shower in the second cabin. While they really only had time to scrub their respective partner's back there was some playfulness and these "short showers" took an hour or more.

Frank could not stick around and chew the facts with the scientists because he had to check in and find out what else was going on in his forest. After a lingering kiss from Megan, Frank reluctantly sped off toward the Ranger station.

"I'm open for ideas, where do we go from here?" asked Jerry as he downed his fifth or sixth pancake, "damn I was hungry. How long were we Gesroh's guests, a week or month? The guy sure wasn't much on handing out food, was he?"

"I don't know how long we were there but I just ate more than my father and big brother combined," smiled Megan as she gulped the last of her stack of pancakes and her second glass of milk.

Lisa, who thought he had been cooking for a crew of lumberjacks or ranch hands was eating standing up and finally shut down the grill as the last of the pancake mix, sausages, eggs and bacon were cooked and just as quickly consumed, "I guess we had better get over to the east slope of Cook's Mountain and see if we can pick up a trail." She held up the sensor that Gesroh had given her for DNA trails, "if they were there in the last day or so this should show us a sign."

Leaning back in her chair Megan groaned, "I think I just went up a pants size, I can hardly breathe," she said unsnapping the top button of her jeans, a glimpse of pink and white lace peeked over the top of the zipper. She threw her cotton shirt over the top just to keep out any prying eyes, herself slightly embarrassed about being so familiar with her colleagues.

"I would like to point out, if I may," added Jerry, "that our ride is not here. Did Frank give you tell you when he was coming back?" said Jerry looking over a Megan, "why did we let him leave anyway, that Ranger headquarters is over in Newport."

"Well, come to think of it I don't know why he left without us and I have no idea when he will be returning," Megan said leaning forward and putting both elbows on the table, "any suggestions?"

Lisa stopped chewing looking first at Megan and then at Jerry. There was a smirk on Jerry's face because he thought he could hear a car coming down the road. A large vehicle, the size of the forestry suburban or pickup stopped in a cloud of dust and crunching gravel. "My guess is that's Frank," said Jerry as he grabbed his day pack and went toward the front door, "and I bet he is just as bewildered about things as we are."

Frank already had the doors open for all of them to get in, "come on we don't have any time to mess around," he yelled revving the big 350 fuel injected engine. Megan slid in neatly next to him with Jerry and Lisa diving into the back seat, the doors closed by themselves when he hit the gas creating big billowing clouds of dust and throwing gravel everywhere. "There are reporters nosing all around this area from a newspaper rag and a T.V. scandal show, my district boss is beginning to ask me some embarrassing questions and I think one of my own Rangers gave an interview to one of them. I think we really need to get over to the east side of Cook's Mountain and pick up the trail. Instead of leaving I should have phoned in but I contacted headquarters by radio and then came back for you all."

"I get no sense as to which direction they may be heading in but I did get a sense that Teer tend to browse familiar territory," said Jerry as all eyes in the vehicle focused on him. Frank was watching a little too much in the mirror and nearly missed the curve. "Frank slow down, I think we may be going the wrong way. Here's my theory, if they do like to roam familiar territory, where did we have so much trouble with them?"

"Huckleberry Mountain," was the group response.

"Right and isn't that close to their safe area?" asked Megan pulling her note book out of her day pack.

"Yes, but the safe area is actually located behind Huckleberry on the north side of Smackout Pass," added Lisa.

"That's right. It is rather a long trek for them but my hunch says Huckleberry Mountain. Let's go back to our old base camp and set up an observation post and, I'm sorry to say, keep a cold camp. Frank, did you get some chow?"

"Yeah, I stopped in Ione and we've got a cooler full of stuff, a few blankets and chairs in the back of the rig and most of our camping gear. I was expecting a day or two of tracking without going home."

"Okay that's great, now Huckleberry Mountain and Big Meadow Lake are only about 10 miles from here. I think our best bet is to go back there instead of driving our butts all over the countryside from Newport to Ione, just to trail them back to the safe area, assuming we could actually find their trail. Covering the roughly 50 square miles of wilderness will be nothing for them and they would probably lead us all over the place anyway."

"But isn't our prime objective to rescue Aaah from where she is in Newport?" asked Lisa.

"We cannot extract her during the day, that would really cause a commotion and besides she may not know we are there to help. Unless she is totally lost she will probably be heading back tonight when it gets dark. I am hoping when she starts moving we will be able to pick up a signal and maybe then that will guide us to her location."

All of a sudden their brains seemed consumed with a powerful transmission, "I agree with your very logical thinking," was the brief blast from Gesroh, "I did not believe you were capable of such logic."

"Talk about instant headache," groaned Lisa as she shook her head from side to side in a feudal attempt to ease the pain, "did any of you get another tidbit of information from Gesroh during that blast?"

"I'm not sure; I am still trying to uncross my eyes. What did you get?" remarked Megan.

"I got an image of them here during one of the ice ages, I don't know which one but I could see them helping early man hunt and make fire. It was a brief image but it was there none-the-less." Lisa quickly recorded the information in her notebook while it was fresh, in case the images and memory might fade sometime in the future.

Frank turned the suburban around and headed for the place they had camped at on Huckleberry Mountain. They decided to make a brief stop for tents and more sleeping bags because the thought of a cold camp was weighing a little heavily on all their minds.

CHAPTER 22

WHILE THE SCIENTISTS were trying to decide where to go to intercept their quarry Grious and Tic-Nar were slogging their way through the forest. It was difficult going during the day with all the prying eyes of the Poc-cin; they seemed to be everywhere. From Cook's Mountain they traversed the northern side of Saddle Mountain heading almost due west to Mountain Meadow Lake, about 5 or 6 miles as the magpie flies but a little boggy in places due to a very high water table. Just past the lake they swung northwest toward Davis Lake. Crossing highway 211 just south of Davis Lake they continued northwest to Grayback Mountain. Their aim was to get back up in the more dense forest and stay as high as possible to avoid Poc-cin at all costs. Their usual pace was going a little slower because when Aaah had made her escape from under the structure in Newport she had climbed the east slope of Cook's Mountain. The two criminals had just awakened and found her easily as she was working her way back toward the safe area and her parents. They captured her again and dragged her with them, a turn of events she was not too happy with but they were going roughly in the direction she had planned to travel so she did not struggle too hard but just enough to make it more difficult for them. By the time they went across the highway near Davis Lake Aaah had given up fighting them, for now, because her acute sense of direction told her they were headed exactly where she wanted to go and even her robust constitution was starting to tire. Her role of being a burden to the criminals was more exhausting than she had imagined.

Finally reaching the edge of the National Forest, near Power Peak, the Teer moved due north again. Grious finally called a rest at Callispell Creek just south of Forestry road 2022. There was heavy cover by the creek and they all wanted a drink. The buck brush was thick and intertwined. They ate wild onions and any other greens they could find, fortunately the males were too tired to frolic so Aaah was also permitted to rest.

Although stout and each having the endurance of a herd of bison their big frames also burn a lot of energy when busting brush all day instead of their normal behavior which is to lounge around during the day and come out in the evening and night to feed and forage. The respite was brief, even for Teer; perhaps an hour and they decided to move on before night fall, when they could rest a little longer, they would probably bed down. Grious wanted to make for the area of Timber Mountain, about two thirds of the way to their intended destination.

With an elevation of 5474 feet they were hoping that no Poc-cin would bother them. They were passing over the path known as the Flowery Trail in the area of Winchester Peak, Dirty Shirt Mountain and Fourth of July road. The huckleberries were just beginning to grow but were not yet ripe. Huckleberries only grow in the years after forest fires and this area had been hit hard in recent years. Moving swiftly through the bushes moving west each was picking handfuls of the not quite ripened berries as they walked. Bear and Elk cleared a path in front of them, as they and their relatives had done for centuries. Ruffled and blue mountain grouse were picked off with rocks and with Aaah turning a disgusted eye the other way looking for greens and more berries, Grious and Tic-Nar at the raw flesh, spitting feathers and small bones for miles.

Timber Mountain is a favorite camping spot for one of the local Boy Scout troops out of Colville, Washington. There is a road to the top, where the troop sets up camp, hikes and works on crafts and merit badges a few days every month. This just happened to be one of those camping out sessions.

The Senior Patrol Leader, Jared Pauley, had the Star Patrol out working on camp improvements that evening and they were also going to have a ceremony to tap out the scouts who were going to the Fall Ordeal at Camp Cowles for the Order of the Arrow. Camp Cowles is located at Diamond Lake about 13 miles west of Newport. The Scoutmaster, Bret Delany, a Vigil Honor in OA (Order of the Arrow) believes strongly that ceremonies are a very important part of a scout's life. He and his assistant, Tom Corbin, were preparing the council fire for the event.

CHAPTER 23

MUCH TO HER delight and surprise Betty got a call from Dennis late in the afternoon. He invited her out to go for a drive and perhaps part-take in an evening picnic. She quickly made arrangements with her sister Elaine to watch her two teenagers for the night. Betty was so excited that Elaine could not say no to her and decided to cancel her own plans of going on a date with her husband. Elaine decided that they would all go out to a movie and eat her gourmet cooking at home. She and her husband would make plans for the following evening for a date.

Dennis had an angle and a definite plan of mixing business with pleasure. He had visited Ranger headquarters and learned that Frank Leonard and the three researchers would be out for a few more days in the area around Huckleberry Mountain. It had only cost him 50 dollars for that information. Dennis knew from his perusal of the forestry map and talking with the locals there was a nice camping area at Big Meadow Lake. His plan was to get to know Betty even better, even if it was in a tent on an air mattress and then try to track Ranger Leonard down to get his side of the story, in his spare time of course.

Dennis' ultimate objected was to beat Mike Turnbull to the story, any story, at any cost.

Mike, for his part of this little drama, had been going around Newport just talking to people and jotting a few notes here and there. He happened to see a nice looking lady in the old fashioned drug store, at the really old fashioned soda counter, sipping a green concoction that gave every indication of being cool and very refreshing.

"May I join you?" Mike asked already having seated himself next to her, glancing down at a pair of great legs.

Elaine looked over at the not unattractive young man and said, "Sure."

"What are you drinking, it looks really good?"

"I'm not sure if you'll like it because it is an old fashioned drink that we small town people have kept alive. Its called a lime phosphate; I love them and I've been coming here to Kimmel's since I was a little girl, just to drink them, back when this store was a five and dime," said Elaine with a lovely smile. Her friendliness was interpreted by Mike as a come on.

Hoping to keep the conversation going Mike turned to the presumed kid behind the counter and said, "I'll have one of those and another for the lady, please."

The not so young "soda jerk" looked over and said, "Mrs. Scribner?"

"Yes, thank you. It's okay Bill I could use another one, it is a hot day."

"Mrs. Scribner? My name is Mike Turnbull, I'm a reporter with the National Star," he said offering his hand that she looked at for a moment then shook it lightly.

"I'm Elaine Scribner, nice to meet you," she said retracting her hand quickly as though it was spring loaded, "What story does the National Star have in this area? We don't have any bat people or werewolves running around that I know of, although I have not read one your papers for years those kind of stories seem to sell to a lot of gullible people."

Mike smiled, his most disarming smile, "I'm following up on another story. Please don't laugh, but it's on a Bigfoot sighting," Mike's expression opting for the shy young reporter angle to further disarm the lady.

The two lime phosphates arrived and after the first sip Mike like it. At Embassy functions he had attended there were non-alcoholic drinks commonly referred to as Lime Ricky's but this had a rather nice tang to it. Very thirst quenching, he thought, "Say this isn't bad."

"What are you following up on? There haven't been any sightings around here for years, and then only by drunken hunters or loggers," said Elaine as a bit matter-of-factly trying to feel him out a little, because there had been some talk across the fences in this small town about the bird watcher and his big score with Bigfoot pictures.

"These sightings have been pretty recent, up in the Ione area. Have you heard anything about what's happening over there?" he figured he'd get what information he could, as long as the lime drink lasted.

"I heard a bird watcher got some pictures of something up in the woods, probably just a grizzly bear. He's been bragging all over our town about them and that he sold them for big money to some idiots from the news media," said Elaine just regurgitating some gossip she had heard from her neighbor, "or so I've been hearing," she said with a sideways glance.

Mike had an amusing thought that he's got a live one here

and with such nice legs too, not a bad combination. Elaine caught him looking at her legs again so she turned the lower half of her body away from him and tugged on the front of her pleated skirt to stop the ogling peep show.

"My sister Betty has recently become somewhat involved with another out of town reporter, Dennis something, whom she met while they were discussing the same subject. I believe it is just another hoax, something just to make money. People around here will do anything these days to get a little more money. Anyway, my sister and her new boyfriend are going on a picnic today, and probably tonight, up in the Huckleberry Mountain area, outside of Ione. I've got her kids for a while; they're all at the movie right now watching yet another remake about the War of the Worlds. I like the first 1950's version so I decided not to go," looking at her watch Elaine swung off her stool, flashing some knee and thigh at Mike as she stood up, "here you are Bill, thank you. Give my best to your sister Katie," she said turning to Mike, "it has been nice talking with you but I have to do a little shopping for dinner. Ep likes fresh lettuce for his salad. Good-bye," Elaine left the store without as much as a backward glance. Happily married she had no interest whatever in this smooth talking reporter; she was small town but not unwise in the ways of wily reporters.

Mike threw 3 dollars on the counter saying, "see you later Bill," and walked out to his car. Bill couldn't believe his good luck; he had gotten paid a handsome tip for 3 lime phosphates, a drink he only charges 35 cents for because it only costs about a nickel's worth of lime juice, a little phosphate and soda water. He now had 3 dollars in his hands and he was thinking seriously about raising the price but then thought better of it. Besides he was the Pharmacist not the soda jerk anyway. The kid he'd hired to do that was on break. Bill, still contemplating his profits was walking toward the back of the store where the pharmacy is located when Deputy Deborah Kent, a sheriff's deputy burst through the door, almost knocking the little bell off the top of the door jam.

"Bill? Bill," inquired the deputy looking all round almost like she was blind.

"Yes Debbie, what can I get you?" said Bill walking back toward the obviously agitated young deputy.

"Bill, give me something for a massive headache, this thing just hit me like a tidal wave and it feels like the back of my eyes are on fire!"

Gorgeous eyes too, thought Bill as he went to the shelf to get her a powerful non-prescription pain reliever, "I've got some stuff back here that should help, just under prescription strength. Do you want to lie down in the back for a few minutes?

"No thanks, I've got to go over to Ione. But, you're sweet," Debbie knew he was attracted her but she had no interest in a married man.

"What's up?"

"A domestic squabble; The Blockers are at it again and I need to have a clear head when I talk with those two, you know Mrs. Blocker can be a handful at times. Debbie downed some of the evil tasting liquid, followed by a half a bottle of water, "Thanks Bill you are a life saver." She kissed him on the cheek, "we'll settle the bill when I get back, OK?"

Deputy Kent went outside to her cruiser, got in, put on her sunglasses and buckled up. She did not notice, why would she really care, the U.S. Air Force staff car going up Main Street that was also headed for Ione. Deputy Kent was a dormant psychic, totally unknown to her, but she was feeling the effects of some powerful mind communications and that was what had given her a double migraine.

In the back of the staff car were a full Colonel and a Captain, faces ashen and like chiseled stone looking neither left nor right. The driver was almost as still as a granite statue, moving only his eyes. Crossing back over to Highway 2 the staff car went immediately to 60 mph and headed toward the sleepy little village called Ione.

CHAPTER 24

FRANK STOMPED HARD on the brakes to keep from going past the old campsite location; his mind was laboring on other matters. They quickly set up their tents and got the bedding laid out; although all of them were quite sure they would not be doing much sleeping tonight, though one never knows what can occur on a camping trip.

With Frank acting as a look out the three scientists began to set up a barrier of cameras. They laid them out in a straight line covering two hillsides and two dry creek ravines that seemed to have a little more than the usual foot and hoof traffic; making sure to cover the well-established trails too. Frank stayed close to their camp using his binoculars to keep track of everyone because he wanted to stay close to the radio in the vehicle; his portable radio had a dead battery that he had put into a charger that was now working off the little generator. He was continuously scanning the forest with his binoculars keeping a close protective eye on Megan as she moved around setting up cameras and battery powered motion detectors that Frank had purchased at the hardware store. Each digital camera would be linked to the laptop in the very Spartan research tent. Most of this technology was through the courtesy of the University of Michigan and Lisa's ability to sell them on the idea of helping out with this project. Jerry had mentioned to her something about the archaic equipment they were using due to his limited budget, and although they had not used the new equipment on the first outing they certainly needed to use it now. Jerry, of course, preferred the old tried and true methods he had always used but it had been his idea to put it all out there and not use trip wires this time. Fortunately they had these additional cameras because of the two cameras that had been stomped out of existence. Lisa had her department head overnight this equipment after he had read the paper submitted to him.

Bone tired, everyone was back in camp around sundown, it was just after 1900 (7 p.m.). Lisa jumped into the portable shower with the amorous assistance of Jerry, who said he had been feeling somewhat deprived. Lisa said it was more like depraved but was not opposed to him washing her back. Frank and Megan worked in the equipment tent, with even more and more amorous breaks in the action. The pheromones of the spray tend to stay in the affected bodies especially in the hair follicles for a long time and the influence is very difficult to ignore. All four tired people settled back to wait now that all the preparations had been completed, although all three were in the limbo land between being awake and in the first stage of sleep but still a bit too tired to sleep to drop into the even the second stage of sleep. Exhaustion could claim four victims later perhaps.

Grious, Tic-Nar and Aaah, continued their part of the drama, as they were involved in what we humans call "scrambling". Each had simply put their head down, gritting their teeth and just kept moving on with hands and feet, moving in multiple yards at a time up the side of a mountain. It was more like three incredible Hulks moving swiftly through the forest, sliding down the hillsides and running up the next hillside and through ravines. It was the Teer version of the Iron Man competition but in the forest. Aaah, the youngest of the three, began getting tired because she had sustained a head injury earlier and it was sapping her stamina. Grious had hit her on the head with a log to stop her flight from them when they captured her on Cook's Mountain. They had been crashing the bush like herd of Grizzly bear ever since throwing all caution to their crude Gods, just trying to get to a place where they could feel safe. Aaah prayed silently to Tybal, their God of the Trees and Land.

This marathon was through almost virgin timber in an area between Boulder Mountain and Parker Lake, as they headed in a northwesterly direction and they were rapidly making their way to the top of Timber Mountain. Their bodies were racked with pain and their lungs were being expanded to the bursting limit; their pain caused inadvertent groans, their pace began to slow. The old stag white tail and elk that seldom see humans moved aside for these creatures.

Just about the time all the camera traps were set at Huckleberry Mountain the three hairy behemoths crashed to a halt just 100 meters from the top of Timber Mountain. The two males quickly killed a deer that was just too slow or sleepy to get out of their way; they tied up Aaah throwing but provided greens for her to eat and then settled down to their gristly feast. They had picked a site to stop on the east side of the mountain; the most remote and rocky side where only deer and bear walk. Angry squirrels kept up their continual chatter at the annoying creatures who stopped in their private scavenging area.

Although the smell of burning wood and the proximity of several Poc-cin was heavy in the air the Teer felt a degree of safety amid the buck brush, clinging to the hillside and in the dark spaces between the rocks.

Aaah, as was her way when unhappy or hurt, began to emit a nasal mewing sound that only served to irritate both males. They leered in her direction but continued to consume the young doe they had killed. Finally, mercifully, Aaah drifted off into an uneasy sleep, tears falling freely from her yellow and amber eyes. She had found a rock shelf where she could lie flat but curled up into a fetal position to conserve body heat.

Grious, having finally eaten his fill had it in his warped mind that he wanted to frolic before going to sleep. He carefully pulled the bows off some of the surrounding trees and made a comfortable bed in a rock hollow. He untied the tired and protesting Aaah and led her to the bed where he performed nothing short of an act of rape upon her. She thrashed and protested in pain but to no avail, as Grious kept his massive hand over her mouth to keep most of the sound from coming forth. Finally he finished, rolled off and went, almost immediately, to sleep. Fortunately for Aaah Tic-Nar was too tired to frolic. He heard the grunting noises and for a moment there was an inclination to join in but he just rolled over on his bed of bows and leaves and went to sleep trying his best be disinterested. In just few minutes he too was sleeping in a rolling growl snore that would strike fear into the heart of a full grown male lion. Aaah made her way, painfully, back to her bed on the rock shelf where she once again fell into a troubled sleep.

The unsuspecting scouts were just concluding the

ceremonial "tapping out" of the new Order of the Arrow candidates and Scoutmaster Bret and his assistant Tom were allowing the council fire to die down for the night. Both standing over the dying embers they had both heard the strange mewing sound carrying through the trees from the east. They also heard something like the cracking of bones or the breaking of large limbs of wood. Both men were looking around and feeling somewhat apprehensive, "There could be a cougar den or a bear den nearby. The adults could be cracking the bones of a deer or something for the nourishing marrow," said Tom, not really believing a word he had just said.

"Sure, yeah, I guess you could be right," answered Brett not wanting to make his new assistant seem foolish, but he was more than a little leery of the situation himself. He had never heard those types of sounds before and certainly not in this their favorite camping spot. "Tom, I've never heard that particular mewing sound before but I've seen cougars and cougar cubs in these woods. The cracking of bones for marrow by a big cat would never be that loud."

"I know, that occurred to me too," answered Tom who was adding dirt and pouring water gently in the fire pit to make sure the fire was truly out. Both men walked the 20 feet back to their camp shining their powerful flashlights into the forest, high and low but seeing nothing out of the ordinary.

"Tom, I think we had better guard the camp tonight. Do you want the first or second watch?"

"I'll take the first I guess. Did we bring a rifle or anything?"

"No weapons, you know we can't have any type of firearms in camp. I do have a can of bear spray that I will put here by the fire. We'll have to use an axe or a hatchet for protection that is about all we have but they can be effective. Chopping wood for the campfire should keep most predators away and you'll need to do that anyway to keep this campfire going.

"Okay," answered Tom whose quivering voice was showing some signs of fear.

"I'll be right here Tom. Wake me about 2."

"Okay, good night."

Little known to the two leaders, who were supposed to be kept informed about such things the Senior Patrol Leader Jared had taken the new OA candidates out to sleep under the stars, like they would have to do at the Ordeal later this summer or fall at the big scout camp at Diamond Lake. In the fashion of the Ordeal the boys were led out into the woods in a brotherhood chain and their sleeping bags were just tossed into the woods. Wherever the bag landed would be where that scout would spend that night until retrieved in the morning. Also like the Ordeal the scouts were not allowed to talk.

The Brotherhood chain had weaved its way around the east side of the camp and soon all the scouts were finally in place. Because it was a large troop they had tapped out six candidates to place. Jared, a Vigil Honor, decided he would remain alert and keep an eye on the campers too. He figured the two adult leaders were already asleep after the long day in the fresh air.

When Jared threw the last bag into the brush he heard a real commotion coming from the steep hillside. Almost like two bear or cougars fighting. It died down fairly quickly, so he figured the animals had settled the problem and moved on, staying down slope, he hoped.

Jared watched as Seth got into his sleeping bag and stayed a moment to make sure he was situated. Satisfied that everything was serene Jared made his way back to camp, about 50 or 60 yards, to tell his Scoutmaster how he had placed the boys and to get his coat and flashlight. Jared felt a chill in the air but he did not smell rain so it should be okay. He hoped that the skunk odor he had detected over where Seth was would not be too strong for him to go to sleep. Jared felt confident that what he had done would be acceptable with his adult leaders; the troop had done this before. When Jared stuck his head into his leader's tent Brett was already levered up on one elbow listening to the sounds of the night. The wind made it sound like cars going down a highway in the distance.

"What can I do you Jared? It's late and you really should be asleep."

"Yes sir. I just wanted to tell you that I put the new OA candidates out to sleep in the bush like they will do at the Ordeal. I'm going to keep a vigil on them and make sure they are safe."

"Jared," began his Scoutmaster who decided to pick his words carefully, "I wish you would have talked with me about doing that before you placed them. There are some really strange sounds on the east side of the camp and Tom and I are going to be doing a vigil of our own, watching the entire camp, just in case something might wander through."

"They are all within a 20 yard square, about 40 or 50 yards out of camp, on the east side. I won't let anything happen to them. This is part of my duty at the Ordeal every year."

"I know you help run the Ordeals," Brett said groaning slightly as he adjusted his arm, "Jared, I can't sleep anyway. Let's go and keep watch together. I don't want anything happening to you either."

Tom stood his vigil at the campfire in the area of the tents; Brett and Jared built a small fire in the center of the sleeping candidates and would keep their vigil there. It was pretty quiet for about 3 or 4 hours when Seth, the scout farthest out started screaming and thrashing around in his mummy bag trying to get out of it. A high pitched continuous scream echoed his great and growing fear. This young man's alarming screams brought the entire troop to instant awake mode. Brett and Jared were standing looking in that direction when all of a sudden Tom went by them on the dead run, not a jog. Brett smiled, he did not know Tom could move that fast.

Seth was still screaming at the top of his lungs and kept trying to get out of the mummy bag when they finally caught up to him. His face was so pale his face seemed to glow in the dark. Seth was a little hard to catch because he was rapidly trying to crawl away, from whatever scared him, like an inch worm, a sight that seemed to take the edge off the situation for a moment and the three responders had a chuckle while trying to catch young Seth and get him out of the bag.

"Seth! Seth! Stop, it's me Jared!" screamed the Senior Patrol Leader. Jared caught him by the feet and rolled him over. Tom reached for the zipper and after a couple of tugs finally opened the bag. Brett had to catch the boy around the waist as he jumped up and was headed down hill, actually he was headed anywhere just away from where he was at the moment.

"Seth! Simmer down son. Easy boy," said the Scoutmaster who rarely if ever raised his voice. Seth finally showed some sign that he recognized his rescuers. By now there was a crowd around them with all types of flashlights showing everywhere. Seth finally stopped struggling, his panic seemed to be abating, and his Scoutmaster set him on his feet between two older boys to steady him on his very shaky legs.

Seth put his left hand on the shoulder of the boy next to him, "I saw a huge, dark shape, go between me and the fire where Mr. Corbin was standing. I thought it was a bear but it was walking on its back legs, walking upright like us, and did I say it was huge."

Looking around at all the lights and scared boys the Scoutmaster said, "Scouts, I want you all to go back to the campfire, now please. I don't want any more damage to this area. In the morning we can come out and look for tracks," pointing in the direction he wanted them to go. "It's about 2 or 3 hours to first light, Mr. Corbin and I will stay up and keep watch, so all of you please go back to your tents. You OA candidates pick up your gear and move back into camp too please."

There was some nervous laughter and a great deal of grumbling. Brett was sure none of them were going to sleep but maybe they would get bored laying there and fall asleep. In about 20 minutes the camp finally began to quiet down. Jared Pauly, the 17 year old SPL asked to stay up and his request was granted. His Scoutmaster could see Jared feeling responsible for the problem and needed to be treated as an adult, not a young scout. It was a real growth opportunity.

The perpetrator of the panic was Tic-Nar who had gotten hungry again and thought the Poc-cin might have left something out for him to eat. He saw the fire and the lone Poc-cin standing nearby. What he had not seen were the six scouts sleeping out in the bushes "under the stars" very near to where he was walking.

When the young Poc-cin began to scream and thrash

about in his cocoon bed Tic-Nar thought at first that he should kill it but there was a stirring in the cloth dwellings so he decided to retreat down the slope and watch. When Tic-Nar got back to Grious and Aaah they were both awake. In moments the three were up and moving northeast around the noisy group of Poc-cin. The yellow/luminous purple eyes of the Teer are perfectly adapted for guiding their movements at night and they moved away like the sound of the wind in the branches. The Poc-cin is a primitive race that has lost their acute senses in the last few hundred years so the Teer knew they could easily move away without detection. There was so much commotion in the camp that the Scouts would not have heard a logging truck go by. The Teer quickly moved away.

CHAPTER 25

THE FOUR RESEARCH campers had a very pleasant and restful night. The playful lovemaking, in separate tents, had lasted for an hour or two then all four literally passed out from exhaustion. The two women felt an odd sense of rejuvenation. They were up early first checking the equipment and quickly realizing that nothing out of the ordinary had passed the cameras during night. The camera images were set up to go directly to the laptop so each image could then be viewed quickly without having to go out to each camera every time there was a flash. Then they set about making breakfast on a gas powered double burner stove. The coffee was first, then water for tea. Lisa and Megan were both famished and they were sure the men would be ravenous, if they ever woke up. They made small jokes, with lots of low laughter, about why the men were sleeping to long. They built a small fire in the portable pit to keep the coffee and tea water hot. They both figured that a fire during the day should not be a problem.

There was a stirring in both tents when the bacon hit the pan and a knowing smile passed between the two women. Men aren't always so predictable but they certainly kept things interesting in the age old "battle of the sexes." Food cooking is a great motivator for getting men out of bed, at least that part is predictable.

Frank emerged first still tucking in his shirt. He headed to the water bucket to wash up. He produced a battery-powered wet/dry shaver and was attempting to mow down the two days' worth of stubble. Jerry emerged, eyes half closed and somewhat unsteady on his feet with a white towel over his shoulder. He walked slowly to the portable shower and began a noisy washing session that included singing of some unrecognizable tunes.

"Hurry up boys, breakfast is almost ready," jibed Lisa looking over her should at the two men toweling off their faces. With the assistance of the generator there was toast from a real toaster and even a couple of blueberry bagel halves. Soon the only sound that could be heard except for the occasional logging truck going by the lake was chewing and "yummy sounds". Sitting back sipping coffee each now felt warmer and, at least for the moment, contented. There was a nagging feeling in the air that this would be a long day, a very long day.

The encounter in the safe area seemed to all of them more like a dream now than something that had actually happened. They began to imagine that they had all shared a dream, a rare phenomenon if it were possible at all. However, just touching the back of their own skulls gave sobering reassurance that each of them had not been dreaming; more like a nightmare in the day time with their eyes wide open.

Down at the lake Dennis and Betty had another wonderful night. They were awakened rather rudely by a logging truck speeding by spewing dust over the entire north end of the camp. Betty, slightly more domestic than Dennis and an avid camper, had fortunately brought instant coffee, tea and some pastry for their breakfast. The Thermos water was still hot enough and the meal was actually quite good. Neither were particularly aware it was Sunday and obviously the over achieving logging truck driver had no idea it was Sunday either.

Suddenly Dennis' cell phone started to play "Saturday Night" by the Bay City Rollers. Betty just smiled at his choice of music for his ringtone. "Excuse me," said Dennis after looking at the readout on the telephone, "I need to take this call, it looks like my editor." Checking his antenna level, which was at one brick, he moved around to see if he could get something better. Down by the lake a second brick appeared and he answered it. "Hey, Max you're up early on a Sunday morning. What's up?"

"Have you gotten anything for all my money?" was the irritated inquiry of the small voice on the squawk box without a hello or any other fanfare.

"Max, buddy, I've gotten a lot of good stuff, I just haven't written it yet. Give me today to write it all down and I'll send you an Email this afternoon. I still have a few leads to track down."

"We go on the air tomorrow morning lame brain; you seem to keep forgetting that little fact."

"But Max, my old friend, you are always a week ahead so my story won't be coming on the air for at least another week, maybe even two," said Dennis as he looked over at Betty who was sitting quietly sipping her tea and looking beautiful.

"I am not your friend, now or ever. It may not come out at all if I fire your butt and let you go back to free-lance again. I've heard that Tom, over at the Star, has gotten a story from Turnbull and they're coming out with a special edition tomorrow. You'd better get off your ass, out of bed or whatever you've been and get me something. We need to scoop this story by the Star and get it on the air. You've already cost be 70 or 75 thousand and I don't have one word or picture ready to put out there."

"Calm down Max, calm down, I'm on it. I'll have something this afternoon just like I said," his mind already racing as to where to start, what byline he wanted and the composition of the topic sentence, as well as the rest of the story. What he would rather write about it how great Betty would look in a bathing suit.

Mike Turnbull, having filed his initial story entitled the "Bigfoot Conspiracy" was typing furiously on his laptop in his hotel room. This story would have everything the public wanted from wild sexual orgies by the research scientists, their run in with the Air Force at the Bjornson farm; sexy married women in a small town and anything else he could think of to juice it up. In his perverted little mind he had enough material to last for years. His only real problem was how he would present it because he had actually obtained some of the pictures illegally; but that never slowed him down before. The only way around the problem was to use other people as models and testimonials from local residents and the professor's college associates. These minor details did not keep him from smiling as he tapped away on the keyboard.

Dennis uncharacteristically was still cuddling with Betty at the campground, all the while his mind racing trying to figure out what he would write about. True he had the pictures and an average interview with Jansen, the bird watcher, which he could embellish but nothing so far really that was truly eye catching.

"Lovely lady, we really need to go up on Huckleberry Mountain and find out what the researchers are doing."

Her answer surprised him a little because all she said was, "No thanks," and snuggled closer.

He squeezed her gently around the shoulders, "No, I mean it. If you don't want to go then I can probably meet you in Newport tonight for dinner. You have your car here and I presume you know your way home." When she looked at him, the disappointment in her eyes made him feel bad, but only for a moment.

"Okay," was all she said, without protest, because she was not feeling like the outdoor hiking type today anyway, Betty got up, kissed him a long, lingering promise of fun later kiss and began cleaning the area. She also wanted him to know he could count on her and she did not want to smother him or make him feel corralled. "Will I see you tonight for sure?" she asked as she climbed into her little red Ford.

"I'm not sure what time, but you have my cell number and I have your number programmed. I'll let you know when I know," he leaned down and gave her another kiss. He watched her drive away. He then gathered his own gear, threw it in the back seat of his rental Explorer and headed up the road to Huckleberry Mountain. He did not know where he was going exactly or where the scientists would be but he had all day to search for them. Turning up hill just a half mile down from the lake he put his foot down, sliding sideways and fishtailing in the loose gravel started climbing the hill. Billowing dust trailed behind his vehicle as he enjoyed a feeling of being in a car rally while speeding up the narrow mountain road.

Three startled Teer watched as Dennis drove by them as they crouched on the side of the road. There were growls all around as the two, with one in tow, turned from their course and ran up the mountain parallel to the road. Curse words in the Teer language are severe and all three were mumbling some of the more juicy ones.

Grious, showing his yellow teeth murmured, "Blac-zop-lin" roughly translated meaning "limp male member"; Tic-Nar grumbled his favorite, "itas-oster" which translates to "belly crawler or coward"; Aaah who was still coughing from the dust simply said, "urs-ida-urd-zop-lin" which very roughly translated means "lizard brain in the male member".

CHAPTER 26

UP ON HUCKLEBERRY Mountain the three researchers and the Ranger were checking the pictures from the previous night. Jerry still had to walk to some of the cameras, replace the disk, and bring them back to load into the computer because something in the remote connection or the program would not allow him to erase the pictures and start over.

"National Geographic would like some of these images, look at that Bobcat, I didn't know there were any of them this low," commented Lisa as she clicked through each image carefully. Not only were they looking at the principle subject of the photograph but they were checking the backgrounds very carefully.

"I've got a whole herd of Elk moving through on this one. It's a good thing these cameras are infrared or we would have had a stampede," chuckled Megan.

"How can we be sure of the path these, okay I'll call them by their own name, Teer, are going to take?" mused Frank.

"Because Gesroh says they would probably come back this way since of the supply ship shuttle is coming in a few days," replied Megan as she sat back and sipped her coveted green tea, "and I would like to be there when it lands, it would be so cool."

Unannounced Jerry entered the tent suddenly causing all of the others to look around very quickly, only slightly startled. Jerry looking at their faces smiled meekly and handed the disks he had retrieved to Lisa to load into the computer. "I think we should launch another hiking expedition. If we get within half a mile from Aaah we might be able to pick up her brain patterns on this thing Gesroh gave us, although it is not specifically programed for her."

Chuckling Frank patted Jerry on the back saying, "Why don't we call it a tri-corder?" Everyone knew where that term started and there was a rolling chuckle going around the tent, "and we'll give you a Vulcan name too, huh? How does that compute Mr. Science Officer?"

"I'd rather be the captain or the ship's doctor if you don't mind. My ears are way too flat and I am not pretty enough to be the communications officer," said Jerry striking a post an awkward hands on hips pose, "and my singing voice wouldn't attract a cold virus, let along wandering Teer."

"Ooh, I'll be the sexy communications officer and you can be the ship's captain later, if you like," remarked Lisa with a big smile.

"Later baby," making Jerry actually blush, "I want you to stay here and monitor the systems. We three are all going to take a day hike and fan out a little to cover more area. Do you still have your pistols?"

Lisa slapped her side and caused a dull metal sound, "Yes Captain phasers have been issued to all the crew on the away party and I have mine right here."

Doing a double take on his companion, "Ah, thank you,"

remarked Jerry reaching for his daypack. "Megan will you and Frank cover the lower east side, on the other side of the road toward the lake? I have a gut feeling you might cut their trail at some point. I want you to take this tri-corder with you to try and locate Aaah."

Looking at each other, Megan answered, "Sure but wouldn't it be better if we split up more, we could cover at least a third more territory?"

"No, because like I said I believe you are going where their best route from Newport and Ione would lead them in. I am going up and over, north of Smackout Pass and then due east from there. I am also going to talk face-to-face with Gesroh to get another tri-corder modified to the criminal's biorhythms which he should have by now, as well as Aaah's to help in the search."

"Once you two hit little Muddy Creek," continued Jerry pointing on the map, "I want you to swing south a little and parallel the road maybe a mile down to here and then back to camp using the overland route. I am hoping you'll cut their trail out there and we can home in on their position or maybe get an idea of their exact route."

"Okay," came in unison as the other two hikers grabbed their own daypacks.

"How come I get left out "captain" shouldn't I get to go on this away mission?"

"I'm sorry, my pretty commander, but you need to be our base station and data collection center. You are the sexy communications officer and hardly get to go on away missions anyway; you've got to stay on the ship."

"Great, thanks," grumbled Lisa, "I guess I can hold down the fort, uh I mean ship."

"If there is some type of emergency or you requiring us to return quickly to camp use the terms "welcome home" on the radio. We will know we need to get back double quick. Your call sign will be "Federation Base"; I'll be the "captain" with Megan and Frank "the away team", is that okay?" Lisa nodded after taking some notes. "Good, give your captain a kiss lovely commander and let's get started," said Jerry as he leaned down swooping in for a kiss. Lisa ducked initially but he kept after her until he found her lips. The kiss was not the peck she had expected but a bit more lingering which brought her hand up to the back of his head. She just sat in her chair smiling as he exited the tent. "Now that will give her something to think about while I'm out" he thought. (Gesroh smiled up in the safe area.)

The morning was just starting to heat up. The dew was burning off the grass and the musty smell of wet pine hung in the air. There was a tang of dust smell in the air too. The three began plodding up the small logging trail. Jerry stopped and silently pointed in the direction he wanted Megan and Frank to break off this trail and head east.

"See you at dinner. I think we should do a radio check. Federation Base this is the captain, how do you read me, over."

"Captain, this is Federation Base, loud and clear."

"Thank you, out."

CHAPTER 27

MIKE TURNBULL HAD decided to follow Dennis because he wanted to see what Dennis was up to. Early in the morning, after sending his story, Mike parked his car at the boat ramp, at the west end of the lake scoping out the camp ground with his binoculars. He found Dennis and his lady friend sitting and cuddling at a picnic table. Mike was a little surprised when the lady departed but Dennis stayed where he was, after all he wanted to know what Dennis was up to not where his pretty lady friend might be going.

Dennis threw his daypack and the rolled up tent into his rental (Mike even took note of the license plate number) climbed in and went at road rally pace the entire half mile to the turn off, took the turn way too fast throwing a cloud of dust and gravel as Dennis headed north up the hill. Mike did wonder why he was in such a hurry but decided to follow at a more leisurely pace. It was certainly not going to be difficult to follow the dust trail as it snaked up the mountain road.

Dennis was enjoying being out in the sun on this crisp summer day and driving like a maniac on a high mountain road. He was thinking of his younger days when he actually drove in and also covered European road rallies. Unaware that there was a huge smile on his face, due mainly to his own exuberance, he tapped the brake, turned the wheel right, hit the gas to slide right round a right turn, immediately he turned the wheel left to compensate and neutralize the turn so the vehicle would make the turn and not go careening down the hillside. Dennis glimpsed something across a small raving that made him ease off the gas pedal and settle the vehicle down.

Mike, following a short way behind, also saw the camp through the thinning dust cloud. He quickly began to formulate a plan, a story, to tell the scientists as to why he was there. He too smiled but not from the exhilaration of being in the mountains, no, he smiled from all the stories yet to be written and people yet to be exploited.

Unknown and unseen by the two reporters, Grious and Tic-Nar were setting a blazing pace and although younger Aaah, because of her head injury, was still having difficulty keeping up. She had to stop frequently to catch her breath much to the irritation of both males.

"Can't you make her go faster Tic-Nar?" growled Grious, slobbering a little through his massive yellow teeth.

"No. She only wants to lag behind and slow us down."

"Tie her up and leave her here. I see a small cave over there we can leave her in it, once we have secured passage on the transport we can come back for her," snarled Grious.

"That could be two or three revolutions (days). Do you think she'll still be alive?" asked the slightly more caring Tic-Nar.

"Who cares? All she is doing now is slowing our progress and leaving us open to detection."

"You are probably right," answered Tic-Nar as they

walked back together to where Aaah was napping. They tied her hands and feet with some stalks of tough plants, picked her up and laid the mildly protesting Aaah inside the small, cool cave. Both then covered the entrance with rocks careful to leave some cracks for air to filter through.

Their work quickly done both of the criminals set off once again. Both were thinking of how they might overpower one or two Teer at the safe area; contact the incoming transport using faked I.D. and get off this ball of dust prison planet for more comfortable digs, or capture the safe area for their own use by getting rid of the others, realizing none of it would be easy.

Aaah struggled in her bonds of woven plants but decided to sleep for a time. She convinced herself that she could break free once the plants dried out and became more brittle making them easier to chew through.

Megan and Frank were not far from the small cave where Aaah lay but they did not see any tracks and kept moving. They were uphill moving southeast where the Teer had not been. Once they circled down toward the road and the lake they might see the trail but it would take sharp eyes to do so.

Scoutmaster Brett, on his cell phone, made a report to the sheriff's office, in Colville, on what had transpired in his camp the previous night, along with pictures of some of the odd footprints that he transmitted from his cell phone camera. He made a full report and then packed up the camp and went back home. He figured the boys would need to sort things out before going camping up here again; even he was a little spooked. He had never seen tracks like that before, and he had been camping and hunting in these woods since he was a boy.

The sheriff's office, as was their normal procedure faxed a copy of the report to the Ranger headquarters. It made some interesting reading for the young Ranger at the desk who quickly decided he could make a few thousand more dollars with this exclusive story. He hid the report from the rest of the staff so he could contact the reporter he had talked with earlier.

The slight altercation with the scout troop had happened several miles west of where the scientific camp was located and of course because the young Ranger stole the fax for his own monetary gain, they would not learn of it for some time. The information in this report would have helped in the search or at least helped estimate where Aaah and her captors had been the night before.

CHAPTER 28

ISA WAS JUST sitting in the lab tent sipping her tepid tea when she heard a vehicle pull up. She, for some reason, made sure her pistol was at her side. She opened the tent flap of the canvas walled tent and had to squint in the bright sunlight to see a man walking toward her. He was smiling and pulling something out of his wallet.

"Hi, I'm Dennis Graham. I'm a reporter with the National Scandal T.V. program and magazine." He showed her his press credentials, which she took, read on both sides and then handed back to him. Her pretty face had a look of pure disgust.

"Okay, but you've got a lot of gall calling it a television program and a magazine. So what can I do for you?" she said wondering to herself if this guy could recognize the rhetorical question; her guess probably not.

"I'm looking for the Bigfoot researcher's camp. Have I found the right place?" he smiled in an effort to disarm the beautiful woman, but he could tell she was not buying any of it.

"Maybe, why?" was her very guarded response.

Re-igniting his fading smile Dennis extended his hand again, "I didn't get your name."

Not extending her hand, but taking a half step away from the man, "I did not throw it. Now answer my question."

Dennis withdrew his hand looking at it briefly like maybe he had forgotten to wash it or his fingernails were dirty, "I've, uh, well I've heard you've actually seen something in these woods, you know, the Jansen pictures and I wanted your take on it."

"My take on it is that the pictures have not been authenticated and all we have are some sketchy reports from excited hikers in this area."

"I see," he said pulling out his notebook, "would you care to tell me about it?"

"No! You really need to leave, I am busy and you are trespassing in my camp and I've got no time to talk with you, nor do I have the inclination to talk to you. Your brand of journalism is, at best, not worth being quoted in or even worth lining the bottom of a birdcage."

Unknown to either Dennis or Lisa, Mike Turnbull the more unscrupulous of the two reporters, was listening and taking his own notes. He had after all broken into the scientist's cabins and would actually stop at nothing to get this, or any other, story. He had sneaked around behind one of the sleeping tents while they were distracted so he could listen in but he knew he would be seen if he tried to go any further right now.

"Is there anything I can say to make you more hospitable toward the press?"

"In your case good-bye would be the best thing. If you were from, the Times or National Geographic or even the Smithsonian, maybe I would give you a sentence or two, but never to a supermarket rag or an idiot's T.V. program. Now move your ass or I get on my radio here and call the sheriff or the Ranger station. In this case filing charges and seeing you in court would be a pleasure."

"Yes ma'am, I'm going," said Dennis as he turned around, walked back down the short road and got back into his vehicle. He backed out to the service road and pointed it downhill. It was at this point he noticed a car parked in the trees that he had not seen when he turned in toward the camp but, as the lady said, it was not his business so he went back down the hill and turned toward Ione.

Lisa followed him down the trail a little way to make sure he left and then went back into the lab tent. She found Mike Turnbull in there viewing her laptop. He had sneaked in while she was distracted. This time she drew her pistol, something he had not expected.

"Easy Doc, I'm not here to bother or hurt you," he said, but her expression was serious and he felt she might actually shoot him. "I'm from the National Star. I don't suppose you'd like to talk to me about what you and your boyfriend are doing up here?"

Lisa was becoming more infuriated by the moment, "In about 5 seconds your natural curiosity is going to disappear along with your manhood," she said as she lowered the pistol to that area, "put your notebook on the table and move or would you like to test my aim?

"You wouldn't actually shoot me, would you Doc," he said not terribly sure of what she was capable of doing.

"Well I guess we'll find out won't we," she clicked the safety off the 9 MM, "if you are not out of here in the next few seconds you might bleed to death before the ambulance can get here from Newport. There wouldn't be anything to put a tourniquet on."

It was obvious he was used to calling people's bluff so she put a round in the chair just an inch or two from the promised target. He jumped like a toad in a hot skillet and backed out of the tent, the same way he had sleazed his way in. The blood had completely drained from his face, exactly opposite of Lisa's expression. She was becoming angrier by the second. His hands were in the air like he was under arrest, something Lisa figured he was not a stranger to.

"Move," she said flicking the barrel of her pistol in the direction she wanted him to go.

"Would it help if I showed you my press credentials?" he asked fumbling in his wallet.

"Fine just drop the card and keep going. In case you haven't figured it out your manhood and your bleeding to death are still a viable option. You are moving way too slow and that makes me nervous; it could spoil my aim too!"

Mike pulled out his press card and a business card and dropped them in the dirt. He was hoping she would be distracted but her eyes stayed on him. He knew then she was serious and that he was in real danger. He picked up his pace, still walking backward, going down the deer trail that he had used to sneak into camp, bumping into trees and he moved toward his car like a pin ball marble.

"You, mister reporter, will now leave my camp. If I ever see you again anywhere I will shoot you under the "Make my day law" in this state because I "felt in fear of my life". Do I make myself clear? It's too bad we're not in Florida I could shoot you now under the "fear and flight" law.

"Crystal clear, Doctor Shields, you are very clear," again he hoped to distract her by using her name and again he did not fall for it.

"You know my name, how nice. If I see my name in print in your rag you'll see me again in court. I don't care how many lawyers you have my father's firm will blow yours out of the water. Now I have just one more thing to say to you," snarled Lisa.

"What's that," said Mike stumbling in a rut in the path. He was till backing up with his hands in the air.

"Git!"

Mike turned and ran. Lisa fired two more shots into a tree not quite in the direction of the fleeing man, just to emphasize her point. She laughed quietly to herself. Her father was not a lawyer; he was a college professor of Geology at the University of Maryland. She was sure the guy, Mike Turnbull (she read his card and press card as she fished it out of the dust) would be researching her. She did wonder though how he knew her name.

Going back into the lab tent, "Federation base to away team," she waited for an answer but only got static in reply so she repeated the call.

"Away team, go ahead."

"What is your ETA to camp, I've had visitors, over."

"About an hour, maybe two, any trouble we heard some shooting, over?"

"Nothing I couldn't handle but I would like some better company, over," she looked around nervously as some shadows danced on the tent wall.

"We'll be there as soon as we can, out." Megan handed the radio back to Frank and they changed their direction of travel quickly and headed toward camp.

CHAPTER 29

IT WAS EARLY in the afternoon when two more visitors arrived at the research camp site. These two had been skulking through the forest quietly making plans for taking over the safe haven. Both knew the risks that were involved, even onto death but they were willing to risk it with their plan.

Both stopped and observed the woven houses of the, sniffing the air, their delicate noses revealed the scent of a female Poc-cin. There were strange smells, and some familiar smells, emanating from within. Grious and Tic-Nar moved a little closer. Their acute senses were picking up something odd; they were feeling her thoughts and emotions quite clearly. The two criminals felt a psychic connection to this female. Although they had been startled by the 3 gun shots they were still curious about this Poc-cin female.

Grious had once tried mating with a Poc-cin female but the union had killed her; she was too frail for frolicking. Suddenly, as both moved even closer to just outside the downhill facing wall, there was a tremendous blast of kinetic energy. Peaking inside they could see the Poc-cin still, very still, as if listening intently; her gaze was away from them.

She was listening to Gesroh as he communicated to her that

Jerry was just leaving the safe area, the force of the computers had drained his radio battery. Slightly startling to Lisa was that Gesroh was also telling her that the two rogue Teer he had been searching for were now just outside her tents. He had finished programming the computer to pick up their brain waves, with or without a device. She reached down and unsnapped her pistol in its holster and drew the 9MM. Realizing what the significance of the gesture meant Grious and Tic-Nar rushed her, collapsing the tent in the process. Gear went everywhere. The 2 Teer fought and ripped their way out of the material and rolled her up in the tent, then scurried off with Lisa kicking and yelling, in the same language that an angry drill sergeant might use with recruits and at the top of her lungs.

Gesroh, sensing what was going on, transmitted a message to the other 3 Poc-cin. Jerry began running in long strides downhill.

The two criminals scurried back toward the cave where they had left Aaah with their struggling prize, although neither really knew why they had taken the Poc-cin. Down the mountain about a mile the two looked at one another and squeezed to hold on to the still weakly cursing and struggling woman. She heard them grunt to one another but in her mind she understood what they were saying, "We do not need to burden ourselves with this ugly Poc-cin female. She has no value except to the Kev-tah'esh who may want her for a banquet. She is too old for breeding stock anyway and probably too frail to frolic," growled Grious.

Lisa heard the conversation and stopped struggling when they said she was too old for breeding stock. She then started screaming with all the force she had left in her lungs about "male chauvinist pigs from another planet" and again began kicking and wiggling as much as she could, but she was getting tired. The two criminals did not get the full translation of her thoughts but they got the idea.

Lisa achieved the desired effect and was dropped unceremoniously while the 2 Teer went back the way they had come. Initially Lisa could not breathe, the air left her lungs from the long drop and it seemed to her that both her lungs had collapsed; moments later she was relieved when she could actually breathe again. She had been gasping for air and nearly passed out before she got a breath. Then she did pass out for about 5 or 6 minutes. When she awoke she was still covered by the canvas tent. She began to fight her way out but was having some difficulty because she was lying between two big rocks and had rolled down an eight-foot bank, slamming into a tree and then careening into the low brushes between the rocks.

The brush popped and cracked as it broke under the pressure of her escape attempt. She had to stop and rest a few times put finally she got her head and one arm out, now that she could see what the problem was she finally broke free a few minutes later. She had to crawl out from between the rocks to be able to stand up. Lisa was exhausted from her struggles. She sat on a stump to recover some of her strength and get her bearings. She felt grateful she had been able to hold on to the pistol that she now put back in her holster. She gently lifted her shirt and looked at her bruised ribs; bruised from the rough treatment and being tossed down an embankment. Looking at the black and blue saucer shaped bruise made her groan. She put her shirt down, stood and began to walk slowly back up the hill toward the camp site. She drug the tent behind her, it was too heavy for her to carry.

Grious and Tic-Nar were moving fast once more. They had returned to the camp and wrecked most of the equipment. They tore the woven houses to shreds and ripped all the sleeping bags apart. It reminded Grious of a time when he had killed a Poc-cin and torn up another camp many, many years before. He still carried the scar of where the Poc-cin had shot him.

Satisfied they had wreaked enough havoc they moved north, into the trees. They stumbled onto a resting white tail doe, killed her and ate her in great gulping mouthfuls. Both then decided, because they were so close to their objective, to hold up until nightfall and sleep away the warm afternoon. They curled up under the low branches of a spruce, easily blending into the dark area below the boughs and slept the dreamless sleep of the Teer.

CHAPTER 30

EARLIER, JERRY HAD spent time with Gesroh learning more about how to find Aaah. He was also learning volumes about the Teer, their world they call Kleek, the Kev-tah'esh, Clot-tor and the Effe. More than once during the session Jerry's mouth dropped open when he learned how the Teer had helped, millions of years ago, buy adding their own DNA to the promising looking "pond scum" they had come across living in the warm water of the volcanic primordial pools. It was something they had done on other planets where they had visited and had found no appreciable intelligent life forms.

One of the things the Teer miss about this planet Strig'et ocouts (we named Earth) was the virgin giant forests that existed before the first amphibians ventured on to the land and their flippers evolved into legs, rather simple an explanation for something that took thousands or millions of years. During those golden years, as Gesroh thought of them, the Teer of old were here in great numbers, always observing and just enjoying their surroundings.

At some point the always hungry planet seeders, the Effe, arrived to add their own designs to the still virgin world of trees, seas and volcanoes. Always thinking with their stomachs the Effe fostered some species and changed the path of other species. The Effe, known for their odd tastes especially liked, and devoured great multitudes of the giant spiders and sea scorpions then just emerging.

When the Effe next returned they saw the giant warm blooded and cold blooded reptilians and they decided to change the direction of the evolutionary strategy and caused a catastrophe to kill them off, leaving the mammals in the underbrush to become more dominate. The Effe knew that the ice flows which covered half the planet every few thousand years would help weed out the lesser species and the mammals would grow in size. Again they made a few changes here and there and went on their way.

On their next visit the Effe were pleased at the strides the mammals had taken, mostly in their size development and took many specimens off world with them. They were also pleased that the warm-blooded reptilians that had survived had morphed into birds and the giant birds of the southern continent were their greatest prizes. The Effe took many healthy ones to their home planet for breeding purposes. The Kev-tah'esh also took many specimens to their planet around the same time.

The Effe noticed a species, which they considered inferior, evolving into the use of tools but still moving in small herds. After further analysis they still considered them weak and unremarkable believing extinction was just a few thousand years away. They found them so inferior that this anthropoid species was not worth saving or changing so they left them on their own to die off.

It was about this time the Clot-tor discovered the system. They especially liked the red planet and the smaller planet further out that was always shrouded in clouds and mist. Up to this point they had not been interested in exploring the blue planet; too many volcanoes; an oxygen hydrogen atmosphere and the life forms were all carbon based something very distasteful to them.

The Clot-tor established colonies on the red and green planets, those colonies flourished for a time, perhaps twenty to thirty thousand years. When the water sources diminished or disappeared from several areas entirely the red plant was then not so appealing. The Clot-tor attempted terraforming the atmosphere to their own special blend but failed, and the factor of the water disappearing had a lot to do with their decision, so they picked up their colony and joined, their established colony on Festu-ang, the green planet.

The green planet colony is still in existence although it is becoming more difficult to maintain a domed, somewhat protected, environment. The supply ships are not as frequent from the home world, Tor because the warrior race has moved farther back into the galaxy leaving the outer rim on its own in the last few thousand years. The only indigenous life form is a worm that uses an acid to tunnel through solid rock. The favorite rock is lava rock that is more porous. The worm digests the minerals as it makes its tunnels and leaves "worm guano" that is harvested and used in the environment reactors to filter the methane gas atmosphere. Somewhat of a symbiotic relationship but the worms are the sizes of your large land roving transports; Jerry's brain interjected semi-trucks with their trailers and Gesroh agreed.

At this point Jerry had to stop the session because his head was radiating pain like a super nova migraine and it was becoming more and more unbearable. Gesroh apologized profusely. He touched Jerry's head, closing his eyes to concentrate and literally took the pain away. Gesroh winced as he transferred the pain to himself, grabbing his skull with both hands and sitting back in his chair.

In a very gentle thought, now because his own pain, Gesroh shot a question to the recovering human, "How can you manage…cope…with this pain…ache…pain?"

"Well this is the worst migraine I've ever had, but we do it with drugs that mask the pain and we are forced to sit in the dark for many hours until it goes away."

"We…I…must show you how to better treat this problem. It is debilitating. No wonder your race is so primitive, thinking and exchanging information causes you such pain."

"I do not yet know your words well enough to explain the process. It is a matter of relaxation and transference. The same way I took your pain, I will send this pain to another place, where it will die."

"Did you say this is something you could teach me, a poor, dumb Poc-cin?"

"Your brains may have evolved enough. Perhaps we can try later," mused Gesroh, "our race has spent time telepathically teaching the holy people in the high places of Strig'et ocouts, Na-tok-lum-ta (the Himalayas) this discipline and they have proven very receptive and have learned well. We taught them astral projection that they believe they have learned on their own," Gesroh paused and his very expressive face became pensive, "I am still trying to connect to Aaah with projection techniques. She, her mother and I, should be linked through…mind link; it is what you call telepathy, a strange word. Aaah is not far, I can feel her, but I cannot connect with her," he said sadly. She may be in deep rest.

"I am not sure if my team has made contact, I must leave here soon to find them and check their progress," said Jerry as he began putting items back in his daypack and making sure he got the second bio-detector.

Closing his eyes Gesroh made contact with the other three Poc-cin, "They have not yet found Aaah but they have had come in contact with the criminals. I must contact your woman, she is in danger as the two criminals are very near and they are observing her movements."

Jerry jumped up and swung his daypack over his shoulder quickly leaving the enclosure. "I'm outta here!" was all he said as he rushed out. Gesroh monitored the emanation of great concern and the very deep protective feelings that that were involved.

CHAPTER 31

T HE TEAMS FINALLY converged on the camp that had been totally destroyed by the 2 rogues. Everyone arrived at nearly the same time, Megan and Frank were the first and furiously searched through the remnants for Lisa's body, as both were convinced that she must have been injured or killed in this vicious attack. Jerry got there just moments after his companions and he slipped in so silently that Megan and Frank were startled to see him appear out of thin air or like he was "beamed in", where he stood. The soft dirt of the path made his footfalls quiet like an Indian on a raiding party. Without fanfare he threw his daypack on an open spot and joined the frantic search for some signs of Lisa. They began to fear that she may have been devoured or buried by these unpredictable Teer.

All three stopped, grabbed their pistols and turned, as one, toward the strange scraping sound coming along the trail, only to so see Lisa dragging a tent and coming from the direction of the service road. She stopped by the coolers and looked at her teammates, covering her eyes with her hand on her forehead, "What'd yah lose?" as she bend over, opened the noisy cooler and fished out a long neck. When she opened it

203

half of the beer foamed all over her hand and dripped to the ground; she did not care she downed the rest of it in one or two swallows.

Jerry took two giant steps and gathered her in his arms, "You!" he said pulling her close and swinging her around. She winced and squealed in pain, so he set her back down very gently and looked into her eyes, "are you alright?" escaped his lips almost before he thought about it.

"I got roughed up by a couple of really Abominable Snowmen. The two bad guys we are looking for were here, rolled me up in this tent and hauled me away," said Lisa as she gingerly lifted her shirt to show some of her bruises. "There were a couple of reporters here to but I ran them off before my other guests arrived," she recoiled from her own touch as she rolled her shirt back down but left her shirt un-tucked.

"I guess staying behind was not as dull as you thought it was going to be," mused Jerry, a comment that put him on the receiving end of a fist to the point of his shoulder. "Ouch, you pack quite a wallop," he said making a show of rubbing his wound and throwing his arm around like it really hurt.

"I am not amused, you big baby. If you really want me to hit you that can be arranged," Lisa came forward with another fist. She was mad now because she thought he was making fun of her.

"No thank you ma'am, I believe you really mean it and I was just having a little tension relieving fun with you. Let me look at those bruises, you may have a broken rib and we might need to get you to a hospital," Jerry said as he reached for the bottom of her shirt.

"No," slapping his hand away, "I am pretty sure nothing

is broken, so can we get out of here now?" Lisa said stepping back a little to look at the wreckage.

"Would you please go sit in the truck and we'll finish up here?" asked Frank. He got no protest from Lisa who grabbed her daypack and crawled into the back seat of the truck. The other three packed up the gear that they could salvage and put it in the back of the suburban. Only the beer cooler and one laptop would make the trip back to the cabins and some of the hard cases that were not too badly dented. They then buried everything else in a hole where a tree had recently been uprooted from, threw dirt on top of it covering it very neatly and then piled into the truck. Frank backed out and pointed vehicle downhill toward Ione and the cabins.

"You know," said Jerry loud enough for everyone to hear but rather to himself, "we came up here for a summer of research, just to do some hiking, day camping and follow some leads," he was digging in his pack for something and a quick look around showed him that everyone was listening, "I thought it would be fun and I was really happy when Lisa said she could make it to spice things up and we've been here, what, six days? To date we have already made contact with the alien race we call Sasquatch, we've been given mind altering technology, have amassed enough information to write volumes of books on a myriad of subjects and we have learned so much about several other species of extra-terrestrials I don't know where to begin; all of this in less than a week," Jerry looked around for a reaction and got nothing but blank stares, but he continued anyway even with such a tough audience, "now we have been enlisted to find a lost alien child; I finally found it; this not the alien child," as he pulled out one of the new scanners and switched it on, "what do we do for an encore?"

"You've got me there, captain. I was looking forward to the relaxing and fooling around part, not all of this. When those two brutes grabbed me I thought my life was over and I really do not want to go through that again," explained Lisa as she grabbed Jerry's arm and laid her head on his shoulder for some comfort.

Megan, as if on cue, snuggled closer to Frank who looked in the mirror at Jerry and smiled, "I'm all for the more lay back summer too but until we find Aaah that's not going to happen, now is it?"

"My guess is that we are somewhat committed to complete this little mission before we can go back to our once mundane, although well educated, lives," said Jerry as he handed Megan the other scanner and suddenly, scarring the life out of everyone, yelled, "Stop!"

A very startled Frank hit the brakes bringing all the equipment in the rear crashing up against the back seat and locked up all four brakes causing the back end of the vehicle to fish tale in the loose gravel; the rear end was trying to be up front with the front end. Everyone lurched forward and then slammed back into their seats fortunately restrained by their seat belts. Frank once again regained control of the suburban and finally skidded to a stop with them all looking down slope over a huge embankment that shown the tops of several trees about 50 yards down a steep incline; the cloud of dust surrounded the vehicle and then slowly dissipated as its momentum flowed over the truck and around the top of the trees, way down the hill.

Jerry looked up quickly with a silly grin on his face at the startled faces of his team and said, "sorry, but I have an alien life sign reading and I think it's Aaah. She may be moving away from us because it's blinking. Frank would you put it in 4 by 4 and let's go up that trail," he said pointing, "to the left there for about 250 or 300 meters. We really need to go quickly I think."

Frank, without comment, put the transmission in neutral, shifted the four wheel lever to 4 low, waited a moment for the light to register, put it in gear and began climbing the steep deer trail on the uphill side of the service road. "Hang on; it gets bumpy from here Lassie! We'll be lucky if we don't lose all of the suspension on this little maneuver," Frank said through gritted teeth. He had to give it more gas to get up the small shale covered bank. The truck lurched at an odd angle like it was going to roll over but it just did hold on and remained upright. Finally cresting the bank Frank had to use all of his experience to begin weaving his way through the lodge pole pines and then head straight into some of the most dense buck brush he had ever seen. It sounded as though all the paint was being scrapped off as they bulled their way through, still following the old deer trail. Jagged rocks kept popping up everywhere trying to puncture the tires. After going about 200 meters up the trail there was a small rocky clearing that looked impassible for the constantly complaining and rapidly aging truck. "I think we should walk from here. Everyone should check their sidearm," said Frank as he turned off the engine and set the brake on the steep incline. "Have you got a fix on her location yet?"

"It's still blinking, I think she may still be moving away," said Jerry throwing on his daypack but still concentrating on the tracker, which he deftly changed from hand to hand to get the pack on his back.

Megan looked at Frank then back at Jerry, "We went through there?" she was pointing to the west, "How did we get up that hill?"

"Only a major 4 wheel drive had a chance and I still do not know how we made it through that brush on such a steep hill. Hell a tank or a bull dozer would have had problems," said Frank scratching his head, "we may not be able to get it back out of here."

"Let's worry about that later, we need to get moving," said Jerry waiving for everyone to follow him heading in a northeasterly direction. It did not take long to find the cave where Aaah had spent her time as a captive.

They found the heavy stalked plants that had been used to tie her hands and feet, both showed that they had been gnawed through but looked more like the work of a chain saw not a set of teeth. There was a trace of blood, which was more orange than red; Megan got a sample and some additional hair too that she carefully packed away in a plastic pouch.

"You have done well my friends," said Gesroh in a powerful mental blast, causing them all to stagger, "she was there and is now moving north…east…and she is wounded, your word is…concussion." All four stood with their hands on the side of their heads, eyes closed to listen to the mental flash; they looked more like protestors at a rock concert now than the secret agent look earlier. The message was still so powerful it almost knocked all of them to their knees.

"Gesroh," thought Megan, "please tone these communications down; the amplified power almost blew the top of our heads off again, thanks."

"I am sorry; due to the distance I did add some power. You are not used to this form of communication nor particularly adept at reception yet. I will turn the power down but it may not reach you as easily due to the interference and the reduced frequencies. I am whispering most of the time. I will adjust our machines to communicate like we do with our infants."

Although all were slightly taken back by this last bit of news about being infant brains, there was a collective, "thank you." Outside the cave Frank picked up Aaah's trail. It was quickly decided that Jerry and Megan were going to trail on foot and Lisa and Frank were going back for the truck. Looking up the hillside the trail was not really too well hidden as the brush and small trees looked like a tractor tire had move through. Just as they were parting company Lisa confirmed that she was not able to walk without a lot of pain so she did not protest the decision. The bruises she had received from the rough treatment had taken their toll.

Completely unknown to any of the four, or to Gesroh, there was an Air Force vehicle sitting on a small logging road nearby. A sergeant, a captain and a Colonel were sitting quietly with their eyes closed, listening to the mental transmissions running rampant through the forest. All three sets of eyes opened suddenly glowing greenish yellow and then slowly transitioned toward more human appearing eyes. The sergeant started the car and drove in a northeasterly direction.

The sheriff's vehicle that had been patrolling near Big Meadow Lake suddenly turned around and headed back toward Ione. The telltale greenish yellow glow in the sheriff deputy's eyes lasting only a few moments before turning back to a set of lovely pale blue eyes.

Aaah after having easily gnawed her bonds and just as easily broken out of the small cave became confused about the direction she needed to travel back to the safe area. Her concussion was giving her a lot of pain; pain she certainly was not accustomed to. Her stomach was now very upset; her eyes were becoming more sensitive to the light, causing her to be nearly blind; this only added to her confusion. She moved northeast angling up in an effort to get her bearings. Her only thought now was that she really wanted to see her parents at the safe area. She no longer cared about being seen. Her long hair was matted and covered with leaves and dirt held together with a generous amount of her orange blood. Her wrists and ankles were also bleeding and sore; she was hungry and her stomach although upset was growling louder than her father when he had yelled at her the last time she saw him. She began her scrambling assent kicking rocks in small landslides down the sloped rock face.

CHAPTER 32

JERRY AND MEGAN, now designated as the away team, were making pretty good time following the swath left by the wounded female Teer through the forest. It was like following a wounded grizzly, hoping to find it and also hoping it won't charge when you do come across it, the way the trees were broken and the brush had been trampled the tracking was not difficult. Jerry could tell the general directions they were headed was not toward Ione, but angling up toward Deer Mountain through Cameron Meadow. They couldn't quite figure out why she was headed away from the safe house, but from the amount of blood loss, both in the cave and on the brush, it was evident she was hurt bad, probably dazed and disoriented.

By late afternoon Jerry and Megan, both winded now from the pace of their pursuit, did not seem to be making any progress on their quarry. How did Aaah have the strength to go on, the silent question passed between them and they both answered with a shrug of the shoulders. They paused at Jim Creek, finding some huge muddy footprints still showing and the direction of travel. The bio-tracker indicated Aaah was still at least 2 kilometers ahead of them and moving at a steady pace away from them.

"Why can't Gesroh come get her now, he must know where she is? Gasped Megan who was really starting to get tired; her energy and pace were fading with almost every step.

"He can't leave the safe area until they capture Grious and Tic-Nar. Those two pose a real danger to the Teer already on this planet. If they manage to get a ride off planet, there is a chance of first contact, something Gesroh also does not want," answered Jerry still concentrating on the bio-tracker, "we need to keep our word on this little chore." It did not occur to him he had not physically said a word.

"How does he plan on catching the two bad guys?" was the mental question from Megan who was just now figuring out physical speech was not necessary and they could all communication with each other.

"He has set some type of a trap for them at the safe area," Jerry said as he looked around without explaining more in case there were any listeners nearby. This mental communication was interesting, tricky, a little frightening, but interesting.

The Air Force staff car pulled into the road junction of Thorson Meadow that was just north of Cameron Meadow, both just down slope from Deer Mountain. The engine was shut off and all three sat in the vehicle with their eyes closed, communing with their ship and each other. They too were acting on the projected path of the injured Teer hoping to intercept her before the Poc-cin could retrieve her. Their motives for the rescue were certainly their own, but Aaah's safety was not their real motive.

The deputy sheriff's patrol car took up a position just southwest of Deer Mountain, closer to Cameron Meadow. The possessed deputy stayed in her vehicle, the creature inside her closed her eyes and communed with the same Effe ship, now orbiting the moon.

"Lisa, I mean Federation Base are you copying?" whispered Jerry into his hand held radio microphone head piece.

"Federation base, what's up?"

"What is your twenty?"

"We limped our way into Ione by the train station waiting to hear from you. Have you had any luck?"

"No, we are still on her trail. We are all still heading northeast. It could be Deer Mountain or Cameron Meadow, then who knows, she has been pretty steadfast in her heading so maybe there is an objective out there somewhere."

"Okay, what do you want us to do now?"

"My best guess is that you both meet us at Cameron Meadow. Do you see the white square in grid 14 where the roads intersect?"

"Copy, we see it," Frank knew exactly where that point was he had tranquilized a grizzly bear by that building just last spring.

"We are easily an hour away, maybe a little less if we hurry, so we'll see you there. Away team out."

"There, at least I have arranged for us to have a nice ride home, I hope. I also hope Aaah stops moving pretty soon," panted Jerry putting the radio in a side pouch in his daypack and fishing out a candy bar. It was a chocolate wafer bar and he gave Megan 2 of the 5 sections.

"Thanks boss, can we get moving now?" remarked Megan

somewhat sarcastically. She still had a colossal headache and she was getting tired from this whole jogging and orienteering chase. Every once in a while she had to grab Jerry and pull or push him so he wouldn't hit a tree or a deadfall because he was concentrating on the bio-tracker so intently.

"We seem to be able to communicate with telepathy here in close range, I wonder if Lisa and Frank have been listening. It did not seem like it when I had her on the radio. Maybe we are just good for short distances between ourselves," thought Jerry.

"Maybe so, who knows and who cares at this point," was Megan's retort.

"I think Aaah may have stopped moving," thought Jerry, as he punched a couple of buttons and there were some odd beeps and bleeps, "there is a structure near that intersection. It shows that it is large and metal, like a pole barn or garage. Yup, she has stopped in the building. It should be pretty easy to make contact if we can just get there. This thing should signal her of our approach and tell her we're friendly, at least that is my hope, providing that her mental faculties have not been too scrambled."

"If I am reading this thing correctly there is an indication of some other minds, powerful minds near her. There is a cluster of three here on one side and a single some distance away; odd Gesroh didn't say anything about other Teer in or around this area. Very curious," mumbled Jerry as he lengthened his stride and picked up the pace.

The going was easier because the buck brush had thinned out a little but there was still a lot of deadfall and stumps to jump over. Megan was nearing the exhaustion point. Her internal energy supply that she always thought would never run out was gurgling on the empty mark. She began to stumble on each deadfall and she could not catch her breath.

"Grab my hand we've got to keep moving," urged Jerry, "we are just about a mile away now," he too was gasping.

"Okay," was all she could manage between gasps for more oxygen. She ran another twenty yards, jerked her hand away and sat down. "I don't know what's wrong here, I'm in good shape." She reached again for his hand but when she stood up she stumbled into him. Jerry was starting to feel real fatigue set in as well. It reminded him of Dorothy and the Lion running through the poppy field toward the city of Oz and falling asleep on the dead run. There was no Tin Man or Scarecrow to carry them and no good witch of the North to make it snow; where was Gesroh when they really needed him.

CHAPTER 33

A BEAD OF SWEAT popped out of the Colonel's brow as he concentrated, it ran down his nose and dripped off the end. Urging the others to concentrate he doubled his efforts. He did not want the Poc-cin, as the Teer called them, to reach the wounded Teer female. He was protecting her for his own selfish reasons and his thoughts were being enhanced by the lesser, although still powerful minds of his compatriots. The male gender was something foreign to this being, but because the human body it inhabited was male "it" began to feel what being a male was all about, raising in his trousers.

These beings, inhabiting the military males and Deborah, the deputy sheriff, are all Effe, beings of pure energy. Ranchers, somewhat like the Kev-tah'esh, the Effe have herds of humans and mammals from all the ages of Earth. Their word for Earth is Pec-ay-na (third world away). They consume flesh to maintain their energy but do not have the more delicate pallet of the Kev-tah'esh, the grays allied with the Teer.

The Effe have meddled in the affairs of other races for thousands of years. They even have secret herds of the warlike Clot-tor who act as their mercenaries to guard and fight for them. They have no taste for the Clot-tor who are silicone-based reptilian creatures.

Of late a newer predator, a warrior race, the Scha-kur have emerged after traveling from across the galaxy to challenge the Clot-tor at every turn and are just now finding this remote, outer ring system. This race of vicious insect based beings have begun attacking anything moving in space in their quest to dominate every race in this sector. At first contact it became evident that diplomacy was impossible because the Scha-kur will fight any race to dominate them or themselves be annihilated. No quarter is ever asked or given. They came to the stars by copying the technology of the Kev-tah'esh who had the misfortune of colonizing one of their planets. The insects are relative new comers to the older star races and are now wreaking havoc among all of the races on this side of the galaxy.

The Effe had a plan to enhance their stock on a distant planet with fresh DNA from this wounded Teer female. Offspring of Teer are always carefully guarded and well cared for making it very difficult to obtain fresh specimens. After two or three thousand years of cloning and interbreeding infusion was needed quickly or their herds would die off and this was their best opportunity to get a specimen like the Teer prime minister's daughter.

As strange as it may seem it is always to the advantage of the Effe that these primitive races like this planet think they are alone in the universe. The unexplained disappearances are soon forgotten, so the Effe can return every few thousand or hundred years and harvest what they need, at their leisure and in any amount they believe necessary.

The vacationing Teer have started things in motion that

could ruin the plans of all the other dominant races now vying for this planet so the secret must be kept from these Poc-cin; they must always think they are alone in the universe, which has always been the arrogant presumption of all minor, non-star travelling, races. It is also seems important that the Teer remain a myth.

Something all the older races know too is that this side of the galaxy is very sparsely populated. The center of the galaxy is where the hot bed of races exists just itching to break out and expand their territories. The Clot-tor and Scha-kur have thus far kept all expansion at bay. All the star races want to hold on to their possessions for themselves in their own little empires and confederations.

Now a few Poc-cin, Earth people as they call themselves, are arrogant little fish in a huge pond, full of predators and are careening through the universe on this blue planet. This small ball of dust on the outer rim just happens to have some value to the other, hungry, races. This planet must remain protected from expanding into the galaxy. Sharing any star race technology with these primitives and showing them they are not alone will ruin their cute little "status quo". It could even cause another interstellar war to erupt. The last one nearly consumed the center of the galaxy.

CHAPTER 34

MIKE TURNBULL SAT at the intersection where the road comes down from the mountain and meets the lake road. He was trying to decide where to go, literally which way to turn. He was typing a few lines into his laptop for his next article on the college professor who threatened him with a gun. He knew Dennis had gone back in the direction of his new girlfriend so he wouldn't have to worry about him for a while. Then he saw the forestry suburban hurrying past him throwing gravel and dust everywhere to get somewhere in a hurry; it had to be important. "Now there is a reason to get up in the morning," he muttered to himself out loud as he set his notebook and computer into the passenger seat, turned the key and followed in the dust trying to keep from being noticed, at a discreet distance. His nose for sleazy news told him they were leading him to another, even better, story. Mike also expected them to go back to the cabins but they surprised him again by speeding by the cabins and not stopping until they reached the old train station tourist trap. A few minutes later they fired up their engine and continued on through Ione, heading north following secondary road 2705. Mike's GPS was keeping him abreast of his precise location. According to the map displayed on the GPS this road went pretty much nowhere, so he knew something must be in the works.

Dennis just happened to be coming out of the drug store about 100 yards from the forestry truck when it started its engine and sped away from the old train station. He took a long drink of his diet cola just thinking about his next move when he saw his old friendly enemy following close behind. Without thinking about it he looked at his watch, it was 1720, which has nothing more than a time hack to get his brain started. He fished out his keys, jumped in his rental Explorer and sped off as the third car in the convoy.

Three vehicles, two in close pursuit but trying to stay back in the billowing dust making them almost invisible in Frank's mirrors, were all heading toward the foot of Deer Mountain. The occupants of the vehicles already there were becoming very aware of all the entities converging upon them.

In the Air Force staff car, the driver starts to writhe and contort. There is an anguished groan and the human host disappears, except for the outer garments. In place of the human host sits a being of pure energy, crackling with white and red sparks, with roughly the same outline and size of the human body it had once occupied. The eyes of the others snap open and two heads turn in the direction of the Effe, now exposed. It was glowing like a yellow 100 watt bug light bulb.

"I am sorry, my energy level was dangerously low and I needed to feed," the being thought to the others.

"That was foolish," was the irritated counter thought from the superior, "You could have waited longer. You must leave us now," was the equally cold, unemotional thought, "one to transport!" Instantly there was a twinkling of blue/green light and the offending Effe departed to the orbiting ship. "Discipline is needed, we must wait to feed on these beings or we will lose our quarry," was the second thought from the superior to the ship's captain. There was a return thought of agreement. In the seat where the young sergeant had been sitting were now just the uniform and shoes. The two Effe both got out and relocated themselves into the front seat of the staff car resuming their concentration once more.

Gesroh saw the transport beam come in from space and plotted where it had originated and then triangulated the point on the planet where it had touched down. He was sure now that the Effe were involved and the beam merely confirmed any suspicions. The point where the beam landed was very near where Aaah was in hiding. Gesroh decided to send out a warning to his Poc-cin allies, "beware the Effe are awaiting your arrival and they are endowed with infinite patience, except when they are hungry. They are very near Aaah. Her life signs are becoming weaker, you must hurry."

Jerry and Megan had regained some of their strength and a little more stamina since the Effe had stopped their concerted effort to put them to sleep by trying to drain every ounce of their strength. Gesroh began to block the thoughts of the Effe to aid his allies and sent positive energy in a greater effort to protect the Poc-cin. The effects of positive energy were having an energizing effect and had both Jerry and Megan speeding along, so much so that Megan began to feel as though she had been awarded super powers. Both had become exhilarated to the point of looking more like steeplechase athletes running through the forest. The deadfall logs, brush and tree branches were no longer obstacles. Their heightened senses allowed them to anticipate several yards ahead the easily find the best path around or over any obstacle.

The Effe, concentration now destroyed and blocked from the minds of the Poc-cin could only sit and wait for all the players to arrive. Unknown to the Earth bound aliens there was a pitched battle raging on the far side of Jupiter. The Clot-tor armada and a flotilla of the Effe were not heavily engaged with the entire Scha-Kur fleet of this sector for the rights to the system and the eventual harvesting of the third planet, Kylch-ulk, in their clicking mandible language. There was no apparent advantage for either side; the effects of the eventual attrition would ultimately decide the winner and loser by which fleet would dis-engage first and run. Attrition would favor the Scha-Kur's larger fleet.

The battle raged so extensively that the Hubble telescope was picking up small distinct explosions coming from the vicinity of Titan, one of the more hospitable moons, where the Clot-tor star base has been hidden for hundreds of years. The scientists who had booked time on the telescope for today had abandoned their observation of the nebula they supposed to study to try and figure out what was going on over and around Titan. At first they thought it was a meteor shower hitting the atmosphere but then they could just discern small points of light darting everywhere in and around the explosions. The scientists were getting as much of it on film as possible.

Gesroh, monitoring the telescope transmissions, thought how ironic it was that his own daughter had somehow started an interstellar war, although he was not exactly sure how or even why. This entire situation was getting out of hand. Gesroh contacted the transport ship of the Kev-tah'esh, who harbor no love for the Effe, the Clot-tor or the Scha-kur, to ask if they could swiftly bring in one of their own fleets in an attempt to put down the problem. Gesroh was hoping that all of the other fleets engaged in the battle would be severely depleted by the time they arrived and be more easily defeated when surprised by the Kev-Tah'esh and their more advanced weaponry. The newest Kev-Tah'esh battle cruisers carry more combined fire power than a fleet of the ships currently engaged. They have even developed a passive weapon that when fired at close range, say 100,000 or 200,000 kilometers attacks the ships computer and electrical systems thereby minimizing the loss of life of the opponent, giving them the chance to surrender or by killing them slowly through loss of their life support systems.

CHAPTER 35

FRANK AND LISA arrived at the intersection near Cameron Meadow. They could not see the Air Force staff car from their vantage point but they could see a county sheriff's car parked about 60 yards north of the only structure in the area, a county pole barn garage. There was a chain link fence surrounding the building, one overhead lamp on a telephone pole and a sturdy looking gate with a chain and padlock. Inside the compound were mounds of gravel and dirt for road maintenance and a crude lube rack on one side. It was overgrown with weeds and tall grass as if it had not been in use for the whole winter season.

They could see a person in the sheriff's patrol car who was just sitting very still. At first, with just the naked eye, it looked empty with just two head rests but when Lisa put the binoculars to use she could see a person's head. Once in a while a yellow-green glow could be detected in the waning daylight, like the occasional glow of someone smoking a cigarette or taking a puff on a pipe or cigar.

"Away team this is Federation Base, over," Lisa whispered into her radio headset, not taking her eyes off the patrol car and its occupant.

"This is the Away team, why are we whispering and what's up?" yelled Jerry hardly able to contain all the energy coursing freely through his once tired body. He was hearing something like an echo when talking on the radio to Lisa but had not yet figured out why.

"We're in position, now what?"

"We have just reached the tree line southwest of the building, we can see your suburban. Did you know there are two cars behind you? There are two men standing in the road who seem to be arguing," reported Jerry as he surveyed the scene. "I also see a car with U.S. Air Force markings, parked on the northwest side of the fence, over."

"We've got a sheriff's patrol car on our side of the building not too far from the gate. The occupant has not moved but keeps glowing on and off like a beer sign in a tavern. I think we have more aliens here than humans, although that isn't counting what may be human hosts for some of them, over," surmised Lisa who was starting to feel a little spooked. All of this was happening far too fast and she was totally overwhelmed and lost as to what to do next or who might make the first move. Would that first move be lethal or were they merely here to talk; she decided that no one was really here to talk.

Jerry and Megan observed that the two, as yet unknown men, by the trailing cars had finished their argument and were now in a fist fight, so they were pretty much out of the problem for now. Jerry had a solid location on Aaah now, although he wasn't sure how he was going to rescue the 1,000 pound "girl". "Gesroh," thought Jerry, "what is happening here? Are those Effe converging on Aaah? Why do they want her so badly?" Jerry suddenly understood something about this mind link and why he had been hearing an echo when talking with Lisa on the radio. It was something he would file away for later discussion however with more urgent matters at hand.

"The Effe are hard to read, but I have learned that Aaah is with child from her frolicking with Ustra and the Effe want to capture her and take her to a colony to add to their herd of Teer that they have hidden on a moon of a planet you call...Jupiter. I have learned, from their cluttered minds, that they have been cloning and growing Teer from two criminal specimens they took from this planet around a thousand years ago. The Effe are currently fighting with other star race to protect that herd. The other race not only want that colony but this planet for harvesting."

"I have caused the two fighting Poc-cin to become... asleep...unconscious; their presence here is a liability to our effort. I am sending a beam of thought to the Effe, who are not at this moment in communication with their ship, in order to confuse their telepathic abilities to help you rescue Aaah. You must hurry and you must make mind contact with her to get her into your large vehicle and bring her to me; she is in a great deal of pain. I will not be with you for a while now as I must attend to the attack of Grious and Tic-Nar here at the safe area, now!"

The mind link abruptly ended. Jerry felt lost and exhausted. Lisa felt helpless. Megan felt so fatigued it was like she had an elephant sitting on her shoulders. Frank was immediately confused, ready to pass out. All four were shaking their heads from side to side in vain in an effort to regain the link, much like hitting the lever on an old telephone trying to reestablish the telephone connection of the person that had become disconnected, all very feudal efforts.

229

The 3 Effe inhabited bodies, still sitting in the cars, had their heads down and their eyes closed, like someone had turned their switch to off. The connection with the ship orbiting the moon had been lost because Gesroh had successfully jammed their signal. All three were frozen in time awaiting instructions from the central core.

Aaah was now lying in the garage, in the back storage room on some old quilted packing blankets and she was getting images like a kaleidoscope in her brain. It was all coming so fast that she was not able to discern reality from fantasy. She hovered between unconsciousness and a painful wakefulness where a Poc-cin was trying to contact her. She did not want the contact because the Poc-cin brain is so primitive and cluttered, but there was a background image of Gesroh, her father with the mind link inquiry lending some credibility to, what she considered a bad dream. Weakly she answered the mind link, which was fortunate for Jerry because it came in pretty loud, "what do you want Poc-cin?" was all she could manage, her eyes fluttering and blood oozing slowing down her matted hair, her life force ebbing away.

"Your father wants me to bring you to him. May I come inside and assist you?" thought Jerry fighting back the now familiar searing pain at the top of his skull; a lightning bold began cutting through the back of his skull.

"My limbs are not functioning well, you may help me..." answered Aaah, and she lapsed into an unconscious state. The mind link had sapped her last ounce of energy.

Jerry looked at his partners in crime as he and Megan walked the short distance to the building and the fence. Frank was already at the chained door having already broken through the gate. The two men finally broke in and found

Aaah passed out in the back among the used tires, on the pile of old moving quilts. Fortunately she, and the quilts, were on a pallet and it seemed to them it might be possible to move her using a rolling pallet jack, unfortunately there was no forklift. They found some respirator masks, like painters wear, to wear while they worked because the smell was unbelievable. They did get her hoisted gently up on the overextended jack that said it had a 2,000 pound capacity, stacked a few tires around her, covered her with a quilt and rolled her slowly out of the building. They were fortunate to have greasy concrete floors. Megan, in the meantime, had backed the suburban into the oil changing rack that had a ramp that seemed strong enough to unload the unconscious Teer into the back of the truck because it was about the same level as the back compartment. It was going to be a tight fit.

Fortunately the ramp where she backed in was a dug out and it was level with the floor of the garage, like a loading dock in the back of a warehouse. After overcoming the difficulty of some gravel interfering with the wheels of the pallet jack, it took all four of them to roll Aaah into the back of the carry all. The smell, even out of the building, was like being confined with fifty angry skunks; it was horrendous. Lisa used the first aid kit on the side of Aaah's head, cleaning and dressing the wound. Lisa was sure it was a concussion, but she at least stopped the bleeding.

From a kit that Frank carried under the front seat he took out some tranquilizer darts and Jerry injected Aaah with about half a dart to ease her pain and let her rest rather than being in a feverish stupor. Aaah stopped moaning after a few minutes. They all decided it was time to hit the road. Frank had to put the suburban into four-wheel drive, because the front end was so high the wheels were hardly touching the ground. In an effort to stabilize the truck so it was more drivable, Frank found an old pick-up truck transmission and chained it to the front of the truck, and although it weighed 150 or 200 pounds the front tires only came back down a few inches and still barely touched the road.

No sooner had the truck revved its engine and gotten on the road did the confused Effe seem to regain their composure. There was twitching and a great deal of jumping around. The two human forms in the Air Force staff car disappeared completely and in their place were beings of radiant greenish golden with white and red sparks of energy popping inside the cab; it had been too long since they had eaten. The Effe inhabiting the body of the deputy sheriff left her body and migrated to the staff car; it had eaten earlier and could safely join its kind, no longer needing to inhabit an energy sapping body and deducing that there was no need for additional coverage on the building where the Teer female had been. The deputy slumped over, completely exhausted, unable to move although she was slightly aware of her surroundings, but very confused. She had been in a conscious nightmare for many hours. She mercifully passed out, just like someone with alcohol poisoning and her hangover promised to be gruesome. She would need a couple of days to recover from the strain of being inhabited, fortunate to have survived the incident.

The 3 Effe watched as the suburban awkwardly ambled down the gravel road in the direction of Ione. Now back in touch with their ship the Effe were communing with the central core collective mind. The Effe are not a hive or a colony culture exactly, they operated more like doing things on the advice of a committee. The collective mind is a group of elder Effe linked together like an electrical circuit, more in series than in parallel, so if one burns out they all tend to end up looking like burnt matchsticks. The central core then quickly sends in more elders. Things do not get accomplished very quickly when dealing with the Effe.

There was a great commotion in the Effe fleet as they watched a Kev-tah'esh ship break out of the atmosphere of the blue planet and head for deep space. A Clot-tor destroyer left the fleet and followed at a distance. The Clot-een'ta (Captain) asked for a plot on the trajectory of the enemy ship. The computer technician quickly reported was bound for the slave moon by the huge gas giant planet. The Clot-een'ta decided to follow without attempting to intercept curious about the cargo and the reasons behind a Kev-tah'esh going to the slave moon. The plasma main gun and armor fields were kept in place just in case it was a trick or a calculated ruse to break up the Effe battle fleet.

CHAPTER 36

GESROH CONTINUED HAVING problems of his own. The two criminals had been able to break into the safe area and even killed some of the Gray's in an effort to commandeer one of their ships. Gesroh and two other Teer males had been able to trap them in the back of the hanger bay, which was inside the hollowed out mountain top.

Ustra, the husband hopeful of Aaah and the father of her child, in his youthful exuberance, wanted to rush the criminals and do them some real physical harm, chain them up and send them back to Kleek for immediate execution. Gesroh was more in favor of just killing them here on Strig'et ocouts (Earth) and have done with it. Pa-Alec, another of the Teer males, suggested they put the two on a ship programmed for the Effe slave colony on the gas giant's moon, citing an old proverb of his people that "It would be more generous to give than to receive."

Gesroh thought it over, "There is a chance old friend that the Effe may then stop chasing Aaah and her unborn." Gesroh gave a yellow toothed grin and slapped Pa-Alec on the back of his shoulder in agreement. A fine joke he thought. This congratulation blow would have killed a 5-ton elephant, but Pa-Alec with a yellow toothed grin of his own set off to program a ship for the journey. The Teer do not like to kill their own species but they are great ones for cruel irony of jokes when it comes to dealing with criminals.

The Kev-tah'esh (the Gray's), having no religious convictions or even mythological beliefs, rites or any deities to pray to, put the bodies of their dead into one of the disintegration machines, log and tag the small containers of particles of their fallen comrades and stack them in their "dead locker". All citizens must be cataloged dead or alive for the census that occurs every 100 standard years. So they busied themselves taking care of their dead while Teer dealt with Teer.

Pa-Alec came shuffling back to Gesroh and whispered in his ear. Gesroh nodded, a single nod, and picked up an object about the size of a Ping-Pong ball, "Grious and Tic-Nar, can you hear me?"

"Yeah, we hear you. We are not giving up!"

"I am quite sure of that. I am not asking that you give up. We have decided to give you both a ship and I have had it programmed to take you to a place of safety and not back to Kleek where you deserve to go for punishment and death."

The two criminals looked at each other quite incredulously. They both said, "Bask-ah!" in unison, their word for trick that led Grious to ask the inevitable question, "Why do you give up so easily and grant our wish?"

"I want you off this planet, it is as simple as that," retorted Gesroh followed by a loud snort; blowing a huge wad of snot all over the side of the ship he intended to give them. "We will back off to the other end of this hanger. All I ask is that you, without further hesitation or argument get on board and depart."

"Do we get a pilot?"

"No, you have killed enough pilots today. As I have said it is programmed with a destination where there are many of our kind and it is not a hostile place, with lots of food to eat." Gesroh waived everyone back to the other end of the hanger without waiting for a reply. He knew that these two criminals would run, not walk, to the ship and take off as quickly as they could shut the hatch, so he wanted everyone out of the way of the blast. As soon as everyone was back to a safe distance he closed the middle blast panels and set the energy field.

Just as he predicted the two criminals broke cover and ran for the ship. They hesitated only long enough to look inside for an ambush and then quickly climbed into the small scout shuttle. As soon as it lands on the distant moon and the two criminals get out it was programmed to begin a short count down, seal itself for flight and return to this planet. The whole process should take about 3 standard days.

Although the blast of the engines is nearly silent the fumes and gases discharged could be seen against the blast panels. Anyone caught inside the blast area without protection would perish quickly from the extreme heat and enclosed noxious fumes. As the small ship was sent racing for the outer atmosphere the blast residue was contained, properly stored and the hanger would then be cleaned of hazardous material. It only took a matter of minutes due to its automation. The Kev-tah'esh would do a final clean up with their detectors and the incident would be just another bad memory.

The only glitch in the entire operations was that Gesroh did not see the unconscious Kev-tah'esh that Tic-Nar had carried aboard. The criminals knew Gesroh had given in too easily and they wanted, no needed, the opportunity to get control of the ship before it went to its destination, wherever that may be. The hostage they had taken was a mechanic not a pilot. They had incorrectly assumed that all the Kev-tah'esh were capable of flying the craft and soon they would find out the error of their wicked ways.

Flying past our moon Grious and Tic-Nar observed the Effe fleet in a non-orbiting formation very near the trajectory of their own small ship. As they pasted they did not see the single Clot-tor ship leave the formation and follow at distance. The 2 Teer did not know how to use or interpret any of the instruments of the craft so they did not know they were being followed. Depositing the unconscious Gray on the deck without ceremony the two criminals sat back to wait out the ride. The destination anticipation was somewhat dissipated when in the distance they saw a black hole that they believed might have taken them back to Kleek, a place they had no real desire to see again anyway. Tic-Nar did feel a minor twinge of home sickness.

CHAPTER 37

DRIVING THE SUBURBAN down a gravel road with 800 to a 1000 pound sleeping Bigfoot in the back end was like trying to drive a tail-dragging plane down the runway with an elephant for cargo. The steering was tedious at best because the front tires were barely making contact with the road and the leaf springs and shocks in the back were groaning pitifully. Frank had to keep zigzagging down the road looking out the side windows just to keep the vehicle on the road; not to mention he was also hanging his head out the window trying to breathe. He was still wearing the painter's respirator but his eyes were watering like fountains and he was gasping mightily.

Lisa was hanging out the passenger side front window trying to give him directions. She had been given the other respirator but she was gasping for breath due to her sore ribs and she was having trouble seeing her eyes were tearing so badly. Megan and Jerry were fishing for items in the first aid kit to help them breathe in the awful stench. To make matters worse Aaah's snoring was like a runaway freight train complete with the bells and whistles. The noise was deafening.

Not too far down the road there were two men lying off

to the side of the road, their cars still running. The noise of the suburban going by brought them back to wakefulness; they both coughed in the dust they inhaled from the passing vehicle making them hack away and wheeze as they sat up. It was a few moments before either man could stand. There was no recollection as to why they were lying in the road or why they were bleeding from their noses. Each decided to follow the dust trail of the truck no matter where it might lead, reasoning it was certainly going somewhere.

Each man got up slowly; racked with pain from the induced fistfight that Gesroh had forced them into and both stumbled on their way to the appropriate car without saying a word to each other. The only noise uttered by either man was a melodious series of groans with each step. Dennis crawled into the driver's seat, closed the door and promptly passed out. Mike could do no better, but he did manage to get his engine shut off before he succumbed to the moment and also passed out. The bruises and small trickles of blood each man had in evidence were not life threatening, nor were there any broken ribs or bones, although there were some cracked and loosened teeth. In their comatose condition neither man saw, nor heard, the second car race by in another billowing cloud of fine powdery dust with the gravel hitting the windshields, in rapid fire staccato succession.

Frank was forced to slow down when they reached the outskirts of Ione, although the decrease in speed did not help the maneuverability of the overburdened, almost un-steerable vehicle. A State Patrol officer looked curiously as the lumbering suburban went by but turned back to his lunch muttering something about the mentality of Forest Rangers.

"Frank we need to get out of town she is starting to wake up already!" Megan yelled as the behemoth turned over in her sleep shaking the vehicle violently. To make matters worse as Aaah turned over she passed gas so loud it was like several balloons of lethal methane all being popped at once; the act of rolling over caused the wheel wells of the beleaguered truck's frame to scrape the tires causing them to heat up and begin to smoke, nearly catching fire from the friction. Even though Jerry and Megan had put surgical masked on they too were hanging out the windows gasping for fresh air. Frank was driving now with half his body out the driver's window with still about 2 or 3 miles to go to get back to the cabins.

The Air Force staff car that had been in such hot pursuit was not able to follow the truck through the west end of Ione because none of the Effe had a host body anymore. Finally giving up the chase the three beings beamed back to their waiting ship, leaving the car to crash down a ten foot embankment into Jim Creek at a speed of nearly 60 miles an hour. This crash would be a mystery that the authorities would work on and wonder about for many years to come.

After what seemed to be the longest trip of their lives the suburban did at long last turn in at the cabins. Frank drove it quickly around back behind the second cabin in an attempt to hide the cargo from any prying eyes. The now wide-awake Teer was smashing her gigantic fists against the back doors in an effort to break out. Jerry and Megan quickly got out to the back doors just in time to open them, allowing Aaah to make her escape. Without so much as a thank you or a backward glance Aaah, in two giant strides, had disappeared into the underbrush and was running headlong uphill toward her father and mother in the safe area at Huckleberry Mountain.

She parted the brush and knocked down small trees like a rogue elephant running through the forest. The popping and cracking of breaking limbs and falling trees could be heard well off in the distance.

Rather than feeling some elation or joy at the culmination of the rescue Frank had made it to the underbrush and was puking his guts out while Lisa was just did not have the strength to go anywhere out of sight and was just leaning out of the passenger seat, hanging on the open door, also spewing her insides out. Jerry and Megan stood leaning against the truck with one hand, holding their stomach's with the other hand and just let everything go right there. Once one started to vomit there was no holding back the other three. None of them could even remember when they had eaten last but whatever was in their stomachs was coming out now and quickly. Soon they could do nothing but dry heave.

Completely drained of strength and vitality all four sat on the back steps of the backside cabin, their heads down, "I don't know if I will ever be able to get the stink out of the vehicle. I think I could fumigate it with a family of skunks and that would make it smell better," wisecracked Frank but everyone was too drained to do more than groan at the awful attempt at humor.

"I don't remember smelling anything that horrible at the safe area," murmured Megan, "I wonder if they all smell like that or do you think it is some type of defense excretion mechanism, like Frank's friends the skunks?"

"An interesting theory but I am not in the mood to pursue any more science today," muttered Jerry as he finally mustered enough strength to stand and stumble up the stairs and go into the cabin. He returned with two black garbage bags.

"Frank, you and Megan go over to that cabin and strip, put your clothes in this bag and if you have the strength take a shower. We do not have any tomato juice so just use soap and scrub. We will do the same over here. Lisa and I will try to find some clothes for you Frank, if you don't have any over there. In the interest of breathing please leave the clothes bags on the porch and tie them securely.

"Thanks Jerry, but I have a clean uniform in the closet," groaned Frank as he stood offering his hand to get the black garbage bag. He then assisted Megan to her feet and together they both stumbled their way to the the cabin. Not wanting to carry any of the stench inside the cabin both stopped on the other side of the truck and stripped; Jerry and Lisa stayed on their side of the suburban and did the same thing. Without glancing around everyone slowly, as if suddenly 90 years old, stumbled up the stairs of their cabin and straight to the showers.

The lovely hot water streaming and steaming on their bodies was more bliss at this point than making love. Each dutifully scrubbed their partner and the men assisted washing their lady's hair. No one wanted to put on any clothing because the intense scrubbing had left them somewhat chaffed. Toweling off as they walked, stumbled and fell into bed and within seconds of their heads hitting the pillow all four were in a dreamless, almost comatose, sleep. They had been up for almost two days and even though it was early afternoon now there would be no stirring until sometime tomorrow. The two combatant reporters continued to sleep in their cars and Aaah continued her steady trek toward the safe area and her father's protection. She had enough recuperative rest and she was in a hurry.

Just after dark a small ship lifted out of the safe area and went looking for Aaah to bring her back. Aaah, who was beginning to tire, was picked up and safely transported but some campers had an encounter of the extra-terrestrial kind while gathering firewood. Two fainted, one was hit partially by the blast of the engine giving a 2nd degree burn on half his face and one seemed to have a near heart attack, at age 36. All four were unconscious for several minutes before they attempted to make a 911 call on a cell phone. Unfortunately the batteries of all three cell phones in their possession were completely drained due to the electromagnetic pulse of the ship's engines. The campers helped one another back to their campsite and just sat there looking at their dying fire, draining beer after beer. The heart attack was forgotten, because it was not an actual heart attack more of an anxiety attack. One of them fished out a bottle of German made Apple Liquor that was kaput (drained, dead) in a matter of minutes; all four passed out in a forgetful drunken stupor from the very strong liquor.

One facet of the rescue operation that may not have been too fortuitous was that, even though the craft had hugged the treetops to and from the safe area, the young Forest Ranger, Max Delecourt had managed to photograph the entire event with his digital video camera. Later, when the film was analyzed, and to his embarrassment, he is trying to narrate the events but he is so scared and excited that all that came out was a great wheezing sound with a few indistinct words. The pictures, however, were quite sharp and clear showing almost every detail of the craft including a brief image of the pilot, whose gray skin and huge dark eyes seemed more foreboding than friendly. The huge female Bigfoot, Aaah, was seen only as a large moving dark mass, so that part of the evidence could not be substantiated or enhanced enough to make out an image of any kind.

One humorous aspect of his video was image of the four campers, shown in the landing lights of the craft, on their knees or lying in the short grass. The two on their knees were clearly praying but in a screaming, confused tearful sort of way.

CHAPTER 38

LOOKING OUT THE small windows of the craft the two criminals watched as they approached the huge gas giant of this solar system that they call Toc-g'last (Jupiter) and they were pleased that the trajectory seemed to be taking them past it, although it was at a pretty close proximity. They could see the violence of the surface storms and with a look conveyed to each other the hope that this was not their final destination. They were both somewhat started when the landing signal began to sound and the ship fired its reverse thrusters to slow down.

In the distance they could see one of the many colorful moons, for which they had no name, starting to grow larger in the view port. It had a light blue shimmering atmosphere and they could see land dotted by the blue green of seas or lakes; the green of trees. It could be freedom or another prison planet as far as Grious and Tic-Nar knew so they began roughly trying to revive the Gray who had not moved even a twitch since being thrown on the metal deck. They then noticed that the head of the creature was at an odd angle to the rest of the body and it was apparent that it was no longer living.

Having no options, the 2 Teer strapped themselves in for

the landing that seemed just moments away. The landing was a little more abrupt than they expected but smooth enough to walk away from. As soon as the craft was down and the engines shutoff the 2 Teer were scrambling down the ladder.

There was a hint of ozone in the air that tickled their senses; a smell that usually meant snow somewhere near. The forests of odd looking trees were bluer than green but there were some actual green intermixed. The atmosphere was breathable although it was richer in nitrogen than oxygen so it hurt their lungs a little, but each knew they were adaptable to such things, but right now it hurt their lungs in little sharp shooting pains. This minor atmosphere problem causes no real adjustments for a Teer as their metabolism can, and has, adjusted to many types of environments that would easily kill other species as soon as they opened the hatch of their ships.

Safely in the forest and having climbed a tree the 2 Teer took stock of their environment. Their keen sense of smell told them that they were not the only Teer on this moon, but they were still not sure of whether it was a prison planet or a colony. They both watched, with a sigh of resignation, as their pre-programmed ship suddenly fired its engines and took off.

The Clot-tor ship only stayed in orbit long enough to make sure that the ship was empty, except for the dead Gray. Satisfied that their quarry was safe on the Effe moon breeding colony, the ship returned to where the fleet was reassembling.

The tree that the two criminals had climbed began to shake violently, so much so that Tic-Nar nearly lost his grip. Looking down they saw several of their own kind and much to their delight all of the adults were female. Thinking that they had been transported to paradise they climbed down to look over the prospects.

"Where are we?" asked Grious to a lovely young female who was giving him the mating eye. She only grunted and grabbed for him, which started a minor scuffle among the assembled females. Grious laughed, in his own hideous way, watching Tic-Nar being carried off by three screeching females with two more in hot pursuit. A particularly lovely young female was now nuzzling him and groping without hesitation. Two other females joined in and he was becoming lost in the pleasure of it all but he was still puzzled because none of them were speaking, but he could hear their erotic thoughts well enough putting him in the mood to frolic.

Grious was nuzzling one of the females in return when he saw the reason why she could not speak. There was a patch of hair missing on her throat and a scar where her vocal cords should have been. This was an Effe means to keep the herd more docile and the females more subservient to the males in all their breeding herds, but it was not something Grious would have known about. The Effe either did not know, or cared to know, that the Teer were able telepaths and could communicate easily.

Grious would find out later that the Effe came to cull the herd every few years. Once Grious and Tic-Nar could no longer produce offspring they too would be culled. All of that put aside Grious did not care about the future he was lost in the moment, with four females. The females were projecting nothing in their minds but erotic thoughts to keep this male in the mood to frolic, now and as often as possible for some time to come. Still young enough to stay in the frolicking mood for many hours Grious thought his prospects good for having a harem and the females too like the idea. They carried their prize to the lush quarters set aside for such activities; lush by Teer standards.

There was a padded platform in the center of the room where the females intended to work this male very hard. The dark room was lined with wooden panels to make it more friendly and conducive to frolic in a forest environment. On each wall were benches for the females waiting their turn could sit and watch his performance. On higher shelves were bottles of the spray to enhance everyone's performance.

Grious, and Tic-Nar, were roughly thrown down on the padded platform and attacked by two females at a time. They did not really have much time to view their surroundings. One other thing the Effe provided was an enhancement drug of their own making to keep the male Teer in the mood, even as robust as their race is, for extended periods. The females would keep them on a strict schedule of frolic, eating, some sleep and feeding now for the rest of their lives. There was the possibility that the two males would not live long enough to be culled from the herd, it has happened in the past, so the females would be careful with these two.

CHAPTER 39

SEVERAL DIFFERENT FORCES were now moving at what could be likened to locomotives all converging from four directions at the same intersection at 60 miles per hour, which meant very little ability to stop the crash. The three scientists and the Forest Ranger were just showing signs of stirring back to life; the two tabloid reporters had finally come back from their forced coma, bruised and battered but very much alive. Each had driven slowly into town. Both men had heads pounding with what could only be described as hangover pain and an aching nausea so bad that they failed to note the staff car in the middle of the creek bed. Dennis limped home to Betty for some T.L.C. and Mike limped back to his hotel room. Neither man would receive any sympathy from their respective editors.

The other forces converging were not the humans but the Effe and their mercenary Clot-tor who were planning an invasion just out of reach of any Earthly sensors. The combined fleets were on the dark side of the moon where no telescope could detect their presence. The battle with the Scha-kur was now over. There was no clear winner but the

251

Scha-kur moved off to the edge of the solar system to regroup and plan a new strategy.

The Teer and the Kev-tah'esh knew that these forces were still in the solar system and gathering for some type of new battle or an actual assault on the planet. The Kev-tah'esh, at the request of Gesroh, requested urgent help from another star race. This particular race of beings had been thought extinct for many thousands of years. So powerful is this race that only one ship, having made its way from the center of the galaxy, was now sitting on the outskirts of this out of the way solar system. One ship from an ancient race straight out of their mythology called, in the Teer language, Basta-nok, literally translated meaning Guardian Lords.

The Basta-nok hardly look the part of a race of super intelligent beings or having no equal in battle. They range from a hue of blue green to bright green; their head resembling that of an Earthly lion with six protruding different colored eyes. A body of 3 heavily muscled segments, four arms with retractable claws on large finger like paws and a barbed blunt tail. The adaptation of the multi-colored eyes enabled them to see in several spectrums of light at the same time. Their powerful weapons had ruled the Galaxy when it was young. They were however never conquers; they were keepers of the peace and trans-dimensional. The Basta-nok had been keeping to their own counsel on a secluded planet near the center of the galaxy since dinosaurs first ruled the Earth. Most of the newer star races had no record of their existence and that was acceptable to the Basta-nok. The overconfident Effe had become too powerful and too hungry; too arrogant to care about any other races that far away from their territory or star races shrouded in fairytales to frighten the young.

The Clot-tor had their own appetites to appease involving creatures that live and breed in salt water; too warlike to care about any other star race but the Effe whom they serve, confident in their ability to overcome all aggressive species they might meet. They have no legends or myths to believe in; no gods to worship.

Now a peace keeper Lord had come to settle this dispute. It was not here to negotiate with races where diplomacy had no meaning. It would settle the situation by force and then retreat back into legend and myth.

It is hard to believe that with all this turmoil in the solar system that the personnel aboard the space station, or the crew of the shuttle that just docked with the space station, were so unaware of what is transpiring. Each is too busy to care about what is happening in the vastness of space; each crew member was more concerned with the resupply, the removal of the garbage and the transferring of experiments to the space shuttle. The loading and unloading taking place with astronauts and cosmonauts working side by side in confining space suits perhaps has caused them to have tunnel vision limiting them to their own problems. There had been no recording of data or checking of instruments that had been operational and recording some of the activity taking place within the solar system.

Even the scientists on the planet's surface were not believing or accepting the data that their instruments were showing. The SETI project, listening for life out in the cosmos, was receiving data and odd transmissions from several sectors in space but the higher powers were discounting the data as false echoes due to the current space mission.

The Human Race, always looking to find its origins

could now possibly be in a struggle with their benefactors, the Teer and to some extent the Effe as both races did add their substance when seeding three planets in this small solar system. No one on the ground believed any of the data being captured by their equipment; it was too much, all at once, so the skeptics were winning the battle in the scientific world. It had not yet been put to the theologians but it was only a matter of time before the religious leaders had their input.

The Effe believed they had originally seeded the three planets in this system that seemed capable of sustaining life, carbon based life forms. The names of the planets, in the Effe language, are Pec-ay-Tan (Venus); Pec-ay-na (Earth); Pec-ay-Tyio (Mars). Venus was a long shot. Mars had been seeded first, as an experiment, to see if anything would evolve or grow on such a barren red planet with limited water. Upon their return the Effe harvested the planet to extinction and feeling happy with themselves performed seeding operations on the other two planets. However, records were lost and the Effe forgot about these last two planets for almost 200 million years. That hurt the colony established on Pec-ay-Tan put there to try terraforming the atmosphere into some more hospitable than the methane atmosphere. Even when given to the Clot-tor to terraforming it was forgotten.

When the supply ships stopped coming to Pec-ay-Tan the colony abandoned their operations and moved to the moon Titan (eke-bal-Som) and re-established their terraforming operations there. A scouting expedition followed a Kev-tah'esh ship to the third planet and saw the lush herds of warm flesh to aid in their feasting. The Effe captured several criminal Teer from their high homes and transported them to the moon to begin a herd for future profit and consumption.

The Effe also tried to transplant several of the large warm blooded lizard animals but found they could not adapt as quickly as the Teer so that project was abandoned.

Back in the present the small Clot-tor armada was making final preparations to invade and capture the lush blue planet with the huge salty oceans teeming with life. The Effe fleet commander was trying to decide how to capture Aaah, because they still wanted this fertile, young female and her child, to infuse the herds of Teer being kept for food on several planets and moons in this part of the galaxy. This plan was being considered by the central core but the debate seemed to go on and on without result. There was the belief by many that the 2 Teer males who were recently dumped on eke-bal-Som were infusing enough new DNA into the colony to preclude starting a war to get one female and a child.

It had also been observed that the Kev-tah'esh were putting together a fleet to thwart the plans of the Effe and their allies. The ratio was two to one against the Effe, not the best odds in any war. The Kev-tah'esh were not yet aware that the Basta-nok had come to their aid. Most of the Kev-tah'esh did not believe that the Basta-nok race even existed any more. The legends had the Basta-nok retreating to the center of the Galaxy where they had colonized and cloaked an entire solar system and the planet which would become their home, so they could retire in peace and not be bothered with all the petty bickering of the fledgling star races. The plea of the Teer race however could not be ignored; the Basta-nok had decided that it was in their best interest to stop the killing even if two star races had be neutralized or made extinct. There were thousands more less aggressive species ready to take their place. This was a distasteful business for the Bastra-nok but the more barbaric races were being gobbled up rather than allowed to flourish, as the Bastra-nok had intended. The Effe had degenerated over the last few million years into a race parasites and scavengers. Originally the Effe were flesh and fluids but evolution had taken them to high energy beings with insatiable appetites.

CHAPTER 40

THE FOUR HUMANS in this galaxy conquest equation were finally awake and just finishing breakfast. They were trying to relax and plot their next move over cups of tea and coffee. Lisa had made blueberry muffins for desert and biting into the steaming muffins with butter dripping on the plate garnered sounds of happiness from everyone at the table.

"These muffins are really hitting the spot. I feel as though I have been in battle with a whole battalion of giant skunks and lost!" said Frank, "I know I'll never get the smell out of the truck but the Vicks I put under my nose before going to bed did help me breathe a little better. Excuse me please," as he pushed back from the table and went outside to blow his nose.

"I am thinking very seriously about shaving my head just to get the smell out. I hope you burned those clothes," said Megan looking at Jerry, in between bits of muffin; butter dripping off the corner of her mouth and on to her plate.

"No, but I will put them in that 55 gallon drum out back and set them off before we go anywhere this morning," explained Jerry as he made eye contact with Lisa, grabbing another muffin before she could swat his hand with the wooden spoon she had just picked up, just for that purpose.

"To whom should we go with the information we have gathered?" asked Jerry, "were any of your dreams as 3D as mine were. I felt as though we were being briefed by a whole gallery of Teer; watching battles in space and seeing invasion plans. Anyway where should we turn with all this information and who will believe anything we have to say? The Department of the Interior, no not really their jurisdiction; the FBI, no they would just complicate things and try to take over; the CIA, no they are even more paranoid than the FBI; how about one of the black operations teams, even if we could contact one they would just come in and try to kill everything or capture and torture everyone and everything involved," he paused to finish off the muffin in two bites and drain his coffee cup. "Should we go to the local police, the sheriff or the State Patrol, no they have the same egotistical problems as all the other law enforcement agencies; I know we could Email all our information to one of our science department heads at one of our Universities; no they would try and hog all the credit. The military then," he said looking around for a reaction of some sort but all he got were groans of disapproval, "I know we can't really trust them either, those Air Force people were really aliens inhabiting human bodies, which frankly is pretty creepy. The really sad thing is we do not have anyone to turn to for help except our friends up in Huckleberry Mountain and I hope they have some sort of plan."

Lisa sat down rather heavily in the old creaking wooden kitchen chair, "I never really thought about who we would go to for help if we actually found something. I do know we are going to have a killer of a jointly authored paper to submit to a few scientific journals and our respective department. Funding should go out the roof for next year!" The other three looked at her just a little taken back by her exuberance.

"Do you really think anyone is going to believe any of this stuff? The scientific communities are all going to think we were up here smoking "wacky tabacky" for the summer and collaborated when we were high," said Megan looking around the room at the gloomy faces. "We have evidence to back up our claims. We have their hair samples, some blood, some footprint casts and a few pictures but still nothing solid enough to be believed or even funded for another expedition." Continuing with her thought, "Let's see we could tell them about the cannibalistic race of energy creatures that only want us for dinner; a race of reptiles that do the fighting for the energy creatures; how the Yeti are criminals and that Bigfoot is actually a race of beings that call themselves the Teer and how their chauffeurs are the Gray aliens, who just happen to like horse and cattle parts for their payment. We would be better off just selling these stories in installments to the sleazy rag newspaper people who have been tracking us all over these woods," said Megan as she rose and rinsed her cup, "at least they pay money for this stuff."

"You know, that may be our only available means of getting this information out. Remember what someone said in that alien movie that "these rags are the best investigative reporting on the planet," said Jerry as he stood up sending his wooden chair across the linoleum floor, "let's go see if we can make a deal with one of those guys!" He put his cup on the drainer by the sink, grabbed his daypack and headed toward the door.

"Hold on there, partner," said Frank, grabbing Jerry at the elbow and spinning him half around, "don't you think we should talk this over, I mean, it seems a little drastic to go chase down one of these guys in the first place and in the second place what is our advantage when no one else will believe anything we have to say even if we do publish it in the tabloids first?"

"It's a marketing ploy, the old push/pull concept, where we get people to start believing in a product before we serve it up to them," responded Jerry putting down his pack and began giving a dissertation on the dry erase board to his captive audience, "we leak it to the press, first the sleazy press then the more legitimate press, but we get some of the population believing in it, that is the push part of the concept; then, we publish the paper and let the legitimate press get a hold of it somehow, that is the pull. Once it is on the national news then that should lend some credence to it and perhaps then some of the scientific communities will read it and accept it. It is worth a try." Jerry looked at his little audience and they were all looking at each other trying to make some sense of what they had just heard, "it sounds a little farfetched but believe me it is our only hope right now."

Before anything else could be said each one of them, as if on cue, closed their eyes to receive a message from Gesroh, "so this is how you will notify your planet of the proposed invasion of the Clot-tor? How long will this method take? Will your armies arise to fight these vicious creatures as their ships move about your planet destroying everything so they can then land their troops to begin the round-up?"

"We did not know such a thing was that imminent Gesroh but you must understand people, they will not believe us. Do you have a plan?" thought Jerry, wincing as the wire crackled with energy and wiggled at the back of his neck.

"I have asked for some help and if we are…lucky, the Clot-tor will not be able to invade. The Effe still want my daughter for their herd and even now are helping plot the invasion of Strig'et ocouts in an effort to capture her," Gesroh's thought path eased up a little.

"Why do they want her so much? Didn't you say they had their herds already on other planets?" was a thought from Megan.

"Because she is…the daughter of…the rulers of Kleek… like a princess in your language. They know that I have been plotting the return of all the Teer herds from the Effe for many years and they feel if she were a hostage at one of their colonies I would be forced to give up my plans of conquest and deprive them of one of their main sources of food," there was a brief pause and easing of the pressure then it started again, "I must go I am being contacted by an ally," and his transmission quit almost as abruptly as it started.

"So we have been working for the leader of the Teer, their King or Prime Minister or something, no wonder he got everything his own way," thought Jerry unaware that the other three were somehow picking up his thoughts, they had all forgotten the connection factor that Gesroh had given them. Jerry now fully understood the echo he had experienced when he had been talking on the radio to Lisa and all the background noise they had all be experiencing.

Lisa looked at him, staring with a cold foreboding look in her eyes, she concentrated and thought, "We are the court jesters then, aren't we?" a tear of pity for herself or from strain quickly ran down her beautiful cheek.

"Maybe so, maybe we are the jesters or pawns in this," Jerry said aloud causing the others to break contact and shake their heads back and forth to dislodge the cobwebs forming in the back of their brains.

"Ole Gesroh has an ally out there somewhere, that's encouraging, but we have to speed things up and warn the Poc-cin of Strig'et ocouts that there are silicone based reptiles getting ready to put on a round-up for their energy being masters. You know we may have to change the name of this planet to Strig'et ocouts because that is how I am starting to think of it, "said Jerry.

"Wasn't there an old Twilight Zone episode back in the 50's or 60's, certainly in re-runs, that had a race of beings coming down with a book entitled, "How to serve man" that finally got translated showing it was a cookbook? This is like that only these beings are not going to play nice before herding the human race on their ships for slaughter," said Megan. She looked at each person in the room, "how are we going to get this planet of idiots up and ready to fight with this story of ours; I wouldn't believe it either," she said walking slowly over to the rocking chair, curling one leg up under her and sitting down gently blowing the steam off her green tea.

"Well, in law enforcement there is always the burden of proof," said Frank trying to get the discussion moving again, "we have to prove to someone with some influence that something is going to happen and that we know what we are talking about. In the movie "The Day the Earth Stood Still" Michael Rene, the space man, went to a scientist who in turn went to an assembled body of scientific minds to convince them before anyone else would listen," he paused looking for some form of approval.

"Yes, but the military shot the guy in the beginning of the movie and shot him again about half way through out of fear," said Lisa.

"True, but when he was in the elevator with Patricia Neal

he set something up to make all the power stop around the world, except planes in the air and hospitals, for 30 minutes. That got people all over the world to be afraid of him but it also got their attention at the same time," said Megan, looking questioningly over at Jerry.

"You are all looking at me for the brilliant idea that will save the world, aren't you?" asked Jerry, "I am sorry to disappoint you but I am fresh out..." he said as his eyes closed rather involuntarily although the pain was not as bad as usual.

"I have a plan my friends," said Gesroh, "it may be time for your people in space, your...astronauts...cosmonauts... to actually see a space craft from another world. Your race is truly not yet ready for this type of contact but it is too late to worry about such things. I believe your race must be preserved and not allowed to be herded away and used as a food colony planet," Gesroh paused to let the primitive minds absorb the information thus far. "Seeing one of our ships, piloted by the Kev-tah'esh, up close should put your planet on alert. It would lend credibility to your story...report too. What do you think of my plan?" he said taking some of the pressure away from his transmission to give them a chance to respond.

"Good plan," responded Frank, "but isn't there some way to get a message across that there is an invasion fleet on its way to the planet?"

"Thank you Frank, but you are thinking as a law officer and very linear in your approach. I believe that we do not want the Kev-tah'esh to be mistaken for the vanguard of the invasion fleet so I intend to transfer some data ship-to-ship showing where the fleet is located. Then our ship will retreat in exactly the opposite direction it came in and away from the position of the invasion fleet. They do have a device to bend light rendering the ship virtually invisible that they can engage and return to the safe area later," replied Gesroh, obviously pleased with himself.

"What would you like us to do?" asked Jerry.

"I would like you to be ready to answer questions. A second stream of information will be sent to the station with your names, pictures and location so that you may be contacted by your government or military officials so you may give them what information they will need to prepare to repel this invasion, if my ally and I cannot stop their fleets in space, the next step is that your people be prepared to fight."

"Well that certainly makes it easier that all of the "bone heads" will be coming to us instead of us trying to sift out the really stupid ones to get the word out. We will just sit tight and wait," thought Jerry as he walked over and poured himself another cup of coffee. "Just how much do you want us to tell them?"

"Please do not talk of the safe area, Kleek or of the Teer. Only tell them what you know about the Effe and the Clottor invasion. I wish no contact with these other Poc-cin and I do not want our secret out. They will see the Kev-tah'esh, the Grays as you call them, when contact is made but limit your information about them especially in relation to the Teer. We do not wish our friends to be thought of as part of the enemy. You may put out your theories when you publish your…tree bark…no…paper, yes, about crop circles, animal mutilations and the UFO lights in the sky but keep the Teer a mystery. In a few hundred more years we may make contact with your primitive culture, again, but the time is not yet right. Only out of necessity did we make contact with you, please do not make me sorry to have befriended you," Gesroh's transmission stopped abruptly as usual.

With that last thought in their minds, the 4 Poc-cin in the room were exhausted from the powerful thought transmissions of Gesroh and all four were again asleep. A gallon of coffee each would not have kept any of them awake for a second longer and it would be another day before they fully recovered. Time enough for Gesroh to put his plan into action.

CHAPTER 41

THE PERSONNEL ON the space station were going about their duties quite efficiently. One was eating, one was sleeping, one was tending the small garden and one was doing the preliminary work to prepare for a spacewalk. After the resupply ship had departed no one had bothered to check any data received during that time, no alarms had gone off which to them meant no interesting data had been recorded.

Vitaly Demitriov was struggling into the suit while, Ivan Petrinovich, now finished eating was assisting him with the checklist and getting everything secured for when the air lock door was opened to space. They didn't want everything floating out.

The station was over the Atlantic Ocean and Vitaly wanted to be in space by the time the orbit took them over mother Russia. He loved looking at his homeland from space and missed his wife and their two boys deeply.

The checklist was finally completed and all the final preparations had been made, Vitaly made a radio check with the tracking station in Great Britain as he moved through the air lock, secured his tether and closed the airlock door behind him. Ivan watched the lights of the indicating that the seal was engaged and signaled Vitaly that he could now open the second door to begin the space walk.

One of the two Americans on board, Tom Sunderland came forward to watch as the outside hatch was opened and Vitaly silently slipped out into space looking like a pure white snowball with arms and legs. Vitaly put down the sun visor just before he went outside the ship otherwise he would be completely blind in seconds from the direct rays of the sun.

Emily Pritchett, tending the small test garden, glanced out the porthole to watch Vitaly floating away toward the aft part of the station where the solar panels were all lined up gathering energy from the intense rays of the sun. One of the panels was showing some type of distress so Vitaly's mission was to repair it quickly and return. This was an unscheduled walk and therefore it should be no more than a couple of hours, but it had taken the better part of two days to get the ground officials to approve it.

Tom decided that their position was good enough to start taking pictures of the moon that was lit up in its full glory; he felt like he could reach out and touch the orb that now seemed so close. While setting up his camera and looking through the view finder to take some test photos Tom noticed a moving object either heavily reflecting the sun or having a light source of its own, coming toward the station. He quickly forgot about the moon and concentrated on taking pictures of the object that seemed to be drawing nearer to the station in a very straight trajectory. As the object came nearer beads of sweat started popping out of Tom's forehead like a fountain geyser in Las Vegas. As the object neared it appeared to be slowing down; Tom was getting excited to the point where his hands began shaking.

"Ivan!" Tom received no answer, "Ivan! Emily!" Tom took his eyes away from the viewfinder long enough to see both people floating toward him. Tom went back to taking pictures. Both Ivan and Emily floated silently up beside Tom and looked out the porthole. Without saying a word Ivan kicked away toward the tracking instruments. Emily just hovered, putting her hand on Tom's shoulder but saying nothing for a few moments.

"What do you think it is Tom?" she said almost sounding like a computer with expressionless words in a monotone. She too was visibly nervous.

"It looks like a space vehicle of some sort, although not a design I have ever seen or even imagined. At first I thought it was a satellite out of orbit but it has been maneuvering. It could be some rich eccentric fruitcake flying up to meet us," Tom thought out loud, "because it came up from below us or below Earth and is on a straight course toward our position." Tom was still unable to control his nervousness although trying to keep his scientific and analytical objectivity.

"It is tracking Tom. It is slowing down?" replied the excited Ivan.

"I sure hope it is a friendly," whispered Tom, "because we don't have anything that would even be considered a weapon, we can't even throw rocks." (Emily just groaned)

Vitaly was busy working on the solar panel and had his back to the object that was now just a hundred kilometers off the hull of the space station and floating toward them, directly between them and the moon. "Vitaly, stop what you are doing and look toward the moon. Tell me what you see?" radioed Ivan.

Vitaly, slightly irritated that he had to stop the repairs for something so frivolous as looking at the moon, kicked away to float up and look over the structure that had been blocking his view of the moon.

"Vat da hell is zat?" yelled Vitaly in his best and clearest English.

"It looks like a real, honest to goodness, space ship to me," said Tom still taking pictures. The craft was almost more oval shaped than saucer shaped with a rotating lower section. It looked something like a jellyfish with no tentacles; the outside hull was a little draped over the cylindrical moving lower piece. There were windows and as the vehicle slowed even further and stopped within 500 meters of the station Tom, through the telephoto lens could see gray colored creatures, with large craniums and large dark eyes. He could feel his knees weaken and if he had been actually standing he would have fallen down.

Emily grabbed the radio head set and sent a message, "Houston, we have a problem," something she had always wanted to say even though she knew it was a tracking station in Finland that answered, "Mir, this is not Houston, this is Lahti, Finland. What is the nature of your problem?"

"Lahti, we are observing and under the observation of a space craft of unknown origin. Do you have it on your scope?"

"Yes, we see something," was the hesitant reply of the night crew technician. "Do you have a visual? Can you take pictures and send them to us? Are you officially reporting a UFO?"

"Affirmative Lahti to all three questions; we are taking stills and I am now putting the video cameras into operation, two angles, are you receiving?"

"Yes! Can you confirm any identifying markings on this craft?"

"No Lahti, we can see no markings on this vessel," replied Emily. "I will zoom in with our highest intensity camera, can you see the vessel clearly, Lahti?"

"Yes we see it!"

"Vitaly, do you see any markings on the side of the craft?"

"Nyet, zere are no markings."

By now people from monitoring stations all over the world were calling in all the technicians available to monitor and track this UFO. Managers and directors were breaking land speed records to get into their duty stations to see what the space station was seeing. The transmissions from the video cameras were going out over the NASA television station, no one thought about turning off the transmission, so people at home were able to get the first views of this UFO, this spacecraft from off world.

"The Kev-tah'esh were nervous about this contact with the primitives and wanted to send the messages and get away, but Gesroh wanted as many Poc-cin to see them as possible, ordering them to stay visible just 500 meters from the space station for one Strig'et ocouts time unit, called an hour by the Poc-cin. After half of the time unit had elapsed the Kev-tah'esh were to send the first of two messages, but remain to be photographed. It was very nerve racking for the crews of both vessels in space.

Vitaly, having quickly done his repair job, had climbed back into the station and had hastily gotten out of the suit. He joined his crewmates at the portholes. Ivan, still at the tracking instruments suddenly called Vitaly over to him, "They are sending a transmission."

"Greetings people of Strig'et ocouts…Earth…we are the Kev-tah'esh, a star race that visits this solar system from time

271

to time. We have come to warn you of an invasion of your world by another star race, something we cannot stop or control. We are warning you to put your warriors on alert, the invasion will be within one or two solar days…about four of your rotations… you must all work together to repel these invaders."

"Lahti, this is Mir, did you get that or do you want a retransmission?"

"This is Lahti; we got the transmission, thank you. We are sending it to all the other stations around the world. Please standby for any further instructions," Lahti out.

"Lahti, are we authorized to talk with the other ship?" Ivan was rapidly trying to set up a return frequency because the transmission from the Kev-tah'esh had come from their computer.

"This is Lahti; we see no reason why you cannot make contact. It is obvious they came to see you."

Ivan had his keyboard out setting up a link through the computer to either transmit voice or keyboard strokes. A few beads of sweat trickled down his forehead and attempted to drip off his nose that he wiped quickly with his sleeve. He stopped however as he observed another transmission was being sent. Instead of an Earth language the screen lit up with alien symbols and attached meanings in English. Ivan stopped to study the transmissions and suddenly a light bulb lit behind his eyes, "I have seen these symbols before somewhere, they are, on my English is so bad, ah…crop circles," he said looking around.

"What?" said Emily as she floated back to where Ivan was seated at the computer terminal, "did you say crop circles?"

"I did. Look at them, they seem to be sending a dictionary of their language and it is taking a long time to load. I am glad this computer has a large memory drive. It will take some study looking at all the old crop circles that have been appearing for the last 40 years and the ancient symbols in South America. They are sending a massive amount of information here, I am going to start saving it on disks, it is like the Rosetta stone or the Dead Sea scrolls. This is so cool, but I have to go to the bathroom, can you take over please?"

"Sure," said Emily with a smirk on her face as to the circumstances that made Ivan float away in such a hurry.

"They may be sending us these language symbols for another message," said Ivan as his voice trailed off into the distance, turning the corner towards the restroom.

Tom, still taking pictures, looked around to Emily, "can you start looking around for any other space craft? If we are going to be invaded the invasion force may already be staging somewhere in our solar system. They could be hiding behind the moon or one of the planets, but maybe if you look for something that is not quite right, like a cluster of stars that should not be there, something like that." Tom stopped taking still pictures but kept the video cameras operating.

"There is a cluster of shining objects just past the moon. We didn't pay attention before because, and I can only guess, there was no movement. There is still no perceivable movement," said Emily concentrating on the screen and moving the scanners here and there. "Just how many blips would be considered an armada?"

Ivan came floating back, "with the power these creatures probably have an armada could be as few as 5 or 10 blips. How many do you see?"

"Right now there are just 4 blips but there is no telling how many are actually hidden behind the moon," said Emily staring at the scanner, "now there are 5, one is moving slowly out from behind the moon to join the cluster."

"Is there any indication that a main body is moving, in any direction?" inquired Ivan, as he floated back to take up his position. Tom watched him moving around and was looking at Ivan with one raised eyebrow. Ivan tried to raise an eyebrow back but he failed so he just looked at him, "well if the blips are getting larger or smaller that would be an indication of movement, yes?"

"I suppose so, Ivan," said Tom hiding a smirk by looking out the port hole. "I cannot dispute such a scientific observation. Maybe we should break out the Space Invaders game to help in our analysis and planning our defense, umm?" Tom looked back as he heard, but did not understand Ivan's reply in Russian.

"What is happening with our friends here Tom?" asked Emily rapidly loading another disk into the system to siphon off more of the data.

"They are putting down the window shades, they may be leaving," said Tom as he rapidly took some additional still shots. "Their craft is falling away from us toward Earth, they are definitely leaving."

"Track them someone, we may be able to trace them back to a base on the planet, or something. This was first contact you know," Tom yelled excitedly as he watched the craft drift away, then the propulsion system kicked on and he expected it to disappear in the blink of an eye. The aliens maneuvered the craft just above the atmosphere over the North Pole and kept going straight, in traceable straight line trajectory out into the solar system, directly away from the moon, but not going anywhere on Earth. Then the ship suddenly disappeared from sight and the tracking scopes.

CHAPTER 42

THE SMALL BALL of energy that had been sitting on the edge of the solar system like a distant sun began moving, slowly, toward the assembled armada. Glowing like a yellow sun but being no larger than the Earth's moon, it moved almost tentatively. The invasion force took no notice of the ship because final preparations were currently underway to conquer and capture this whole planet of food beasts.

Meanwhile the small team of scientists, trying not to ignore the wishes of the Teer, laid out the whole story for the two rival reporters. The two reporters sat and listened, their small tape recorders taking notes for each of them as the team took turns laying out the entire situation to them. Although experienced in listening to and writing about some of the most unbelievable stories their jaws dropped open and stayed open during all parts of the fantastic saga. Especially interesting were the food farms on the moons of Jupiter and the impending invasion. There were even furtive looks of disbelief between the reporters as the whole story was finally revealed. Mike decided to start smoking again as soon as he could get to a store.

Two items that especially peaked Dennis' interest were the parts of the saga about the seeding efforts by the Effe and another race; how an ancient star race was slowly making their way into our solar system to try to stop the massive invasion. The ancient race is known as the Bastra-nok to most of star races, they live in the center of the galaxy on a hidden planet; they consider themselves protectors not conquerors. The lion shaped heads, 6 sets of eyes, different shades of green, segmented bodies and a barbed tail really set off the story well.

For all their ferocious appearance the Bastra-nok are a peaceful race who would rather keep to themselves than become embroiled in these tiny territorial disputes. However, and this should make the people of Earth feel somewhat special, the Bastra-nok directed two of their seeding comets directly at this out of the way galaxy, about 4 million years apart, one destined for the red planet and the other the blue planet. They knew that carbon based life forms would not survive too well on the other, less hospitable, planets.

Mike and Dennis were almost speechless when these long winded scientists, and a freaking Forest Ranger, finally stopped rambling about all the troubles currently associated with this galaxy.

Dennis had to tap Mike on the shoulder to snap him out of his daze, "What do you want us to do for you, exactly?" asked Mike, leaning over to look at his tape recorder to make sure there was still enough tape for the answer. Dennis checked his machine as well and then they both sat back and just stared at Jerry, patiently waiting for a response.

"We want you to get on all the wire services with this story as soon as possible," said Megan, she was leaning in to emphasize the point, "the people of this planet need to know what is going on and you two can share the Pulitzer Prize."

"The Kev-tah'esh have already made contact with the

International Space station, so the governments know but they might do their usual cover up believing that the general populations cannot handle the information and go running panic stricken in the streets, or some other 1950's nonsense. We need to get this news out to the people. If, for some reason, the Bastra-nok cannot stop the Effe armada then the Effe and their hired guns, the Clot-tor are going to hit this planet harder than an NFL defensive line," said Lisa who had picked up the knife she had been washing and shook it in the direction of the reporters.

Jerry, smiling because of the passion shown by his colleagues, turned his chair around and straddled it, "Have you got any questions gentlemen?"

"I do," said Mike who had almost raised his hand, "any idea when the invasion is going to start?" His eyes were flicking back and forth looking at the faces of the scientists and the Ranger.

"Our source does not know for sure, but is sure it will happen in the next 24 to 48 hours. The fleets are massing just on the other side of the moon and the scouts have already broken off the main body and are headed toward Earth."

Mike and Dennis began gathering their items and were whispering to each other giving the group furtive looks.

"Gentlemen, what is the problem now?" asked Frank who already had an idea what was coming. These two journalists thought they were being duped into something although neither knew exactly what.

"Well, we think you people are trying to make us look as foolish as possible and cooked up this elaborate story for us to file, essentially to the world, so that we would at the very least lose our jobs and not bother you anymore," said Dennis.

"Just who in the hell do you think is capable of making up a story like this?" Lisa fired back throwing her apron on the table. "This planet is really in danger; it is going to be attacked and we are all going to be herded off to be raised as food for this voracious star race called the Effe. We are not kidding," she yelled, her lovely face getting a bright almost florescent red. "Now get your butts in gear and file this story. If you lose your precious jobs I will pay your salary for the next 5 years. Now move it."

Jerry grabbed her gently and pulled her to him holding her with one arm around her shoulders, "Easy there Dr. Shields," he was not trying to be condescending or scolding in any way, "they have been led astray before, I am sure. Well boys what kind of proof do you need to believe our rather elaborate story?"

"I know," said Frank as he took off his hat and turned his back to them, "I'll bet they want to see our communications device, am I right?" he said looking over his shoulder at Dennis and Mike.

"Yeah, that would be nice, I guess," said Dennis with a sly grin, matched only by the grin of Mike's cynical expression.

"Well here it is," as Frank turned his head back he grabbed the dangling antenna between his first two fingers and kind of flipped it up for them to see. "What do you think of that?"

"May I examine it please?" said Mike stepping forward. Dennis was grabbing his camera.

"Go ahead; just don't pull on it because it is attached inside my body."

"Dennis will you take a look at this thing? This is obviously some type of monofilament device with this round unit here at the bottom that must be the sender and receiver." Dennis took several close-up pictures. Still holding the device Mike asked, "Do you know the range of this thing?"

"It is attached to my mind and the mind of several others on this planet. For all I know it has the range of across the galaxy." Frank gently grabbed Mike's fingers and pulled them away. "Now, you have some proof that what we have told you is true so start writing or dictating or make a phone call to your editor but get the story on the wires!"

Jerry smiled at Frank's thought transmission, "Frank you are correct, these guys are a little thick."

"Okay, we'll get at it as soon as we get to town. My cell is dead and so is Mike's, so we will have to use the landline and wireless system at the hotel," answered Dennis, who had Betty on his mind. "We had better get going. Mike and I will call you here at the cabin when we get the stories filed." Then both men were out the door, down the steps and into their respective cars. In just a few seconds they sped away.

Dennis, safely back in the arms of a surprised and pleased Betty, he was having second thoughts about filing the story. Looking like a fool in the AP and UPI news networks was not exactly something that was career enhancing. Not that his career had gone anywhere in the last 15 or 20 years anyway, he just could not decide whether to believe the fantastic fairy tale he had just been fed or let it lose on the world. But, on the other hand, Dr. Shields said she would pay his salary for the next 5 years and he had it on tape, so he was very tempted.

Mike was lying in his bed at the motel listening to the recording when he received a call, "Hello?"

"Hey, this is Dennis. Can we talk?"

"Yeah, what do you want to talk about?"

"Have you filed the story yet?" asked Dennis trying to justify his lack of guts.

"No, not yet how about you?" inquired Mike who was feeling the fool.

"No, I guess I haven't got the guts to commit job suicide today. Why haven't you gotten this hot story off to your editor?"

"Do you believe them?"

"I don't know yet. Betty and I have listened to the tape a couple of times and even she is having trouble believing all this stuff. One of those scientists or maybe all of them has a very vivid imagination. Has there been anything on the news?"

"There was something on the NASA channel about a UFO sighting at the space station, then there was a blackout and suddenly re-runs of the last spacewalk came on," saying that made Mike stop and think that maybe there was some small particle of truth to the story. "Do you think that lends any credibility to their story? They did tell us about that UFO thing."

"Some, I guess, but I still don't know what we should do. If it is true then we are going to be heroes, although somewhat late, but if it is not true then both our organizations will have to close because of all the panic it will cause."

"Oh well, why don't we just get this thing filed and let the editors worry about it. We haven't ever had a story this good either of us. Let's get it on the wire and take our chances," said Dennis as Betty was getting her coat to take him to her office where there was a stronger Internet connection for him to transcribe and email it to his editor.

"I guess we better cut the crap then and get to it," said

Mike as he reached over and switched on his laptop. "You heard what the pretty lady doctor said!"

The ball of light began to slow again as it came closer to the Armada. The Effe, on the scanners, were reading a comet so they were not paying closer attention. The Grand Illusion, the Central Core, had given the order at long last to attack.

The Grand Illusion, Central Core is the ruling council of the Effe consisting of 15 beings combining their minds to form one entity, but still a committee of minds. The Grand Illusion was located on the flagship of the Armada and it was also preparing to announce to the entire population of Effe, on several worlds, of the upcoming acquisition of the succulent creatures of the blue planet, they call Pec-ay-na, in their eerie language.

The small ball of light, the Bastra-nok vessel, itself still hidden from the International Space Station, did not attempt to mask its movement from the Armada scouts or the main body as the vessels began to clear the far side of the Moon.

The cold blooded Clot-tor began to disperse to their pre-planned coordinates. Forgoing the small concentrations on the planet where there were fewer inhabitants each heavily armed and armored ship headed for the greatest concentrations of the Pec-ay-na (the Clot-tor Effe adopted word for human food sources).

Suddenly in the flagship, in the council chamber, several blinking lights began to appear as the combined mind received a message from the Bastra-nok. The message was short with just a hint of the old rage, "Stop this, now or be destroyed!" sent in the Effe language.

Instant confusion ruffled through the Grand Illusion

Central Core until it reached the entity recognized as the Na'gat (the quorum). The Na'gat sent a mind spike to the other members that sent them into a quivering state of lighted jelly with sparks coursing through their rather fragile bodies. Turning its attention to the Bastra-nok message the Na'gat caught the message and returned it like a baseball fielded on the short hop and hurled to first base, "No!" was the short reply mind blast. The Na'gat could in times of strife override the Grand Illusion Central Core. Feeling invincible the Na'gat sealed the fate of the Effe.

So powerful were these transmissions that a circuit breaker on Gesroh's computer popped, sparked and sent smoke to the ceiling of the room. The Teer and Kev-tah'esh in the room were scurrying to make repairs, reset and trying to keep everything from short circuiting from the power of the minds in conflict.

The Bastra-nok, not known for their eloquence in these situations replied, "Now!" without threat, warning or posturing. The glowing ship began to slow once again coming within 5,000 kilometers from the flagship. It dwarfed the flagship and the Armada like a moon next to a planet. The reply was sent with such force that the Na'gat lost almost a lethal amount of energy in just seconds. The Grand Illusion Central Core was unable to respond, becoming less creatures of energy and more solid, glowing squares of stacked glowing jell. The controls in all the ships of the Armada, including the Clot-tor, were frozen as was each warrior immobilized, statues inside their armor and stalled ships. The Effe in the Armada suffered the same fate as the Grand Illusion Central Core becoming blocks of glowing jell. The progress or lack of progress, of the ships was all being recorded by the cameras of the space station and the satellite telescopes. The world governments were watching the outcome of this odd, silent and strangely beautiful confrontation. Hackers were breaking into the secure channel networks and broadcasting the information to the world. There were mixed emotions around the world from fascination to fear lightly mixed with terror and helplessness.

CHAPTER 43

THE EDITORS AT the respective media were leery about running the fantastic stories that their reporters had sent in but recent events tended to lend an eerie credibility to the stories. Each story was backed up by the actual tapes used to transcribe the articles. From the events seen unfolding in space every government on the planet had already declared martial law; the articles were put out in a special edition both on the air and in print.

When a 3 star General Officer from the U.S. Air Force's Space Command showed up at the remote cabin just a day later Jerry and the others decided that they had been taken seriously.

Gesroh, still in contact after some rapid repairs on his computer system decided to stay with his decision not to meet any other Poc-cin, he did not like their smell and their brains were so primitive he wondered how his technology had ever been able to operate properly.

Aaah had finally made it to the safe area, she had spent a lot of time in the woods but she still did not like the safe area, it meant getting away from nature and she had come on this expedition to enjoin nature to her soul and mate with Ustra. She found when she had lost track of herself and after being chased by the Effe and captured by the Poc-cin it had all been a very traumatic experience for her, she wanted and needed to rest where she felt safe. After being picked up by the scout ship and taken to the safe area she had been sleeping for nearly 3 days, a power nap to her species.

Gesroh had been monitoring the Poc-cin frequencies and the Armada for the last few days he could not decide whether, without the intervention of the Bastra-nok, if the humans would have been able to survive. Already there were groups forming to welcome the invaders and other groups forming to fight for their lives alongside their government forces.

Poc-cin believe they are superior to these star races, it seemed to him, and this delusion of being superior had many factions believing that the story could not be true, about enslaving the human race for food. These misinformed factions believed that the star races were afraid of the humans and that is the reason why they did not attack.

After fixing the General and her aide a cup of coffee and everyone was finally seated around the small cabin, the General took a sip of her green tea, looked at the four faces and asked, "So why did you start all this talk about being invaded and just how are all these elements connected?" Before anyone could answer, "and I have got to tell you the crop circles around the world have been appearing at an alarming rate. There is no doubt anymore that they are created for extraterrestrials and not a hoax."

Jerry, looked at Lisa, then responded, "As we said in the interview we are here on a government and university grant to study sightings of Bigfoot in this area of northeastern Washington. That simply is why we are here. We have already explained how we got caught up in these other events."

Lieutenant General Sarah Jennifer Vandervert simply said, "I see." Her aide was typing furiously on a laptop trying to capture everything that was being said. The Lieutenant was pretty fast but Jerry found the constant tapping on the keys to be very irritating.

"You military people should really invest in a tape recorder, it is much more efficient," commented Lisa also slightly irritated at how the General was dragging her feet. "General why are you here, exactly?":

Raising an eyebrow and setting down the tea the General sat back in her chair, "I have been sent here to find out how, just exactly how, you four people found out all the information that you stated in that interview and why the government was not notified sooner. I have been sent here by the Joint Chiefs of Staff just for that purpose." She looked at all four people alternately and picked up her tea and took another sip.

"General, just who do you think would have believed any of this?" asked Frank, feeling slightly incredulous that such a question was even asked.

"I can't believe this," said Megan looking at Lisa with wonder in her eyes, "we came to do scientific study, we found some evidence that Bigfoot may actually exist and then the whole situation blew up in our faces. Just how much of that do you think anyone, military or civilian, would have believed our story? We had visions of 1947 Roswell, New Mexico, where the military barged in hushing up and threatening people and putting out bogus stories about weather balloon crashing."

"I see so I am to conclude then that you do not trust

the government or the military in these matters?" asked the General who could not hold back a wry smile.

"Just what kind of a game are you playing her, General?" asked Jerry who was really becoming irritated at these *"when did you stop beating your wife"* style of questions. "The government and military track records speak for themselves. Dr. Hanley is right; no one would have believed us, not for a second. By the way, when we investigated that landing site at the cattle mutilation we thought we had made contact with the military and they turned out to be aliens, Effe to be exact, so what is your game?"

"Game, this is not a game. Have you seen the news lately or been on the Internet with the pirated copies of the NASA alien contact?" asked the General she saw genuine puzzled looks on all four faces. "Well I have a copy of it here and what happens here and in this interview confirms that there may be an impending invasion. Would you like to see it?"

The Lieutenant stopped typing and took a disk out of his computer carrying case and put it in his laptop. Everyone watched with interest and in silence except for a chuckle here and there. When the disk had finished playing the General added, "The Joint Chiefs wanted me to make contact with your "source"; one of you called the source a Teer, to help coordinate the response effort. We do not have much time; according to our information the invasion may already be beginning."

In each one of their heads there was a resounding, "NO!" and as a group they all grabbed the side of their heads and closed their eyes, reeling from pain.

"Well, General, get used to disappointment because it is not going to happen," said Lisa, the first to recover from the blast. "Our contact has declined your request. Does anyone want something for the headache?" Everyone nodded to the affirmative, including the Lieutenant.

"Our anonymous benefactor does not want any more contact with humans. He is telling us that whatever preparations our world makes for this invasion will be feeble at best," was Jerry's very guarded response.

"That doctor is why the Joint Chief's want "his?" help," there was a nod confirming the gender, His technology may be able to upgrade our weapons; there is a real opportunity here for joint cooperation," said General Vandervert.

"That story never changes does it," chimed in Lisa. "You see a real opportunity here for a weapons upgrade but seem to be falling short on other humanitarian concerns. Do you really want to know what our biggest problem was? It was finding a way to get this story out there so someone would believe it and you are sitting her telling us we should have gone to the government for help. General that is one of the three great lies; this particular one I am referring to is, "I'm from the government and I am here to help you"; the first great lie is, "check's in the mail"; but we won't go into the third one right now. Revealing our source, we already knew, would invoke the response we are receiving today."

"So then General now I suppose we are all traitors for withholding information from our government?" asked Frank. He received a very guarded glance but no reply from the General. The Lieutenant even looked up but quickly back to his computer.

"What exactly are the President and the military doing to get ready for this invasion of the Clot-tor?" asked Jerry, who had decided to see what she, knew about the situation.

"The Clot-tor? What are you talking about aren't a race called the Effe going to invade?"

"No, the Clot-tor are a silicone based life form that do all the dirty work for the Effe, they look like big lizards wearing armor and just love to fight, or so we have been told. The Clot-tor are a mercenary race that has allied themselves with the Effe for their own edification and profit. You did not answer my question, General," pushed Jerry.

"The major cities are being evacuated as a precaution; the military is on full alert status and has moved into the field so they will not get trapped on their bases; 75% of all intercept aircraft is kept in the air at all times. These precautions are being taken worldwide."

"Well then General you need to report back to the Joint Chiefs that they're stupid. Yes, you heard me correctly, stupid and very predictable. This invasion is for food and if the food is not in the cities then they will head to the country, wherever you have them stashed. The food, General, is mainly the human race. This situation is not like the movie about extermination to exploit the planet and planet resources; this is taking over the planet and start raising human food crops. They like other animals too but humans seem to be the tasty morsels they really want. Warm blooded and carbon based seems to be their main requirement."

The Lieutenant stopped typing and looked at the General. She had become paler than she was when she walked through the door. Her face softened, "Is you benefactor going to help us?"

"Well, yes and no. He has asked that another star race to intervene on our behalf. This is a powerful race that the Effe should but no longer fear."

"Tell her more," interjected Gesroh.

"I have been told to tell you more, so I will tell you that this is a race everyone out there calls the ancients, the Bastranok; literally translated means Guardian Lords. They were the actual seeders of the galaxy and one of the first races to evolve to the stars. Although powerful they have been reclusive and not dealing with the other star races for several hundred centuries. They have come out of retirement to help our friend reclaim some lost property and to deal with the Effe, and Clot-tor, threat. I don't know if you agree with me or not General but I think we have some pretty powerful help on our side."

The Lieutenant, who had been listening intently to Dr. Paulson, all of a sudden began to type with great purpose. The General was speechless just sitting there looking at Jerry and glancing at the clouds in her tea.

Abruptly the General stood, straightened her uniform and said, "Thank you" and headed for the door followed by the lieutenant clutching all of his equipment that he scooped up without bothering to pack.

The team and the Forest Ranger just sat there looking at one another, "Well, I have the same question now that I had yesterday, what the hell do we do now?" asked Jerry. There were no takers on giving him an answer. Jerry noted that the disk of the space station episode was still lying on the table so he slapped it into the DVD player and they watched in rapt fascination what had transpired at the International Space Station yesterday while they were all sleeping.

Out in space the Grand Illusion Central Core was struggling for self, Id and ego and a separation from the Na'gat in order to hope to survive. Each perceived that the Bastra-nok intended to kill not just immobilize them. Feeling alone, as the other life forces pulled away, the Na'gat was more susceptible to influence.

"Our race has the right to survive. Who are you to interfere with our existence?" responded the Na'gat.

"A fair question," was the initial response from Kag, the Bastra-nok pilot. There was a terrible, prolonged silence that caused the Na'gat and its entire race to feel a shiver of fear.

"We, who you call the ancients, were the first; the creators and seeders for a relatively lifeless galaxy. As the creators we claim that the true destiny of this primitive planet was not to provide a food source for your race of parasites and your conquests must cease here."

The Na'gat now totally alone, now a single mind, still tried to remain defiant, "we claim the right of conquest, whatever we need is ours for the taking, and it has been the law of the universe since the great inception."

"We say we created your race for another purpose and now, seeing the error of our ways, have decided that your race has no useful purpose in the galaxy, or in the universe. Your race will be eliminated. We will seed another planet to develop your race along another path."

Had it been possible the Na'gat would have committed suicide at this moment but it was too weak to move in its current jell like form. The Clot-tor will be sent to another quadrant to fulfill their destiny in battle with other warlike races. The Scha-kur have already gone into deep space, away from this sector. The ships of the Clot-tor began to blink out of existence one-by-one until only the Effe flagship remained with a few other transports carrying a small majority of the

Effe population, along on vacation and new food venture expeditions.

"You have the right of creation but you do not have the right for genocide of a star race," said the Na'gat defiantly, but it could feel itself weakening quickly.

"We bear the responsibility of creation and now must bear the right of genocide. From the great inception we have not relished the genocide of any races but there have been times when it was unavoidable. We feel this is one of those rare times where a race carries more detriment than positive contributions to the common good. We feel we have waited almost too long in this case. Your race has been judged and sentenced; the verdict is genocide. There is no appeal. The sentence is to be carried out now."

The glowing orb glowed brightly, as though carrying the power of a sun. When the glow subsided the Effe had become nothing more than a memory everywhere in the galaxy. The orb ship then left the rim of the solar system in less than a blink of an eye in a direct traceable line for the center of the galaxy cluster.

The people of Earth, poised for an invasion that never came, felt like they were let down, totally lost in the anti-climax. At times like this people will start pointing fingers to shift the blame as quickly as possible, the only problem being that when someone points a finger at someone else they tend to forget that there are three fingers pointed back at themselves. Now that nothing happened the blame spin-doctors would be out in force.

CHAPTER 44

"THE BASTRA-NOK HAS *left the solar system," thought Gesroh to the 4 Poc-cin he had befriended against his better judgment. "They have taken the Effe out of the universal equation, not to bother us again. The Clot-tor have been sent to the other side of the galaxy to do what they love, fight other savage races. We can reclaim the Teer from their food herds on several planets and moons, if they wish to be reclaimed."*

"That's wonderful, Gesroh, but where does that leave us,: thought Jerry, the others monitoring, "This small team of scientists have made some significant discoveries and we all have questions as to how you want us to handle the information."

"What discoveries do you want to...handle?"

"Just for starters we have discovered that Bigfoot does exist; we are certainly not alone in the universe and the belief in a supreme being may have some complications," added Megan's thoughts.

"Not to mention we have pretty much solved the mysteries of crop circles, UFO's, and the existence of not one visiting star race but several," thought Lisa. "Bigfoot is not the hulking beast haunting our woods that we thought before. The Teer are intelligent, as well as caring and loving parents, who use our planet as a vacation spot and a prison."

"I feel that you do not believe that your primitive race is ready for all of this revelation. I know there are those out there who would wish to exploit this type of information and make contact with the star races."

"Judging from the visit of General Vandervert the only reason most military personnel and governments want to make contact is to further our stature as an advance race in the galaxy through advanced weaponry. We are not advanced, and getting up to the level of the star races by asking for help in technology from whoever will give assistance is not the solution."

"This will not happen, do they not realize that it has always been the rule of the universe that each race must precede at its own pace. Many races have come as far as this "human race" of yours only to destroy themselves in matters of supremacy. We believe, as do many of the older races that yours is far too young to handle any of the knowledge known to the stars. The Poc-cin must evolve into more trustworthy beings before any formal contact is made. The Kev-tah'esh only made contact at my request and only because it was an emergency. I see now I may have acted rashly, I was not sure the Bastra-nok would intervene because we have not seen them for centuries," though Gesroh. *"I do not know how we may fix this problem."*

"The only way," thought Frank "is that we make this whole incident somehow a work of fiction. I believe if worked correctly there still may be a way of saving some careers here, after all there is a lot of evidence that suggests that something may have been discovered here this past week, but we are going to have to go on record as prevaricators of fiction or we are going to have to tell the truth, which is sometimes infinitely more strange than any work of fiction."

"An interesting idea Frank, but I think we will go with the truth instead of retracting our newspaper story. If we put out everything we have <u>learned</u> but not everything we have discovered along the way, there may be a way of saving grace and finishing out the summer in relative peace and quiet," was Jerry's response to Frank's very interesting idea.

"I see your plan, but do you actually believe it will work?" asked Gesroh.

"If humans are still human, it has a good possibility of working," said Jerry.

"I, for one, cannot read your conniving little mind so you are going to have to lay out this master plan of yours, so we can all get our stories straight at the trial," said Lisa sitting down next to Jerry and looking over his shoulder.

"First, we only publish our findings and photographs from the initial investigations we have been doing since day one. We do not mention anything about the safe area, its location or any technology we ran into. We do not talk about any actual contact we had, except the pictures, including the mauling Lisa took at the hands of the two criminals Grious and Tic-Nar, whose mention would serve no purpose.

We include the landing site investigation and the contact with the military but nothing after that, nor anything about the sheriff's deputy who was obviously possessed for a short time by an Effe. This must be the last time Effe is ever mentioned, or for that matter, any other of the alien names and words for things we have learned.

As for our interview with the so-called journalists we simply tell them we concocted the story to get them off our backs because we thought we were on the verge of actually discovering Bigfoot and they were in the way. Discrediting them is the least of our worries; I am sure they will survive when they start digging into the government cover-up of the happenings at the space station. As long as they keep their jobs Lisa should not have to pay their salary for the next 5 years, I hope.

Lastly we go back to being just three scientists and a Forest Ranger that are working on Bigfoot sightings and try to drop out of the spotlight. I do not believe we gave General Vandervert anything to go on even if we do see her again we can deny everything. After all she has not recordings of the interview with us.

As for the actual story of all these events, we can all collaborate on a work of science fiction, changing the names of course, to sell for fun and profit. We can all write under an assumed name and find an obscure publisher to handle that for us," said Jerry as he sat back to take a breath.

"Whoa, I am impressed, I had no idea your mind was so dark and mysterious," said Lisa giving him a kiss on the cheek, 'we might even be able to keep our own jobs if we work this right."

"Just keep thinking tenure, my good doctor," said Megan.

"What about that interview my young ranger gave at the tower, he does not know I know about it, but he did have an interview to one of those reporters?" asked Frank draining the last of the coffee in his cup.

"We will just have to let it ride, I guess. If someone wants to follow up on the story there has got to be some sort of proof that might not be that easy to come by. Frank you may still need to have a session with the young man. Anything we have found will be for our eyes only and not for publication until our scientific papers and book on science fiction come out," Jerry raised an eyebrow and there were no dissenters to the suggestion.

"Frank, I do suggest you get that suburban of yours fumigated before we have to spend any more time in it," suggested Megan as she gently put her hand on his shoulder. Frank smiled.

"It is starting to get dark, why don't we get some dinner going and start fresh in the morning?" suggested Jerry. Megan and Lisa went into the lab section of the cabin and the two men started the charcoal for grilling steaks and put on a big pot of beans on the stove.

The next day, early in the morning, using a different vehicle Frank and the three scientists were up into the woods checking out a site where campers had seen something. It was near Big Meadow Lake at the foot of Huckleberry Mountain.

As they walked through the early morning brush everyone was getting soaked from the waist down from the dew on the vegetation and dripping from the trees. The sun was starting to come out with warming rays, so by mid-morning at their first break steam was raising everywhere, including from their clothes. There wasn't much discussion just people doing their jobs collecting samples and taking temperature readings.